For Luca

Copyright © 1997 by Nord-Süd Verlag AG, Gossau Zürich, Switzerland.
First published in Switzerland under the title *Kapitän Jonathan*.
English translation copyright © 1997 by North-South Books Inc.

All rights reserved.
No part of this book may be reproduced or utilized in any form
or by any means, electronic or mechanical, including photocopying,
recording, or any information storage and retrieval system,
without permission in writing from the publisher.

First published in the United States, Great Britain, Canada,
Australia, and New Zealand in 1997 by North-South Books,
an imprint of Nord-Süd Verlag AG, Gossau Zürich, Switzerland.

Distributed in the United States by North-South Books Inc., New York.

Library of Congress Cataloging-in-Publication Data is available.
A CIP catalogue record for this book is available from The British Library.
ISBN 1-55858-813-2 (trade binding)
1 3 5 7 9 TB 10 8 6 4 2
ISBN 1-55858-814-0 (library binding)
1 3 5 7 9 LB 10 8 6 4 2

Printed in Germany

For more information about our books, and the authors and artists
who create them, visit our web site: http://www.northsouth.com

Captain Jonathan Sails the Sea

By Wolfgang Slawski

Translated by Rosemary Lanning

North-South Books

New York / London

Captain Jonathan had a peaked
cap and a smart navy-blue uniform.
He was the captain of a ship—not
a very big ship, but a sturdy little
tugboat called *Santa Maria*.

When the huge cargo ships were ready to start their voyages, Captain Jonathan's little tugboat towed them out to the open sea.

Jonathan watched wistfully as the ships steamed away over the horizon. How he wished he could go with them, across the ocean to distant lands! But he always had to turn back. There were more ships waiting to be helped on their way.

Then, one sunny day, Captain Jonathan suddenly announced, "We're not going back today. Let's sail around the world instead!"

The crew clapped and cheered. They had always wanted to see the world.

And so the *Santa Maria* steamed boldly out to sea.

Soon the bustle of the port was far behind them, and the little tugboat was the only ship to be seen out there on the great, wide ocean.

That night there was a party aboard the
Santa Maria.

The cook made a huge pot of spaghetti for
the hungry crew. The sea air had given them
all an appetite—except for Captain Jonathan.

He just stared at his plate, saying nothing.

Only Luke, the cabin boy, noticed how sad the captain looked.

"He must be homesick," Luke said. "I'll paint some pictures to cheer him up."

Luke got out his paints and brushes. He painted pictures of every ship he had ever seen, and pinned them up in the captain's cabin.

Captain Jonathan thanked Luke for the pictures, but when he looked at them, he felt even sadder than before. They reminded him of the ships he had left behind. Would they all be stuck in port, waiting for the *Santa Maria* to return?

"What we need is a bit of excitement," thought Luke.
"Something to take the captain's mind off home."

"Ship ahoy!" the lookout suddenly shouted.

A huge ocean liner loomed on the horizon.

"Full steam ahead!" cried Luke. "Let's have a race!"

It was a thrilling race, and the little tugboat just
managed to pull ahead. The crew whooped with
excitement, but Captain Jonathan didn't join in.
He looked as glum as ever.

Soon the *Santa Maria* arrived at a foreign port. "Now the captain will be happy," said Luke. "He always wanted to explore a foreign country." The people were friendly, the buildings were picturesque, but when Captain Jonathan looked around the little port, it reminded him so much of home that he couldn't bear to stay and explore.

Every day Luke thought of something new to make the captain happy, and Captain Jonathan tried very hard to look cheerful. He didn't want to spoil the trip for everyone else, but the longer he stayed away from his duties, the worse he felt.

One day Luke set up an acrobatic competition, with a prize for the highest jump. Luke bounced higher and higher until . . .

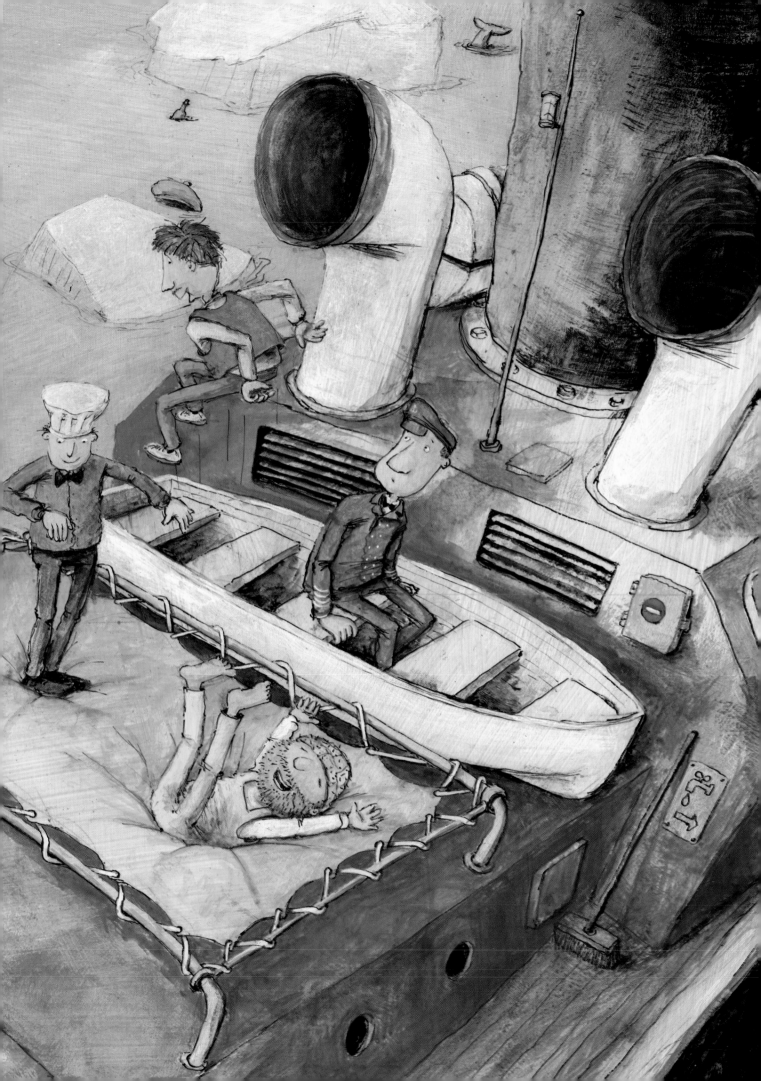

. . . a huge wave tipped the tugboat sideways and he tumbled into the sea.

"Man overboard!"
"Stop engines!"
shouted the crew.

Fast as lightning, Captain Jonathan plunged into the icy water to rescue Luke.

Make Meal Preparation Easier. Chop the vegetables into uniform-sized pieces so that everything will cook evenly. Besides that, please follow the recipes instructions because some pieces of food cook faster than others.

Never Overfill your Cooker. Don't fill your pressure cooker more than two-thirds full with ingredients. If you do not follow this rule, your cooker can not operate properly and this is important for safety reasons.

Always Use Some Liquid. Therefore, make sure to prepare some water, wine, broth or some juice. You should follow the recipe instructions, and you can freely use more liquid, but never use less liquid than recommended.

The Heat is Very Important. Therefore, start cooking over high heat for the best results. Once your cooker comes up to pressure, turn the heat to a low setting so that it maintains pressure.

How Long Do I Pressure-Cook? You can find pressure-cooking time tables on the Internet. However, each and every recipe in this cookbook contains this information and you shouldn't worry about that. You can always taste your food for the doneness, but keep in mind that it's better to undercook your meal than overcook it.

Pressure cooking is an amazingly useful way to cook old-fashioned and modern dishes for a short time and with a minimum of effort. How to find the best one? Just a little searching on the Internet will bring up a lot of information, stories, and testimonials. You can choose the size according to your personal preferences. You can purchase Conventional Pressure Cooker or Electric Pressure Cooker. However, your own experience is the best teacher. So, you can immediately purchase your pressure cooker and start cooking like a pro. However, before embarking on this extraordinary culinary experience, you should read the manufacturer's instructions thoroughly. It is extremely important to make sure to follow all safety precautions. After that, roll up your sleeves and let's get down to work!

Are You Ready for The New Fast Food?

If you are considering buying a new kitchen gadget, think twice before buying a new pot, sauté pan, or electric cooker. Instant Pot is ideal for busy households and everyone who values convenient cooking. Instant Pot will turn your ordinary meals into amazing treats for your family and guests. Enjoy trying a completely new version of your favorite recipe. These delicious recipes will show you a whole new way of cooking! And remember, great cooks are not born – you have to learn and practice. It will be easy and fun with this cookbook!

Instant Pot is a multi-functional cooker that works as a pressure cooker, steamer, slow cooker, yogurt maker, rice cooker, sauté pan, and warmer. Long story short, this is programmable pressure cooker that can replace even seven kitchen appliances! This is a new approach to cooking that has a lot of benefits.

Instant Pot saves the time and energy. The meals are cooking faster with less energy. This cooker is highly energy efficient and it has a lot of functionality. The Instant Pot saves up to seventy percent of energy. The Instant Pot is also easy to clean appliance, which makes it very suitable for everyday use. This innovative intelligent programming will save your time in the kitchen and help you to achieve the best cooking results ever! You can plan your meals with this fully automated cooking process because you can take advantage of delayed cooking.

7-in-1 Multi-Functional and kitchen friendly cooker. This power cooker will surely save your hard earned money as well as your space in the kitchen. Actually, Instant Pot has twelve buttons for the most important cooking tasks. These are Multigrain rice, Rice, Porridge, Sauté, Soup, Poultry, Beans/Chili, Slow Cook, Steam, Meat/Stew, Yogurt, and Keep Warm. As a multi-cooker, the Instant Pot keeps your kitchen organized and clean. This is very quiet piece of equipment so you will enjoy this pleasant experience.

Your meals will be healthy, nutritious and adorable. This way of cooking retains nutrients because your foods cook in a sealed environment. Pressure cooking is one of the best cooking methods for maximizing nutritional value and taste of the vegetables and fruits.

Pleasant and Safe. Instant Pot comes with stainless steel cooking pot, digital display, convenient lid bracket, stainless steel steam rack with handle, and an instruction manual. The Instant Pot is great for the summer time because it works without heating up the kitchen and surroundings. This multifunctional programmable cooker comes with nine level safety protection (e.g. pressure control, temperature control, safety valves, and fool-proof operation detection).

Check out our Instant Pot recipes and enjoy this new fast food. You will find something for everyone, from main courses and snacks to old-fashioned desserts and kid-friendly dinner recipes. Make delicious steel-cut oats for breakfast, slow cook traditional stew and grandma's soup for lunch, treat your family with fast vegetarian dinner, or make festive sweets for crowd… almost everything you could imagine. There are traditional, vegan, vegetarian recipes, and much more.

Remember – Never be afraid to try something new! Even after a lot of years of experience, we should learn new ways to improve our life. Each and every recipe contains the list of the ingredients, step-by-step directions, cooking time, and the number of servings. So, learn these handy and practical techniques to save your time in the kitchen and achieve the best cooking results. Add some "wow" factor to your old recipes! The future has arrived with Instant Pot Electric Pressure Cooker!

PRESSURE COOKER BREAKFAST RECIPES

Biscuits with Bacon Gravy

(Ready in about 15 minutes | Servings 8)

Ingredients

2 bacon strips, finely diced

1 pound sausage

1 teaspoon rosemary, chopped

1 teaspoon dried thyme, chopped

1/2 cup vegetable broth

1/4 cup wheat flour

1 ½ cups whole milk

1/2 teaspoon salt

1 teaspoon cracked black pepper

Prepared biscuits

Directions

First of all, make the sauce. Set your pressure cooker to HIGH. Then, place bacon strips and sausage in the bottom of your cooker; sauté until they are browned, approximately 7 minutes.

Sprinkle with rosemary and thyme. Pour in vegetable broth. Now securely lock the lid and set on HIGH for about 5 minutes. Now release the cooker's pressure.

In a bowl or a measuring cup, whisk the flour and milk. Add this mixture to the cooker; let simmer for 3 minutes, or until the juice has thickened.

Season with salt and black pepper. To serve, spoon the bacon gravy over prepared biscuits and enjoy.

Cheese Spoon Bread

(Ready in about 20 minutes | Servings 6)

Ingredients

1 cup whole milk

2 cups vegetable stock

2/3 cup cornmeal	2 teaspoons sugar
1 cup baking mix	1/2 teaspoon black pepper
1 cup sharp cheese, shredded	1 teaspoon salt
2 eggs	1/2 teaspoon onion powder
2 tablespoons butter, melted	1 teaspoon granulated garlic

Directions

Brush the inside of the cooker with nonstick cooking spray.

In a bowl, combine all the above components. Now add this mixture to the pressure cooker. Securely lock the lid and set for 8 minutes on LOW.

Then, leave steam valve open. Set the cooker to "Brown" and let it cook approximately 5 minutes. Turn off the heat and let stand for 5 minutes before serving.

Super Creamy Potato Salad

(Ready in about 20 minutes + chilling time | Servings 6)

Ingredients

8 small-sized red potatoes, scrubbed	1/2 teaspoon dried rosemary
1 cup water	3/4 teaspoon sea salt
1 medium-sized onion, chopped	1/4 teaspoon black pepper, freshly cracked
1 carrot, chopped	
1 stalk celery, chopped	3 whole hard-boiled eggs, chopped
1 teaspoon cayenne pepper	1/2 cup mayonnaise
	1 teaspoon apple cider vinegar

Directions

Place potatoes together with water in your pressure cooker. Then, you should cook them on high pressure for about 3 minutes. Now let steam release for 2 to 3 minutes.

Now, quickly release the pressure in order to open pressure cooker. Allow the potatoes to cool enough to handle. Peel and slice them. Place a single layer of potatoes in a bowl.

Alternate potato layers with onions, carrot, and celery layers. Sprinkle each layer with cayenne pepper, rosemary, salt, and freshly cracked black pepper. Top your salad with the eggs.

In a mixing bowl, mix together the mayonnaise and apple cider vinegar. Now fold this mayonnaise mixture into the vegetables. Allow the salad to chill in a refrigerator before serving. Serve chilled.

Protein Lentil Salad

(Ready in about 20 minutes | Servings 6)

Ingredients

1 cup dried lentils, rinsed

2 cups chicken broth

1 bay leaf

1 medium-sized carrot, diced

1 medium-sized onion, finely diced

2 tablespoons olive oil

2 tablespoons white wine

1 clove garlic, minced

2 tablespoons fresh cilantro, chopped

1/2 teaspoon dried basil

3/4 teaspoon salt

1/4 teaspoon pepper

Directions

Add lentils, chicken broth, and bay leaf to the pressure cooker.

Securely lock the lid and then, set on HIGH for 8 minutes. Remove the lid; then, drain lentils and discard the bay leaf.

Combine prepared lentils with the remaining ingredients. Serve warm or at room temperature.

Apples and Pears in Strawberry Sauce

(Ready in about 25 minutes | Servings 4)

Ingredients

2 medium-sized pears, peeled, cored, and halved

2 medium-sized apples, peeled, cored, and halved

1 cup water

1 pint strawberries

1 vanilla bean, sliced lengthwise

1/2 teaspoon grated nutmeg

1/4 teaspoon ground cardamom

1/2 cup light brown sugar

1 tablespoon cornstarch

Directions

Put all ingredients, except for brown sugar and cornstarch, into the pressure cooker. Now securely lock the pressure cooker's lid.

Set the cooker on LOW for 7 minutes. Then, remove pears and set aside.

Next, mash the strawberries with a heavy spoon. Combine the sugar and cornstarch with 1 tablespoon of water.

Now, set cooker to "Brown,"; stir in dissolved sugar-cornstarch mixture. Allow it to simmer for 3 to 5 minutes, or until strawberry sauce has thickened.

Divide the pears and apples among serving plates. Top with strawberry sauce, serve and enjoy.

Peach and Cottage Breakfast

(Ready in about 20 minutes | Servings 4)

Ingredients

4 peaches, pitted and halved

1/4 cup water

1/4 cup apple juice

1/4 teaspoon vanilla extract

2 tablespoons brown sugar

1/8 teaspoon grated nutmeg

1/4 teaspoon ground cinnamon

1 cup cottage cheese

2 tablespoons maple syrup

Directions

Add all the above ingredients, except for cottage cheese, to your pressure cooker. Securely lock the lid and cook on LOW for 4 to 5 minutes.

Release pressure, and adjust the seasonings. Remove peaches from the cooker and reserve.

Combine cottage cheese with maple syrup.

To serve: place one peach on each serving plate. Serve topped with a dollop of cheese mixture. Enjoy!

Quick and Easy Aromatic Oatmeal

(Ready in about 10 minutes | Servings 4)

Ingredients

3 tablespoons butter

1 cup steel-cut oats

3 ½ cups water

1/4 teaspoon grated nutmeg

1/2 teaspoon ground cinnamon

A pinch of salt

1/4 cup low-fat milk

1/4 cup light brown sugar

Directions

Warm butter on HIGH until melted.

Then, add the steel-cut oats, water, grated nutmeg, cinnamon, and salt. Seal the cooker's lid and cook under HIGH pressure for 5 minutes.

Next, release pressure and uncover. Add the milk and brown sugar; stir to combine and serve right away.

Fruit Steel-Cut Oats

(Ready in about 25 minutes | Servings 6)

Ingredients

1 ½ cups steel-cut oats

1/2 cup dates, chopped

1/2 cup dried currants

3 apples, cored and diced

1 teaspoon pumpkin pie spice

6 cups water

1 cup soy milk

Directions

Prepare the ingredients according to the manufacturer's directions. Then, transfer them to a pressure cooker.

Now set your cooker to HIGH and cook for 18 minutes.

Sweeten with some honey if desired. Enjoy!

Holiday Eggnog Rice Pudding

(Ready in about 15 minutes | Servings 6)

Ingredients

2 tablespoons butter

2 cups water

1 cup rice

1/2 teaspoon rum extract

1/4 teaspoon ground cinnamon

1 ½ cups eggnog

1/4 cup honey

Directions

First of all, warm butter on HIGH or "Brown,".

Add the water, rice, rum extract, and cinnamon. Then, lock the pressure cooker's lid and set to 7 minutes on HIGH. Now release the cooker's pressure.

Stir in eggnog and honey; divide among serving plates and serve.

Apricot and Almond Bread Pudding

(Ready in about 45 minutes | Servings 8)

Ingredients

Non-stick cooking spray

6 cups stale bread chunks

1 cup apricots, pitted and chopped

1/3 cup almonds, chopped

5 whole eggs

1 ½ cups whole milk

1/2 cup heavy cream

1/2 cup sugar

3 tablespoons butter, melted

1 tablespoon flour

1 teaspoon vanilla extract

1/8 teaspoon cardamom

1/4 teaspoon ground cinnamon

Directions

Coat cake pans with cooking spray. Then, add the bread, apricots, and almonds to the pans and toss to combine.

In a mixing bowl, whisk together the rest of the above ingredients; pour this mixture over top of the bread mixture in the pans; press the bread mixture down to saturate. Allow it to sit for about 10 minutes.

Place a metal rack at the bottom of a pressure cooker. Pour in 2 cups of water. Cover cake pans with an aluminum foil; then, place them on the metal rack.

Now set the cooker to HIGH for 25 minutes. Let the pressure release for 10 minutes. Allow bread pudding to rest 10 to 15 minutes before serving.

Date and Walnut Bread Pudding

(Ready in about 45 minutes | Servings 8)

Ingredients

5 cups stale bread chunks

1 cup dates, pitted and chopped

1/3 cup walnuts, chopped

5 whole eggs

2 cups whole milk

1/4 cup honey

3 tablespoons butter, melted

1 tablespoon flour

1/42 teaspoon ground cinnamon

1/2 teaspoon almond extract

Directions

Brush your cake pans with non-stick cooking spray. Toss together bread chunks, dates and walnuts, and drop them into the pans.

In a bowl, combine together the remaining ingredients; add the mixture to the pans. Let it soak for about 10 minutes.

Place a trivet at the bottom of your pressure cooker. Then, pour in 2 cups of water. Cover the pans with a foil and place them on the trivet.

Set the cooker to HIGH for 25 minutes. Serve warm or at room temperature.

Banana and Cranberry Croissant Pudding

(Ready in about 45 minutes | Servings 8)

Ingredients

6 cups croissants, torn into pieces

1/2 cup dried bananas, chopped

1/2 cup dried cranberries

5 large eggs

1 ½ cups milk

1/2 cup heavy cream

1/2 cup sugar

2 tablespoons butter, melted

1/4 teaspoon grated nutmeg

1/2 teaspoon ground cinnamon

Directions

Brush a soufflé dish with non-stick cooking spray.

In a bowl, combine together torn croissants, dried bananas, and cranberries; toss to combine. Then, add this croissants mixture to the soufflé dish.

In a bowl, combine together the remaining ingredients; stir to combine. Let it soak for 10 minutes.

Lay a trivet at the bottom of a cooker. Pour 2 cups of water to create a water bath. Cover the dish with a foil, and place on trivet in the cooker. Bring to HIGH pressure and cook for 25 minutes.

Release pressure and allow your pudding to rest for 10 minutes before serving.

Healthy Strawberry Jam

(Ready in about 1 hour 20 minutes | Servings 16)

Ingredients

2 pounds strawberries, hulled and halved

1 vanilla bean, halved lengthwise

1 ½ pounds honey

Directions

Put all the above ingredients into the pressure cooker. Then, place the uncovered cooker over medium-high heat, bringing it to a boil; make sure to stir frequently.

Now lock the cooker's lid into place and bring it to pressure. After that, lower the heat to medium-low for 10 minutes. Take your pressure cooker off the heat; allow pressure to release naturally.

Uncover the cooker and place it back on medium-high heat; bring to a boil for about 4 minutes, stirring constantly.

Spoon the jam into hot sterilized jars. Seal the jars properly. Serve with your favorite biscuits. Enjoy!

Breakfast Dessert Oatmeal

(Ready in about 15 minutes | Servings 2)

Ingredients

3⁄4 cup water

1 cup coconut milk

1 cup quick-cooking oats

2 pears, peeled, cored, and diced

1/2 teaspoon vanilla essence

1/2 teaspoon cardamom

1 teaspoon ground cinnamon

2 tablespoons almonds, chopped

Directions

Put all of the above ingredients into your pressure cooker. Now lock the lid. Bring to HIGH pressure and maintain for 5 to 6 minutes.

Remove the cooker from the heat; allow pressure to release gradually.

Serve with some extra milk if desired.

Banana Pecan Oatmeal

(Ready in about 10 minutes | Servings 2)

Ingredients

3⁄4 cup water

1 cup soymilk

1 cup toasted quick-cooking oats

2 bananas, sliced

1/4 cup golden raisins

2 tablespoons honey

2 teaspoons cinnamon

2 tablespoons pecans, chopped

Directions

Drop all of the ingredients into the cooker.

Lock the lid. Bring it to HIGH pressure and maintain for about 5 minutes. Remove from the heat and bring pressure down

Uncover and stir the mixture. Serve with some extra dried fruits or milk if desired.

Vegan Cranberry Oatmeal

(Ready in about 15 minutes | Servings 2)

Ingredients

3 cups water

1 cup steel-cut oats

2 teaspoons vegan margarine

1 cup apple juice

4 tablespoons dried cranberries

1-2 tablespoons brown sugar

1/4 teaspoon cardamom

1⁄4 teaspoon ground cinnamon

Directions

Place a metal rack in the pressure cooker; pour in 1⁄2 cup of water.

Add all the above ingredients to a metal bowl that fits inside the pressure cooker. Stir to combine.

Cover and bring to LOW pressure. Then, maintain pressure for 8 minutes.

Next, allow pressure to release naturally. Serve right away!

Maple Apple Oatmeal

(Ready in about 15 minutes | Servings 2)

Ingredients

3⁄4 cup water

1 cup milk

2 tablespoons dried apricots

1 apple, cored and diced

1 cup toasted quick-cooking oats

2 tablespoons maple syrup

2 tablespoons walnuts, chopped

Directions

Simply throw all the above ingredients into your pressure cooker.

Now lock the lid into place. Then, maintain HIGH pressure for 5 minutes.

Next, remove the cooker from the heat; allow pressure to release. Serve right now and enjoy!

Sausage Breakfast Casserole

(Ready in about 15 minutes | Servings 4)

Ingredients

2 tablespoons canola oil

1 yellow onion, diced

1 small-sized red bell pepper, seeded and chopped

1/2 pound sausage

3 cups potatoes, shredded

6 eggs, beaten

1 cup Ricotta cheese

2 cups Cheddar cheese

3/4 teaspoon salt

1/4 teaspoon ground black pepper

Directions

Warm canola oil in the pressure cooker; now sauté the onion and bell pepper until they are tender. Add the sausage and cook for about 3 more minutes.

Add the remaining ingredients to the pressure cooker. Lock the lid into place; then, maintain HIGH pressure for about 5 minutes.

Remove from the heat. Serve warm and enjoy!

Mom's Berry Jam

(Ready in about 1 hour 20 minutes | Servings 16)

Ingredients

1 pound raspberries

1 pound blackberries

1 vanilla bean, halved lengthwise

1 ½ pounds honey

Directions

Throw all the above ingredients into your pressure cooker. Now place the cooker over medium-high heat, bring it to a boil; stir often.

Cover and bring it to pressure. Next, lower the heat to medium-low for 10 minutes. Allow pressure to release naturally.

Uncover the pressure cooker and place it back on medium-high heat; bring to a boil for 4 to 5 minutes, stirring frequently.

Lastly, ladle your jam into hot sterilized jars. Seal the jars. Serve with English muffins if desired. Enjoy!

Old-Fashioned Grits

(Ready in about 15 minutes | Servings 4)

Ingredients

4 cups water

A pinch of salt

1/4 teaspoon grated nutmeg

1 cup stone-ground grits

1 tablespoon ghee

Directions

Bring the water, salt, and nutmeg to a boil in your pressure cooker over HIGH heat.

Gradually stir in the grits and lock the lid into place. Bring to high pressure over high heat; maintain pressure for 10 minutes.

Allow steam to release naturally. Lastly, stir in ghee just before serving. Serve and enjoy!

Winter Spiced Grits

(Ready in about 15 minutes | Servings 4)

Ingredients

2 cups water

2 cups vegetable broth

A pinch of salt

1/4 teaspoon dried thyme

1 cup grits

1/2 tablespoon cayenne pepper

Directions

Bring the water, vegetable broth, salt, and thyme to a boil in your pressure cooker over HIGH heat.

Slowly add the grits to the cooker. Put the lid on and bring to pressure over high heat; maintain pressure for about 10 minutes.

Cool down and remove the lid. Divide the grits among four serving plates; sprinkle with cayenne pepper and serve.

Breakfast Hash Browns

(Ready in about 15 minutes | Servings 4)

Ingredients

2 tablespoons vegetable oil

2 tablespoons margarine

6 russet potatoes, peeled and grated

1/2 teaspoon paprika

3/4 teaspoon sea salt

1/4 teaspoon freshly ground black pepper

Directions

Warm vegetable oil and margarine in the pressure cooker over medium heat.

Add the russet potatoes to the pressure cooker. Then, cook for 5 minutes, stirring periodically, until the potatoes are just browned. Season with paprika, salt, and black pepper.

Next, press the potatoes down firmly with a wide metal spatula.

Cover the cooker and bring it to LOW pressure; maintain pressure for about 6 minutes. Afterwards, quick-release the pressure. Serve warm.

Hash Browns with Sausage and Apples

(Ready in about 20 minutes | Servings 4)

Ingredients

3 tablespoons butter

1 (12-ounce) bag frozen hash brown potatoes

3/4 teaspoon sea salt

1/4 teaspoon freshly ground black pepper

6 ounces cooked sausage, chopped

2 apples, sliced

1 tablespoon maple syrup

1 teaspoon granulated garlic

Directions

Add the butter to the pressure cooker and warm it over medium heat.

Add the hash brown potatoes and cook for about 5 minutes, stirring occasionally. Season with the salt and black pepper.

Use a wide spatula to press the potatoes down. Add the chopped sausage and apples. Then, drizzle with the maple syrup and sprinkle with granulated garlic.

Now lock the lid in place and bring to low pressure for 6 minutes. Afterwards, quick-release the pressure. Divide among four serving plates and serve.

Bacon Hash Browns

(Ready in about 20 minutes | Servings 4)

Ingredients

2 tablespoons canola oil

1 pound russet potatoes, peeled

2 tablespoons fresh chopped parsley

2 cups crumbled bacon

3/4 teaspoon kosher salt

1/2 teaspoon freshly ground black pepper

Toast, for serving

Directions

Warm canola oil over medium heat in the pressure cooker. Add the potatoes to the pressure cooker.

Sauté for 5 to 6 minutes, stirring occasionally, until they are browned.

Add the parsley, bacon, salt, and black pepper. Mix well to combine. Then, press the potatoes down with a wide spatula.

Cover the pressure cooker and bring it to low pressure; cook for 6 to 7 minutes. Now remove from the heat; quick-release the pressure, and serve with toast.

Saucy Morning Ham

(Ready in about 20 minutes | Servings 4)

Ingredients

1 tablespoon lard

4 slices ham

3/4 cup coffee

1 tablespoon sugar

Directions

Heat the lard in a pressure cooker. Stir in the ham slices and fry them for 2 minutes on both sides. Pour in the coffee.

Lock the lid into place. Then, bring to low pressure; maintain for 7 to 8 minutes. Now quick-release the pressure. Remove prepared ham to the plates.

Add the sugar to the pan; stir until it dissolves. Pour dissolved sugar over the ham. Serve with fresh fruit juice if desired and enjoy!

French-Style Vegetarian Sandwiches

(Ready in about 30 minutes | Servings 6)

Ingredients

1 (13-ounce) package tempeh, cut into strips

3 cups vegetables broth

3 cups water

2-3 green garlics, minced

1 cup soy sauce

2 tablespoons canola oil

1 red onion, sliced

1 small-sized bell pepper, sliced

Salt and pepper, to taste

6 French rolls

6 slices Mozzarella cheese

Directions

Add the tempeh, vegetable broth, water, green garlic, and soy sauce to your pressure cooker. After that, lock the lid into place; bring to HIGH pressure approximately 20 minutes. Then, quick-release the pressure. Reserve the tempeh.

Warm canola oil in a saucepan; sauté the onion and bell pepper until they are softened and caramelized. Add the tempeh, salt, and black pepper.

Preheat your oven to 450 degrees F. Now divide prepared mixture among 6 French rolls. Add Mozzarella cheese. Bake your sandwiches in the preheated oven for about 5 minutes, or until Mozzarella slices have melted. Serve right away and enjoy!

Pumpkin Steel Cut Oats

(Ready in about 20 minutes | Servings 6)

Ingredients

1 tablespoon butter

1 cup steel-cut oats

3 cups water

1 cup pumpkin puree

1/4 cup honey

1/2 teaspoon cardamom

1 teaspoon cinnamon

1/4 teaspoon grated nutmeg

A pinch of salt

Directions

Select 'Sauté' and warm the butter in your pressure cooking pot until it's melted. Now add the oats; toast the oats, stirring often, about 3 minutes.

Add the rest of the above ingredients. Select HIGH pressure and maintain it for 10 minutes.

After that, release the pressure for 10 minutes. Then, carefully remove the cooker's lid.

Serve warm with some extra milk if desired. Enjoy!

Smoky Tofu Sandwiches

(Ready in about 20 minutes | Servings 6)

Ingredients

1 (16-ounce) package firm tofu, crumbled

1/4 cup mustard

3⁄4 cup brown sugar

1⁄4 cup water

3⁄4 cup apple cider vinegar

1 tablespoon chili powder

1 tablespoon soy sauce

1 teaspoon smoked paprika

2 tablespoons butter

A few drops of liquid smoke

1/2 teaspoon salt

1/4 teaspoon black pepper

6 burger buns

Directions

Press the tofu for 5 minutes. Then, crumble the tofu and transfer to the pressure cooker.

In a bowl, whisk the rest of the ingredients, except for buns. Now pour the mustard mixture into the pressure cooker.

Lock the lid into place, and bring to HIGH pressure; maintain for 5 minutes. Use a natural pressure release. Serve with your burger buns.

Quick and Easy Hard-Boiled Eggs

(Ready in about 40 minutes | Servings 6)

Ingredients

2 cups water

8 eggs

4 cups cold water

Directions

Fill a pressure cooker with the water according to the manufacturer's directions. Put the eggs into the steamer basket above the water. Now seal the lid. Bring the pressure cooker to LOW pressure.

Cook for about 6 minutes. Then, allow the pressure to drop for 5 minutes.

Replace the hot eggs to the cold water. Allow the eggs to cool completely. Serve.

Chia and Raspberry Oatmeal

(Ready in about 25 minutes | Servings 4)

Ingredients

1 tablespoon ghee

1 cup steel-cut oats

3 cups water

1/2 cup heavy cream

2 tablespoons maple syrup

1/4 teaspoon kosher salt

1 cup raspberries

1/4 cup chia seeds

Directions

Add ghee to pressure cooking pot, and select "Sauté"; warm ghee and add steel-cut oats. Toast the steel-cut oats until they smell nutty, or 3 to 4 minutes.

Add water, cream, maple syrup, and kosher salt. Select HIGH pressure and cook for 10 minutes. After that, turn off pressure cooker; gradually release the pressure.

Stir in raspberries and chia seeds. Then, let sit until your oatmeal reaches desired thickness. Serve with a splash of milk if desired.

Coconut and Chili Tofu

(Ready in about 25 minutes | Servings 6)

Ingredients

1 (16-ounce) package firm tofu

2 green chilies, seeded and minced

2 green garlics, finely chopped

4 green onions, chopped

1 tablespoon soy sauce

1/2 cup fresh cilantro, chopped

2 tablespoons water

2 tablespoons olive oil

1 (13-ounce) can coconut milk

Salt and pepper, to taste

4 cups hot cooked rice

Directions

Wrap the tofu in the paper towels and press for 10 minutes. Then, cut the tofu into pieces.

In your food processor, puree green chilies, green garlic, green onions, soy sauce, cilantro, and water. Puree until you get a smooth paste; add extra water as needed.

Warm the oil in the pressure cooker; sauté the tofu pieces until they are lightly browned. Now add the coconut milk and the prepared chili paste.

Select HIGH pressure and maintain it for 5 minutes. Turn off pressure cooker and allow pressure to release gradually and naturally. Sprinkle with salt and black pepper, as needed. Serve over hot cooked rice.

Sweet and Spicy Tofu

(Ready in about 15 minutes | Servings 4)

Ingredients

1 (16-ounce) package extra-firm tofu

2 cups water

2 tablespoons cornstarch

2 scallions, minced

1 teaspoon ginger, minced

1/4 cup soy sauce

2 tablespoons maple syrup

1/4 cup sherry wine

2 teaspoons paprika

2 tablespoons canola oil

2 cups broccoli, blanched and chopped

Directions

First of all, press the tofu for about 5 minutes by adding weight on top. Cut into chunks.

To make the sauce: In a bowl, whisk together 1 cup water, cornstarch, scallions, ginger, soy sauce, maple syrup, sherry wine, and paprika. Set aside.

Heat canola oil in your pressure cooker; now sauté the tofu until it is browned on all sides. Add the blanched broccoli and continue sautéing for 1 minute more. Add the reserved sauce. Season to taste.

Cover and bring to HIGH pressure; maintain for 5 minutes. Afterwards, turn off pressure cooker and allow pressure to release naturally. Serve with quinoa if desired.

Coconut and Pumpkin Oatmeal

(Ready in about 20 minutes | Servings 4)

Ingredients

1 tablespoon vegan margarine

1 cup steel-cut oats

2 cups water

1 cup coconut water

1 cup pumpkin puree

1/4 cup maple syrup

1 teaspoon cinnamon

1/4 teaspoon grated nutmeg

A pinch of salt

Coconut shreds, as garnish

Directions

First, melt the vegan margarine in a pressure cooker. Next, add steel-cut oats and toast them, stirring constantly, for about 3 minutes.

Add the remaining ingredients, except for coconut. Select HIGH pressure and cook for 10 minutes.

Next, release the pressure for 10 minutes. Afterwards, remove the cooker's lid.

Serve warm sprinkled with coconut shreds. Enjoy!

Family Grape Jelly

(Ready in about 15 minutes | Servings 12)

Ingredients

5 cups grape juice

2 (1 3⁄4-ounce) packages dry pectin

1⁄2 cup sugar

Directions

Add grape juice and pectin to your pressure cooking pot; bring to medium-high heat.

Lock the cooker's lid and maintain HIGH pressure for 1 minute. Remove from the heat and remove the lid. Add the sugar and stir to combine.

Now discard any foam. Replace your jelly to hot sterilized glass containers. Seal the containers and allow them to cool at room temperature.

Serve with peanut butter if desired.

Everyday Tomato Chutney

(Ready in about 15 minutes | Servings 12)

Ingredients

4 pounds tomatoes, peeled

2 red onions, peeled and diced

3 cloves garlic, peeled and minced

1 ¾ cups white sugar

1 cup wine vinegar

1⁄4 cup raisins

1⁄2 teaspoon ground coriander

1⁄4 teaspoon ground cloves

1 teaspoon ground ginger

1 teaspoon chili powder

1 tablespoon curry paste

Directions

In a food processor or blender, purée the tomatoes.

Add the puréed tomatoes to the pressure cooker. Stir in the rest of the above ingredients. Stir to combine, lock the lid, and cook at LOW pressure for 10 minutes.

Afterwards, turn off pressure cooker. Let pressure release naturally. Serve chilled over flat bread and enjoy.

Green Tomato Chutney

(Ready in about 15 minutes | Servings 12)

Ingredients

2 pounds green tomatoes, diced	1⁄4 cup dried cherries
2 garlic cloves, peeled and minced	1 tablespoon fresh ginger, grated
1 leek, thinly sliced	3⁄4 cup brown sugar
1 jalapeño pepper, minced	3⁄4 cup white wine
2 bell peppers, diced	3/4 teaspoon sea salt

Directions

Put all ingredients into the pressure cooking pot; stir to combine well. Cook on LOW pressure for 10 minutes. Remove from the heat and allow pressure to release gradually.

Place in a refrigerator before serving. You can spread your chutney over pizza crust if desired. Keep in your refrigerator for 2 months. Enjoy!

Homemade Peach Jam

(Ready in about 10 minutes | Servings 20)

Ingredients

4 cups peaches, pitted, peeled and chopped	1 teaspoon lemon juice
4 cups sugar	1 (1 3⁄4-ounce) package dry pectin
1 teaspoon orange juice	

Directions

Add the peaches, sugar, orange juice, and lemon juice to the pressure cooking pot. Stir until the ingredients are well combined.

Bring to low pressure and maintain pressure for 3 minutes. Remove from the heat and allow pressure to release.

Uncover and place over medium-high heat. Then, stir in the pectin; bring mixture to a boil, stirring often, for 1 minute.

Spoon into the sterilized glass containers. Keep in the freezer for up to 8 months.

Fruit Breakfast Risotto

(Ready in about 15 minutes | Servings 4)

Ingredients

2 tablespoons margarine

1 ½ cups rice

1 large apple, cored and diced

1 large pear, cored and diced

1/2 teaspoon cinnamon

1/8 teaspoon grated nutmeg

1/8 teaspoon salt

1/3 cup brown sugar

1 cup apple juice

3 cups milk

1/2 cup dried cranberries

Directions

Melt the margarine in the pressure cooking pot for about 3 minutes. Add rice to the cooker; cook, stirring frequently, approximately 4 minutes.

Add the apple, pear, cinnamon, nutmeg, salt, and brown sugar. Add the apple juice and milk. Select HIGH pressure and cook 6 minutes. Then, turn off your cooker and use a quick pressure release.

Afterwards, stir in dried cranberries. Serve topped with a splash of milk if desired.

Sunday Bread Pudding with Cherries

(Ready in about 25 minutes | Servings 4)

Ingredients

5 cups bread chunks

1 cup dried cherries

2 cups evaporated milk

2 whole eggs

1 egg yolk

1/4 cup sugar

1/4 teaspoon allspice

1/4 teaspoon ground cinnamon

1/2 tablespoon butter

2 ½ cups water

Directions

Fill a metal baking dish with bread chunks. Then, add dried cherries and toss to combine.

In a mixing bowl, combine the milk, eggs, sugar, allspice, and cinnamon. Combine until it becomes frothy. Pour this custard mixture over bread-cherry mixture. Push the bread down.

Spread butter on an aluminum foil. Cover dish with the foil, butter side down; make sure to wrap tightly.

Add water to pressure cooker. Lay baking dish on a cooking rack in your pressure cooker. Allow it to cook about 15 minutes at 15 pounds pressure. Remove foil and serve warm.

Fig and Walnut Bread Pudding

(Ready in about 25 minutes | Servings 6)

Ingredients

2 tablespoons butter

4 slices day-old bread, crusts trimmed and cubed

1/2 cup dried figs, chopped

1/2 cup walnuts, chopped

1/2 cup packed light brown sugar

1/2 teaspoon ground cinnamon

1/4 teaspoon grated nutmeg

A pinch of salt

2 cups warm milk

2 eggs, beaten

3 cups water

Directions

Butter a soufflé dish that fits into your pressure cooker.

In a mixing bowl, combine the bread cubes, chopped dried figs and walnuts. In a separate mixing bowl, combine together the sugar, cinnamon, nutmeg, salt, milk, and eggs.

Pour the wet mixture into the bread mixture; stir to combine well; transfer the mixture to the prepared soufflé dish. Cover your soufflé dish with an aluminum foil.

Now pour the water into your cooker. Put the soufflé dish into the cooker steamer basket. Lock the lid in place; bring to pressure and cook for 20 minutes under HIGH pressure. Remove the lid and serve warm.

Grandma's Sweet Cornbread

(Ready in about 30 minutes | Servings 8)

Ingredients

2/3 cup flour

1 1/3 cups cornmeal

1/4 cup brown sugar

1 teaspoon baking soda

2 teaspoons baking powder

1 teaspoon kosher salt

1/2 stick butter, room temperature

1 cup buttermilk

2 whole eggs

Directions

In a mixing bowl, sift the flours; add sugar, baking soda, baking powder, and salt. Mix to combine well.

In a separate bowl, whisk together the remaining ingredients.

Add dry mixture to the wet mixture, mixing well.

Pour your batter into a greased pan. Cover with a glass lid. Place the pan inside the pressure cooker, in a steamer basket.

Pour about 2/3 cup of water into the bottom of your cooker. Lock the lid, and bring to HIGH pressure. When the pressure is reached, reduce temperature to lowest setting, and cook for about 22 minutes.

Lastly, carefully open the lid; transfer your cornbread to a wire rack to cool for 5 minutes before serving.

Morning Sausage with Gravy

(Ready in about 20 minutes | Servings 8)

Ingredients

2 pounds sausage

2 tablespoons lard

1/4 cup flour

2 cups half-and-half

3/4 teaspoon sea salt

1/4 teaspoon freshly ground black pepper

Directions

Stir the sausage into your pressure cooker. Now fry over medium-high heat for 5 minutes.

Lock the lid into place; bring to LOW pressure and maintain for 8 minutes. Then, quick-release the pressure.

Return the pressure cooker to medium-high heat. Add the lard and cook until it is melted.

Sprinkle the flour and cook, stirring continuously. Whisk in the half-and-half, stirring continuously. Bring to a boil.

Now reduce the heat and simmer for about 3 minutes or until the gravy has thickened. Season with salt and pepper. Serve warm with buttermilk biscuits if desired.

Sausage and Corn Delight

(Ready in about 20 minutes | Servings 4)

Ingredients

1 pound sausage links

1 medium onion, peeled and diced

2 green garlic, sliced

4 potatoes, peeled and sliced

1 (16-ounce) can corn

3/4 cup tomato paste

Salt and black pepper, to taste

Directions

Add the sausage to your cooker; brown the sausage over medium flame. Reserve.

Lay the onion, green garlic, potatoes, and corn in the bottom of the cooker. Place reserved browned sausage on top of the corn in the cooker.

Pour the tomato paste over the layers in the pressure cooker. Lock the lid; then, bring to HIGH pressure, and maintain for about 7 minutes.

Season with salt and pepper to taste. Lastly, allow to sit for about 10 minutes.

Delicious Sausage with Veggies

(Ready in about 20 minutes | Servings 6)

Ingredients

1 ½ pounds pork sausage

1 cup shallots, sliced

4 potatoes, peeled and sliced

1 red bell pepper, seeded and sliced

1 yellow bell pepper, seeded and sliced

3/4 cup tomato paste

1/2 teaspoon granulated garlic

Salt and black pepper, to taste

Directions

Throw pork sausage into your cooker; then, sauté the sausage for 4 to 5 minutes. Set sautéed sausage aside.

Place the shallots, potatoes, and bell peppers in the bottom of the pressure cooker. Top with the prepared sausage.

Pour the tomato paste into the pressure cooker. Sprinkle with granulated garlic, salt, and black pepper. Lock the lid; then, bring to HIGH pressure, and cook for about 7 minutes.

Let it rest for about 10 minutes before serving. Serve and enjoy!

Country Cornmeal Mush

(Ready in about 20 minutes | Servings 6)

Ingredients

4 cups water

1 cup cornmeal

3/4 teaspoon kosher salt

2 tablespoons butter

Directions

In a mixing bowl, whisk together 1 cup water, cornmeal, and kosher salt.

Pour the remaining 3 cups of water into your pressure cooker. Bring to a boil. Then, stir cornmeal mixture into the boiling water.

Add butter to the cooker and stir frequently. Lock the lid into place. Bring to LOW pressure and cook for 10 minutes.

Then, quick-release the pressure. Serve warm with your favorite milk.

Yummy Sesame Congee

(Ready in about 40 minutes | Servings 8)

Ingredients

12 cups water

2 cups brown rice

3-4 cloves garlic, peeled and minced

1 large-sized shallot, finely chopped

2 tablespoons mirin

2 tablespoons toasted sesame seeds

3/4 teaspoon salt

1/4 teaspoon freshly cracked black pepper

Directions

Throw 10 cups of water together with brown rice into your pressure cooker. Then, cook for 25 minutes on HIGH; allow pressure to release naturally.

Next, stir in the rest of the above ingredients; continue cooking until the flavors have married, or approximately 15 minutes.

Serve with sliced cucumber and avocado if desired. Enjoy!

Scallion Rice Porridge

(Ready in about 40 minutes | Servings 8)

Ingredients

2 cups long-grain rice

10 cups water

3-4 scallions, finely chopped

3 slices fresh ginger

2 tablespoons sesame oil

1/2 teaspoon ground black pepper

3/4 teaspoon sea salt

Directions

Add long-grain rice to your pressure cooker. Pour in the water and cook for about 25 minutes on HIGH; then, allow pressure to release.

Add the remaining ingredients; continue cooking for 10 to 15 minutes or until the scallions have softened.

Serve sprinkled with fresh chopped chives and enjoy!

Chocolate and Raisin Bread Pudding

(Ready in about 35 minutes | Servings 8)

Ingredients

1/2 cup golden raisins

1/4 cup brandy

1 ½ cups milk

3/4 cup heavy cream

3/4 cup bittersweet chocolate pieces

6 tablespoons sugar

1 whole egg

3 large-sized egg yolks

A pinch of salt

6 cups bread, torn into pieces

1 tablespoon butter

Directions

In a small-sized mixing bowl, combine raisins and brandy; let soak overnight, at room temperature.

Press "Warm" and set the timer to 10 minutes. Pour the milk and heavy cream into your cooker; bring just to a boil. Remove the pot from your cooker.

Stir in the chocolate pieces and 2 tablespoons of sugar. Stir with a spoon until chocolate is completely melted.

In a separate mixing bowl, whisk together the eggs and the remaining 4 tablespoons of sugar. Then, whisk in cooled chocolate mixture; add the salt; add the soaked raisins.

Add bread pieces and stir to combine using a large spoon. Butter a cake pan.

Transfer prepared mixture to the cake pan. Place a rack in the bottom of the pot; add 2 cups water. Place the cake pan on the rack and lock lid in place. Next, set the timer to 20 minutes.

Allow the pressure to release gradually and naturally. Serve warm and enjoy!

Veggie and Wheat Berry Salad

(Ready in about 35 minutes | Servings 8)

Ingredients

2 tablespoons margarine	1 small-sized onion, peeled and diced
6 ¾ cups water	1 1/3 cups frozen peas, thawed
1 ½ cups wheat berries	1 bell pepper, peeled, grated, and drained
1 teaspoon sugar	1 large-sized carrot, chopped
1/2 teaspoon freshly ground black pepper	2 stalks celery, finely diced
1 teaspoon sea salt	1 red bell pepper, seeded and diced
1/4 cup apple cider vinegar	1/4 cup sun-dried tomatoes, diced
1/2 cup olive oil	1/4 cup fresh parsley, chopped

Directions

Add the margarine, water, and wheat berries to your pressure cooker. Lock the lid into place; bring to HIGH pressure and maintain pressure for 50 minutes. Now quick-release the pressure.

Make the dressing by processing the sugar, black pepper, salt, apple cider vinegar, olive oil, and onion in a blender.

Toss prepared wheat berries with remaining ingredients. Dress the salad and refrigerate for up to 3 days.

Bean and Cherry Salad

(Ready in about 35 minutes + chilling time | Servings 12)

Ingredients

Water

2 cups dried cannellini beans

1 teaspoon lemon zest

3 tablespoons sherry vinegar

2 tablespoons tamari sauce

2 teaspoons honey

1 teaspoon chili paste

2 cloves garlic, peeled and minced

2 teaspoons sesame oil

1 cup frozen corn kernels, thawed

1 cup frozen peas, thawed

3 carrots, thinly sliced

1 medium zucchini, peeled, grated, and drained

3/4 cup dried cranberries

3 green onions, peeled and diced

Salt and freshly cracked black pepper, to taste

Directions

Place water and beans in a bowl. Let it soak overnight.

Now prepare the dressing by whisking lemon zest, sherry vinegar, tamari sauce, honey, chili paste, garlic, and sesame oil. Refrigerate the dressing overnight.

Drain the beans and cook them in your pressure cooker along with 3 cups of water for 25 minutes. Remove the cooker from the heat and allow pressure to release.

Next, drain cooked beans and transfer them to a bowl. Toss the beans with the rest of the above ingredients. Drizzle with chilled dressing. Taste and adjust the seasonings. Serve.

FAST SNACKS RECIPES

Hummus with Pita Chips

(Ready in about 1 hour | Servings 16)

Ingredients

1 cup chickpeas

2 teaspoons canola oil

4 cups water

1 tablespoon fresh cilantro

1 teaspoon dried parsley

2 cloves garlic, peeled and minced

2 tablespoons tahini

1/4 teaspoon dried spearmint

3/4 teaspoon salt, to taste

2 tablespoons lemon juice

1/4 cup sesame oil

Pita chips, for garnish

Directions

Add the chickpeas, canola oil, and 4 cups of water to your cooker. Cover and bring to HIGH pressure; maintain for 40 minutes. Then, allow pressure to release naturally.

Uncover, drain the chickpeas and cook on HIGH pressure for an additional 10 minutes.

Add the prepared chickpeas to your food processor (or a blender). Now stir in cilantro, parsley, garlic, tahini, spearmint, salt, and lemon juice. Pulse until everything is well combined. Make sure to scrape down the sides of the food processor bowl.

Lastly, add the sesame oil with the machine running and pulse until it is smooth. Serve with pita chips and enjoy!

Fastest-Ever Corn Cobs

(Ready in about 10 minutes | Servings 6)

Ingredients

3 cups water

6 ears sweet corn cobs, halved

Directions

Pour the water into your pressure cooker; insert the steamer basket.

Place the corn cobs in the steamer basket.

Seal the lid. Set the timer to 2 minutes under HIGH pressure. Run the cooker under cold water. Serve warm.

Traditional Baba Ghanoush

(Ready in about 15 minutes | Servings 16)

Ingredients

1 tablespoon sesame oil	3/4 teaspoon salt
1 large-sized eggplant, peeled and diced	Cracked black pepper, to taste
5 cloves garlic, finely minced	1 tablespoon lemon juice
1/2 cup water	2 tablespoons tahini
3 tablespoons fresh cilantro	1 tablespoon olive oil

Directions

Add the sesame oil to the pressure cooker; heat over medium heat. Stir in the eggplant. Sauté the eggplant until it is tender. Add the garlic; sauté for 30 seconds more.

Pour in the water, and lock the lid. Bring to HIGH pressure; maintain pressure for 4 to 5 minutes. Then, quick-release the pressure, and uncover.

Add the eggplant mixture to a food processor along with the cilantro, salt, black pepper, lemon juice, and tahini. Process it, scraping down the sides of the container.

Add the olive oil and process until smooth. Transfer to a serving bowl. Serve with your favorite pita wedges or veggie sticks.

Artichoke and Spinach Dip

(Ready in about 15 minutes | Servings 12)

Ingredients

2 cups canned artichoke hearts, coarsely chopped

1 ½ cups frozen chopped spinach, thawed and well drained

1/2 cup sour cream

1/2 cup mayonnaise

1 ½ cups mozzarella cheese, shredded

1/2 teaspoon paprika

Sea salt and ground black pepper, to taste

Directions

Combine all the ingredients together in a baking dish that fits in the pressure cooking pot. Cover it tightly with a foil. Make sure to prepare a foil sling.

Place the rack at the bottom of the cooker. Pour about 2 cups of water into the cooker. Place the baking dish on the rack.

Seal the lid and select HIGH pressure for 10 minutes. After that, turn off the cooker; use a quick pressure release; then, carefully remove the lid.

Serve warm with tortilla chips if desired. Enjoy!

Amazing Steamed Artichokes

(Ready in about 10 minutes | Servings 6)

Ingredients

3 medium artichokes

1 medium-sized lemon, halved

1 teaspoon yellow mustard

3 tablespoons mayonnaise

1/2 teaspoon cayenne pepper

Salt and ground black pepper, to taste

Directions

Pour 1 cup of water into the pressure cooker. Now place the steamer basket in your cooker. Add the artichokes; drizzle with lemon.

Close the lid and turn the heat to HIGH; Cook for 10 minutes at high pressure.

Then, open the pressure cooker with the natural release method. Check for the doneness. If it is not done, cook for an additional few minutes.

Then, make the sauce. In a mixing bowl, combine the mustard together with mayonnaise, cayenne pepper, salt, and black pepper. Serve with prepared artichokes. Serve warm.

Bacon and Bean Dip

(Ready in about 30 minutes | Servings 12)

Ingredients

2 cups water

1 cup dried beans

4 slices bacon, finely diced

2 cloves garlic, peeled and minced

1 onion, peeled and diced

1 (14 ½-ounce) can tomatoes, diced

2 teaspoons chili powder

1/2 teaspoon dried basil

Sea salt and black pepper, to taste

1/4 cup fresh parsley, finely chopped

1 cup sharp cheese, grated

Avocado slices, for garnish

Directions

Add the water and beans to a container and let it soak overnight. Drain the beans and set aside.

Throw the bacon, garlic, and onion into your cooker. Sauté for 3 to 4 minutes or until the onions are translucent.

Then, stir the beans into the pressure cooker together with the tomatoes, chili powder, and basil. Lock the lid into place. Bring to HIGH pressure and maintain pressure for 12 minutes.

Turn off the heat and allow pressure to release for 10 minutes. Uncover and transfer the prepared bean mixture to your food processor. Add the sea salt, black pepper, and parsley and blend until smooth.

Transfer the dip to a fondue pot and add cheese. Stir to combine and garnish with avocado. Serve immediately with your favorite dippers.

Caribbean-Style Relish

(Ready in about 30 minutes | Servings 12)

Ingredients

7 cups water

1 ½ cups kidney beans

2 teaspoons olive oil

Salt and ground black pepper, to taste

2 tablespoons tahini paste

1/4 cup pineapple, drained and crushed

1/2 teaspoon dried cumin

1 teaspoon garlic powder

1/2 cup fresh cilantro, finely minced

Directions

Add 3 cups of water and kidney beans to your cooker; let it soak overnight. Drain and replace to the pressure cooker. Pour in the remaining 4 cups of water. Add the olive oil and lock the lid into place.

Bring to HIGH pressure and maintain this pressure for 10 to 15 minutes. Remove from the heat. Then, quick release any remaining pressure.

Add the cooked beans to the bowl of your blender or a food processor. Stir in the rest of the above ingredients and pulse until it is well combined but still a little chunky.

Place in a refrigerator to chill, and serve as a dip for chips if desired.

Glazed Carrots with Cranberries

(Ready in about 5 minutes | Servings 6)

Ingredients

1 cup water

2 pounds carrots, sliced diagonally

1/4 cup dried cranberries

A pinch of kosher salt

3/4 teaspoon black pepper

2 tablespoons butter

2 tablespoons maple syrup

Directions

Put the water, carrots, and cranberries into the pressure cooker. Close the lid of the cooker. Cook for 3 to 4 minutes at LOW pressure.

While the carrots are still warm, add the salt, black pepper, butter, and maple syrup. Gently stir to combine. Serve right now.

Bacon and Chicken Dip

(Ready in about 10 minutes | Servings 24)

Ingredients

3 bacon slices, cut into strips

2 tablespoons lard, softened

3 cloves garlic, peeled and minced

1 onion, peeled and diced

1 red bell pepper, cut into strips

1/2 cup salsa

1/4 cup tomato paste

1/2 cup vegetable stock

1 pound chicken breast, boneless and diced

1/2 cup sour cream

1 cup Mozzarella cheese, grated

1/2 teaspoon dried dill

Salt and freshly ground black pepper, to taste

Directions

Add the bacon strips and lard to the pressure cooker. Then, sauté the garlic, onion, and bell pepper for 3 minutes or until they are tender.

Next, stir in the salsa, tomato paste, vegetable stock, and chicken. Lock the lid into place; bring to LOW pressure; maintain pressure for 6 minutes.

In order to thicken the sauce, uncover and continue to simmer over MEDIUM heat.

Reduce the heat; fold in the sour cream and Mozzarella cheese; stir to combine well. Lastly, sprinkle with dill, salt, and black pepper to taste. Serve warm with tortilla chips.

Asparagus with Yogurt Crème

(Ready in about 10 minutes + chilling time | Servings 4)

Ingredients

2 cups plain yogurt

1 cup water

1 pound asparagus, trimmed

1 teaspoon dried basil

Kosher salt, to taste

Black pepper, to taste

Directions

To prepare yogurt crème: Put the yogurt into a fine mesh strainer over a bowl; transfer it to the refrigerator for about 4 hours.

Add the water to the pressure cooker; place the steamer basket.

Place the asparagus in the steamer basket. Sprinkle with basil, kosher salt, and black pepper. Close the lid.

Turn the heat to HIGH; when your cooker reaches pressure, lower the temperature to the minimum. Allow to cook for 3 minutes at HIGH pressure.

Afterwards, open the pressure cooker by releasing pressure. Serve with prepared yogurt crème.

Amazing Red Potatoes

(Ready in about 10 minutes | Servings 12)

Ingredients

1 cup water

1 teaspoon vegetable oil

3 pounds whole and unpeeled red potatoes, washed and cubed

Salt and black pepper, to taste

Paprika, to taste

Directions

Put the water and vegetable oil into your pressure cooker. Place a rack in your cooker; load the cooker with potato cubes.

Close the lid and bring to pressure over HIGH heat. Cook for 3 minutes; turn off the heat; use quick release method to depressurize your cooker.

Season prepared potatoes with salt, black pepper, and paprika. Enjoy!

Party Eggplant Dip

(Ready in about 10 minutes | Servings 12)

Ingredients

1 tablespoon sesame oil

3 cloves garlic, minced

1 large eggplant, peeled and diced

1/2 cup water

3 tablespoons fresh cilantro

1/2 teaspoon salt

1/4 teaspoon ground black pepper

2 tablespoons fresh lemon juice

2 tablespoons tahini

1 tablespoon extra-virgin olive oil

Directions

Warm the sesame oil in the pressure cooker over medium heat. Add garlic and eggplant and sauté until they begin to get soft. Pour in the water.

Lock the cooker's lid and bring to HIGH pressure. Now maintain pressure for 4 minutes. After that, quick release the pressure and remove the lid.

Pulse the eggplant-garlic mixture in your food processor along with the cilantro, salt, black pepper, lemon juice, and tahini.

Then, pour in the extra-virgin olive oil and process until the mixture is smooth. Garnish with fresh chopped chives if desired and serve.

Stuffed Potato Shells

(Ready in about 40 minutes | Servings 6)

Ingredients

2 cups water

6 Idaho potatoes, washed

2 tablespoons olive oil

1/4 cup bacon bits

1 cup Cheddar cheese, shredded

1 teaspoon garlic powder

1 teaspoon onion powder

1/4 cup sour cream

Directions

Preheat your oven to 400 degrees F. Pour the water into your pressure cooker.

Slice the potatoes in half lengthwise. Place the steamer basket in the cooker. Then, arrange the potatoes in two layers in the steamer basket.

Then, lock the lid into place. Bring to HIGH pressure and cook for 10 minutes. Next, quick-release the pressure, and uncover the cooker. Then, scoop out the inside of the potatoes, leaving 1/4-thick shells.

Grease the scooped-out shell of each potato with olive oil. Layer them on a baking sheet. Bake them for 15 minutes; remove from the oven.

Stuff prepared potato skins with the bacon bits and cheese. Sprinkle with garlic powder and onion powder; then, bake for 10 minutes longer. Serve with sour cream.

Spicy Pea Dip

(Ready in about 15 minutes + chilling time | Servings 16)

Ingredients

8 cups water

2 cups dried black-eyed peas

1 red onion, diced

2 cloves garlic, minced

1 pickled jalapeño, finely chopped

1 ripe tomato, seeded and diced

2 tablespoons fresh parsley

1 tablespoon fresh cilantro

1/4 cup wine vinegar

2 tablespoons vegetable oil

1/2 teaspoon celery seed

1 teaspoon sea salt

1/2 teaspoon ground black pepper

Directions

Place 4 cups of water in a deep container along with the black-eyed peas; let it soak for 1 hour. Drain, rinse the black-eyed peas and add them to the pressure cooker.

Add the remaining 4 cups of water to the cooker. Lock the lid and bring to HIGH pressure; maintain for 11 minutes.

Remove the cooker from the heat; allow pressure to release gradually. Drain the black-eyed peas and transfer them to the large bowl.

Stir in all remaining ingredients; stir to combine well. Refrigerate your dip at least 2 hours before serving.

Zesty Pearl Onions

(Ready in about 10 minutes + chilling time | Servings 6)

Ingredients

1/2 cup water

1 pound pearl onions, outer layer removed

1 bay leaf

3/4 teaspoon black pepper, freshly ground

1/4 teaspoon salt

4 tablespoons balsamic vinegar

2 tablespoons maple syrup

1 tablespoon all-purpose flour

Directions

Throw the water and pearl onions in your pressure cooker along with the bay leaf, black pepper, and salt. Now lock the cooker's lid.

Turn the heat up to HIGH. When your cooker reaches pressure, cook for about 6 minutes at low pressure. Afterwards, open your cooker by releasing pressure. Transfer pearl onions to the bowl.

In a saucepan, combine the rest of the above ingredients. Cook over low heat about 1 minute. Pour the sauce over the pearl onions in the bowl. Serve chilled and enjoy.

Jalapeño and Cheese Dip

(Ready in about 10 minutes | Servings 12)

Ingredients

2 tablespoons butter

2 tablespoons all-purpose flour

1 cup milk

16 ounces Monterey Jack cheese, shredded

2 pickled jalapeños, minced

1/4 teaspoon cayenne pepper

1/2 cup tomatoes, canned

1 teaspoon basil

1/4 teaspoon black pepper

Sea salt, to taste

Directions

In your cooker, warm the butter over medium flame; slowly stir in the flour and stir until you have a paste. Pour in the milk and stir until the mixture has thickened. Bring it to a boil.

Add the cheese; vigorously stir until it is smooth. Add the rest of your ingredients; secure the lid on your cooker. Cook on medium; lower heat and cook for about 3 minutes.

Afterwards, remove the lid and serve right away.

BBQ Chicken Wings

(Ready in about 25 minutes | Servings 6)

Ingredients

12-15 chicken wings (about 2 pounds)

3 cloves garlic, minced

1/2 teaspoon ground black pepper

1 yellow onion, chopped

1 teaspoon cayenne pepper

1/4 cup flour

1 ¼ teaspoons salt

1/2 cup BBQ Sauce

2 tablespoons olive oil

Directions

Season chicken wings with black pepper, cayenne pepper, and salt.

Warm olive oil and sauté the garlic and yellow onion. Stir in seasoned chicken wings and cook until they are browned.

Then, dust the chicken wings with flour. Pour in the BBQ sauce. Place the lid on your cooker and lock the lid. Press the "Soup/Stew", and cook for 15 minutes. Release the pressure value to open.

Lastly, test the chicken wings for the doneness. Taste and adjust the seasonings. Serve warm.

Hot Party Wings

(Ready in about 20 minutes | Servings 6)

Ingredients

1 cup water

2 pounds chicken wings

4 tablespoons hot sauce

1/4 cup honey

1/4 cup tomato paste

1 teaspoon ground black pepper

1 teaspoon dried basil

2 teaspoons sea salt

Directions

Pour the water into your pressure cooker; place a steamer basket in the cooker.

Place the wings in the steamer basket. Close and lock the cooker's lid. Cook for 10 minutes at HIGH pressure.

While the chicken wings are cooking, prepare the dipping sauce by mixing the hot sauce, honey, tomato paste, black pepper, basil, and salt.

Then, open the cooker by releasing the pressure. Transfer the prepared wings to the bowl with sauce and coat them evenly. Cook under the broiler for about 5 minutes, until they become crisp. Enjoy!

Beets with Walnuts

(Ready in about 15 minutes | Servings 6)

Ingredients

6 medium-sized beets

2 ½ cups water

1 tablespoon apple cider vinegar

1 tablespoon honey

1/2 teaspoon paprika

1 teaspoon dried basil

1/2 teaspoon freshly ground black pepper

3/4 teaspoon salt

3 tablespoons extra-virgin olive oil

2 tablespoons walnuts, finely chopped

Directions

Scrub your beets. Transfer them to a pressure cooker; pour in the water. Close the cooker's lid and bring to HIGH pressure. Reduce heat to medium; cook for 10 minutes.

Remove from heat and release pressure through the steam vent. Remove the lid. Drain the beets and let them cool. Then, rub off skins and cut into wedges. Transfer them to a serving bowl.

Whisk the vinegar, honey, paprika, basil, black pepper, salt, and olive oil in a small-sized bowl. Drizzle the vinaigrette over the beets in the serving bowl. Scatter chopped walnuts over the top and serve.

Beets and Carrots with Pecans

(Ready in about 15 minutes | Servings 6)

Ingredients

2 ½ cups water

4 medium-sized beets, peeled

4 carrots, trimmed

1 tablespoon fresh lemon juice

1 tablespoon maple syrup

1 teaspoon cumin

1 teaspoon dried dill weed

1 teaspoon salt

1/2 teaspoon freshly ground black pepper

3 tablespoons extra-virgin olive oil

2 tablespoons pecans, finely chopped

2 tablespoons golden raisins

Directions

Place water, beets, and carrots in your pressure cooker. Close the lid and bring to HIGH pressure. Now cook for 10 minutes.

Turn off the heat and release pressure through steam vent. Drain and rinse beets and carrots. Cut them into wedges and replace to a bowl in order to cool completely.

In a mixing bowl or a measuring cup, whisk the lemon juice, maple syrup, cumin, dill, salt, black pepper, and olive oil.

Drizzle the dressing over the vegetables. Scatter pecans and raisins over the top and serve.

Herbed Bean Spread

(Ready in about 30 minutes | Servings 6)

Ingredients

2 tablespoons olive oil

2 green onions, thinly sliced

1 ½ cups dried beans, rinsed

3 cups water

1 tablespoon apple cider vinegar

Salt and black pepper, to taste

1 teaspoon cumin

1 thyme sprig, chopped

1 rosemary sprig, chopped

Directions

Warm olive oil in the preheated pressure cooker; then, sauté green onions. Stir in the beans and water; lock the lid.

Turn the heat up to HIGH; maintain pressure approximately 30 minutes.

Open with the natural release method. Drain the beans and allow them to cool. Purée them in your food processor. Add the rest of the above ingredients.

Purée until it is uniform and smooth. Transfer to a serving bowl and drizzle with some extra olive oil if desired.

Amazing Garlic Dipping Sauce

(Ready in about 10 minutes | Servings 10)

Ingredients

1 cup water

2 whole heads garlic, peeled

1/2 cup butter, softened

1 tablespoon fresh oregano

1 teaspoon dill weed

Ground black pepper, to taste

1 teaspoon salt

Directions

Pour water into your cooker; then, place the steamer basket in the cooker. Add the garlic.

Cover and bring to HIGH pressure; maintain for about 2 minutes. Remove from the heat; allow pressure to quick-release.

Then, mash the garlic cloves; add the rest of the ingredients. Serve chilled.

Artichoke Bean Dipping Sauce

(Ready in about 20 minutes | Servings 20)

Ingredients

1/2 cup dry kidney beans, soaked overnight

1 cup water

6 medium-sized artichokes, outer leaves removed

1 small-sized lemon, freshly squeezed

2 cloves of garlic, smashed

1 cup non-fat yogurt

1/4 teaspoon pepper

1 teaspoon salt, or to taste

1 cup Cheddar cheese, grated

Directions

Throw the beans and water in your cooker.

Then, cut off the top about 1/3 of each artichoke. Slice your artichokes in half lengthwise; remove the "choke". Drizzle with fresh lemon juice and put into the cooker cut-side up.

Close and lock the cooker's lid. Turn the heat up to HIGH; when your cooker reaches desired pressure, maintain pressure.

Cook approximately 20 minutes at high pressure. When time is up, open the pressure cooker and wait for the pressure to come down.

Add the rest of the ingredients. Lastly, mix the content by using an immersion blender. Serve warm or at room temperature with dippers of choice.

Favorite Prosciutto-Wrapped Asparagus

(Ready in about 5 minutes | Servings 4)

Ingredients

2 cups water

1 pound asparagus spears

8 ounces Prosciutto, thinly sliced

Directions

Add the water to your cooker.

Then, wrap the asparagus spears in prosciutto slices.

Next, place the prosciutto-wrapped asparagus in a steamer basket. Insert the steamer basket into the pressure cooker; close the cooker's lid.

Cook for 2 to 3 minutes at HIGH pressure. Then, open your cooker with the Normal release method.

Transfer your prosciutto-wrapped asparagus spears to the serving platter, serve and enjoy!

Egg and Ham Appetizer

(Ready in about 5 minutes | Servings 4)

Ingredients

1 ½ cups water	4 large-sized eggs
1 tablespoon olive oil	4 slices Gruyere cheese
4 slices ham	1 tablespoon fresh cilantro, chopped

Directions

Prepare your cooker by adding the water and the trivet.

Coat the bottom and sides of your ramekins with olive oil. Then, lay the ham slices at the bottom. Break an egg into each ramekin.

Top with Gruyere cheese. Lay ramekins in the steamer basket in your pressure cooker.

Close the lid and set the pressure level to LOW. Cook for 4 minutes at LOW pressure. After that, release pressure. Sprinkle with fresh cilantro. Serve right away!

Mustard Baked Beans

(Ready in about 1 hour | Servings 6)

Ingredients

2 cups white beans	6 strips bacon, diced

3 cloves garlic, minced

1 onion, diced

3 cups water

2 tablespoons olive oil

1/2 teaspoon cumin

1/3 cup ketchup

1/3 cup molasses

3 tablespoons Dijon mustard

Directions

Soak white beans for 30 minutes. Drain and rinse your beans and reserve.

Then, cook the bacon, garlic, and onion until bacon is crisp and the onion is tender, or 4 to 5 minutes.

Add the soaked beans, along with the water, olive oil, and cumin; now lock the cooker's lid. Cook for 20 minutes under HIGH pressure.

Let the pressure release naturally. Set the cooker to HIGH, and stir in ketchup, molasses, and Dijon mustard. Continue to cook at least 5 minutes. Serve warm.

Cheesy Potato and Bacon Appetizer

(Ready in about 15 minutes | Servings 6)

Ingredients

4 slices bacon

2 cups water

6 potatoes, peeled and quartered

1/2 cup sour cream

1/4 cup Parmigiano-Reggiano cheese, grated

3 tablespoons butter

Sea salt and freshly ground black pepper, to taste

1/2 cup Colby-Jack cheese, shredded

Fresh sliced chives, for garnish

Directions

Sauté bacon on HIGH until it is browned and crisp. Crush the bacon, and set it aside; make sure to reserve 1 tablespoon of the bacon grease.

Place the water and potatoes in the pot; now securely lock the cooker's lid; set for 6 minutes on HIGH.

Then, release the cooker's pressure. Drain the potatoes and add them back to the pot. Then, mash potatoes, adding the rest of the ingredients and reserved bacon grease, except for chives. Taste and adjust the seasonings.

Top with crushed bacon; garnish with fresh chives and serve.

Parmesan and Polenta Appetizer

(Ready in about 10 minutes | Servings 6)

Ingredients

4 tablespoons butter, melted

1 sweet onion, finely chopped

4 ½ cups vegetable broth

1 ½ cups coarse cornmeal

3⁄4 teaspoon kosher salt

1/2 teaspoon cayenne pepper

1⁄2 teaspoon ground black pepper

1⁄3 cup Parmesan cheese, grated

Directions

Melt 2 tablespoons of butter on HIGH. Then, sauté sweet onion for about 1 minute, until it is translucent.

Add the vegetable broth, cornmeal, salt, cayenne pepper, and black pepper. Now lock the cooker's lid and cook for 9 minutes under HIGH pressure.

Stir in Parmesan cheese and the remaining 2 tablespoons of butter before serving.

Bacon and Collard Greens Appetizer

(Ready in about 20 minutes | Servings 4)

Ingredients

4 strips bacon, diced

3 cloves garlic

1 onion

2 bunches collard greens, chopped

2 cups chicken stock

Sea salt and black pepper to taste

1 teaspoon cayenne pepper

Directions

In your pressure cooker, sauté the bacon over HIGH heat for about 5 minutes.

Stir in the remaining ingredients; lock the pressure cooker's lid. Set for 15 minutes over HIGH pressure.

Let the pressure release naturally and serve right away.

Bacon and Polenta Appetizer

(Ready in about 10 minutes | Servings 6)

Ingredients

2 tablespoons olive oil

2-3 cloves garlic, finely minced

1 cup green onions, finely chopped

4 strips bacon, chopped

4 ½ cups chicken stock

1 ½ cups coarse cornmeal

Sea salt and black pepper, to taste

1 teaspoon dried rosemary

1/2 teaspoon dried thyme

1/3 cup Parmesan cheese, grated

Directions

Warm the oil over HIGH heat. Sauté the garlic, onion and bacon for about 2 minutes.

Add the rest of your ingredients, except for Parmesan cheese. Now lock the lid and cook for 9 minutes on HIGH pressure. Gradually release the pressure.

While the polenta is still hot, stir in Parmesan; stir until Parmesan cheese has melted and serve immediately.

Broccoli and Potato Appetizer

(Ready in about 20 minutes | Servings 6)

Ingredients

2 cups water

6 potatoes, peeled and quartered

2 cups broccoli, broken into florets

3 tablespoons extra-virgin olive oil

1/4 cup half-and-half

1/2 cup sharp cheese, shredded

1/2 teaspoon dried dill weed

1/2 teaspoon cumin powder

Sea salt and ground black pepper, to taste

Directions

Add the water, potatoes, and broccoli to the pot. Securely lock the lid and set on HIGH for 6 minutes. Use a quick release to release the pressure.

Drain the vegetables, and add them back to the cooker. Now, mash them with a potato masher; add the remaining ingredients and mash until smooth and uniform.

Taste and adjust the seasonings. Serve right now or as a cold appetizer.

Brussels Sprouts with Bacon

(Ready in about 10 minutes | Servings 4)

Ingredients

1/4 pound bacon, diced

1 pound Brussels sprouts, trimmed and halved

1 tablespoon mustard

1 cup chicken stock

Salt and ground black pepper, to taste

1 teaspoon dried sage

1 teaspoon dried basil

2 tablespoons butter

Directions

Set your pressure cooker over medium-high heat; add the bacon and cook for 2 minutes, stirring periodically. Now add the Brussels sprouts, mustard, and chicken stock; cover the cooker.

Bring the pressure to HIGH and cook for 4 more minutes. Then, release pressure using cold water method.

Uncover the cooker and add the rest of the above ingredients. Taste, adjust the seasonings and replace to a serving platter. Enjoy!

Easiest Salsa Ever

(Ready in about 10 minutes | Servings 8)

Ingredients

1 pound tomato, quartered

2 poblano chili peppers, chopped

1 medium-sized leek, chopped

1/2 cup cold water

1/4 cup fresh basil, chopped

1/4 cup fresh cilantro, chopped

1 tablespoon fresh sage, chopped

Freshly cracked black pepper, to taste

1 teaspoon kosher salt

Directions

First, place the tomatoes in your pressure cooker. Pour in enough water to cover them. Lock the cooker's lid into place. Bring to HIGH pressure and maintain for 2 minutes.

Turn off the heat; use a quick release to release the pressure.

Add the drained and cooked tomatoes to your food processor. Now add poblano peppers, leek, cold water, basil, cilantro, sage, black pepper, and salt to your food processor. Mix until everything is well combined.

Serve chilled with corn tortilla chips.

Yummy Cayenne Peanuts

(Ready in about 50 minutes | Servings 16)

Ingredients

2 pounds raw peanuts

12 cups water

1 teaspoon cayenne pepper

1/3 cup sea salt

Directions

First, place raw peanuts in the pressure cooker. Add the water, cayenne pepper, and sea salt.

Close the lid; bring to a medium setting and cook for 45 minutes. Turn off the heat; allow pressure to release gradually.

Allow the peanuts to cool. Drain and transfer them to a serving bowl.

Cajun Garlic Peanuts

(Ready in about 50 minutes | Servings 16)

Ingredients

2 pounds raw peanuts

12 cups water

1 teaspoon Cajun seasoning

1 teaspoon garlic powder

1/3 cup sea salt

Directions

Throw green peanuts in the pressure cooker. Add the remaining ingredients; stir to combine.

Cover and bring to a medium setting; let it cook for 45 minutes. Afterwards, allow the pressure to release gradually.

Allow the peanuts to cool. Drain and serve.

Butternut Squash with Pine Nuts

(Ready in about 1 hour 15 minutes | Servings 6)

Ingredients

1 butternut squash, peeled and sliced

2 tablespoons extra-virgin olive oil

Salt and freshly ground pepper

3 ½ ounces pine nuts

1/2 cup green onions, chopped

2 tablespoons tomato paste

1 cup vegetable broth

1 teaspoon grated lemon rind

1/2 cup wine

1/2 cup sharp cheese shavings

Directions

Begin by preheating your oven to 350 degrees F. Now spread the butternut squash slices on a baking sheet; drizzle with 1 tablespoon of olive oil; sprinkle with salt and black pepper.

Cover with an aluminum foil; roast butternut squash slices until they are tender, or about 45 minutes. Add the squash to a food processor; puree until it's smooth.

In the meantime, toast the pine nuts on a baking sheet for about 4 minutes.

Then, warm the remaining 1 tablespoon of olive oil in a pressure cooker. Add green onions and sauté until they are softened, 4 minutes. Add the roasted pine nuts and tomato paste; cook, stirring constantly, for about 2 minutes.

Add the vegetable broth, lemon rind, and wine; cover and cook for 7 minutes. Remove the lid and release the pressure.

Add the cooker back to medium heat; bring the contents to a boil. Cook for about 4 minutes. Add the reserved squash puree; cook until it is warmed through. Serve with cheese shavings.

Zesty Appetizer Meatballs

(Ready in about 15 minutes | Servings 12)

Ingredients

1/2 cup sugar	2 tablespoons cornstarch
2 tablespoons apple juice	1 pound ground beef
2/3 cup water	2 cloves garlic, minced
1/3 cup white wine	1 yellow onion, diced
2 tablespoons tamari sauce	1/2 cup bread crumbs
2 tablespoons Worcestershire sauce	

Directions

Add the sugar, apple juice, water, white wine, tamari sauce, Worcestershire sauce, and cornstarch to a pressure cooker. Then, bring to a boil over HIGH heat.

Stir the mixture continuously until it has thickened; remove from heat.

In a mixing bowl, combine ground beef, garlic, yellow onion, and bread crumbs; mix until it is well combined.

Roll the mixture into 12 equal meatballs; add meatballs to the sauce in the cooker. Lock the lid into place. Bring to high pressure; maintain pressure for 5 minutes.

Quick-release the pressure. Transfer to a large serving platter and serve warm.

Meatballs in Herbed Sauce

(Ready in about 15 minutes | Servings 12)

Ingredients

2 tablespoons pineapple juice

1 tablespoon maple syrup

1 tablespoon dried thyme

1 cup water

2 tablespoons soy sauce

1/2 pound ground pork

1 pound extra lean ground beef

2 cloves garlic, minced

1 cup shallots, diced

1/2 cup bread crumbs

Fresh parsley, for garnish

Directions

In your cooker, place pineapple juice, maple syrup, thyme, water, soy sauce; stir to combine. Bring to a boil over HIGH heat.

Cook until the sauce has thickened; turn off the heat.

In a bowl, combine ground pork, ground beef, garlic, shallots, and bread crumbs; mix until everything is incorporated.

Now shape the mixture into 12 equal meatballs; carefully transfer meatballs to the pressure cooker. Lock the lid into place and bring to HIGH pressure; maintain pressure for about 5 minutes.

Release pressure quickly. Transfer to a large serving platter. Sprinkle with fresh chopped parsley and serve warm.

Fast and Easy Carrot Coins

(Ready in about 5 minutes | Servings 6)

Ingredients

1 cup water

1 pound carrots, peeled and sliced into thick coins

Directions

Fill the cooker's base with water. Place the carrot coins in the steamer basket; put the basket into the pressure cooker. Close the lid.

Turn the heat up to HIGH and maintain the pressure for 1 to 2 minutes at HIGH.

Afterwards, open the pressure cooker by releasing pressure. Replace to a serving platter and serve.

Butter and Maple Carrot Coins

(Ready in about 10 minutes | Servings 4)

Ingredients

1 cup water

1 pound carrots, trimmed and cut into thick coins

2 tablespoons butter, softened

1 tablespoon maple syrup

1 teaspoon balsamic vinegar

Sea salt and freshly ground black pepper

2 tablespoons fresh cilantro, chopped

Directions

Pour the water into your pressure cooker. Throw the carrots into the steamer basket and lay it in your pressure cooker.

Cover and maintain the pressure for 1 to 2 minutes at HIGH. Then, open the pressure cooker by releasing pressure.

Warn butter in a saucepan over medium heat. Then, add carrots, and cook stirring occasionally, for about 3 minutes. Add maple syrup, balsamic vinegar, salt, and black pepper; cook for 1 more minute.

Remove to a serving platter and serve sprinkled with fresh cilantro. Enjoy!

Cabbage and Mushroom Spring Rolls

(Ready in about 10 minutes | Servings 12)

Ingredients

1/2 pound cabbage, shredded

1 cup bamboo shoots, sliced

1/4 cup fresh parsley, chopped

3 cloves garlic, minced

1 cup mushrooms, sliced

1 onion, finely chopped

1 tablespoon rice wine vinegar

12 spring roll wrappers

2 cups water

Directions

In a bowl, mix together the cabbage, bamboo shoots, parsley, garlic, mushrooms, onion, and rice wine vinegar; stir to combine.

Lay the wrappers on a flat surface. Then, divide the cabbage mixture among wrappers. Roll up the wrappers, and transfer them to the pressure cooker steamer basket.

Pour the water into the bottom of the cooker. Place the steamer basket in the cooker. Lock the lid into place. Bring to HIGH pressure and maintain pressure for about 3 minutes. Serve warm with your favorite dipping sauce.

Herby Tomato Sauce

(Ready in about 15 minutes | Servings 16)

Ingredients

2 tablespoons olive oil

1/2 cup green onions, sliced

3 cloves garlic, peeled and minced

2 ½ pounds tomatoes, peeled and diced

1 teaspoon dried oregano

1 teaspoon dried basil

1 teaspoon dried sage

1 teaspoon granulated sugar

Salt and freshly ground black pepper, to taste

Directions

Warm the olive oil in your pressure cooker over medium heat. Then, sauté green onions and garlic for about 30 seconds.

Add the tomatoes to the pressure cooker along with the remaining ingredients.

Lock the lid into place; bring to LOW pressure and maintain for 10 minutes. Turn off the heat and let pressure release naturally. Use immediately or refrigerate for up to a week. Enjoy!

Old-Fashioned Peanuts in Shells

(Ready in about 1 hour | Servings 6)

Ingredients

1 pound raw peanuts in shells

8 cups of water

1/4 cup salt

Directions

Rinse the peanuts in cold water. Transfer them to a pressure cooker and add the water.

Seal the cooker's lid and turn the heat to HIGH.

When the pressure comes up to pressure, reduce the heat to LOW. Cook for about 30 minutes.

Turn off the heat; allow the pressure to release gradually, or for about 20 minutes. Add the salt and serve.

Spiced Artichokes in Wine

(Ready in about 15 minutes | Servings 4)

Ingredients

4 fresh artichokes, tops and stems removed

2 tablespoons canola oil

2 large-sized garlic cloves, minced

1 white onion, peeled and finely minced

Sea salt and freshly cracked black pepper, to taste

1 teaspoon cayenne pepper

1 cup white wine, best you can afford

Directions

Put the prepared artichokes into your pressure cooker. Drizzle with canola oil.

Sprinkle the artichokes with garlic, onion, salt, black pepper, and cayenne pepper. Pour white wine over the artichokes.

Cook in your pressure cooker approximately 10 minutes. Serve mayonnaise on the side for dipping if desired.

Artichokes with Hot Hollandaise Sauce

(Ready in about 15 minutes | Servings 4)

Ingredients

6 artichokes, tops and stems removed	1 teaspoon dried dill weed
2 tablespoons extra-virgin olive oil	2 tablespoons lemon juice
1 cup scallions, finely minced	1 cup water
1 teaspoon salt	Hot hollandaise sauce, for garnish
1/4 teaspoon freshly cracked black pepper	

Directions

Lay the artichokes in your pressure cooker. Drizzle the artichokes with the olive oil.

Sprinkle them with scallions, salt, black pepper, and dill weed. Drizzle the lemon juice over the artichokes. Pour in the water.

Cook the artichokes in the pressure cooker for about 10 minutes. Serve with hot hollandaise sauce and enjoy!

Yummy Healthy Caponata

(Ready in about 10 minutes | Servings 8)

Ingredients

1 large-sized zucchini, cut into thick slices	1 medium-sized eggplant, cut into thick slices

1 leek, sliced

1 red bell pepper, seeded and sliced

1 yellow bell pepper, seeded and sliced

1 green bell pepper, seeded and sliced

Salt and black pepper, to taste

1 teaspoon dried basil

1/2 teaspoon dried oregano

1/2 teaspoon garlic powder

1/2 teaspoon onion powder

Extra-virgin olive oil, to taste

Directions

Add all the ingredients to your pressure cooker, except for olive oil. Cook for about 5 minutes.

Transfer to a serving platter. Drizzle with olive oil and serve. Enjoy!

Easy Veggie Appetizer

(Ready in about 10 minutes | Servings 6)

Ingredients

1 large-sized zucchini, cut into thick slices

2 bell peppers, sliced

1 red onion, sliced

2-3 cloves garlic, peeled

Salt and black pepper, to taste

1 teaspoon paprika

A few drops of smoked liquid

Salt and black pepper, to taste

1/2 teaspoon dried basil

Extra-virgin olive oil, to taste

Directions

Throw all the ingredients in your pressure cooker, except for olive oil. Cook for about 5 minutes.

Drizzle with extra-virgin olive oil and serve.

Sesame and Honey Chicken Wings

(Ready in about 20 minutes | Servings 6)

Ingredients

12 chicken wings, cut apart at joints

1/2 cup chicken stock

1/2 cup honey

3 tablespoons sesame oil

2 tablespoons tamari sauce

2 garlic cloves, crushed

1 teaspoon cayenne pepper

1 teaspoon grated ginger

1/4 cup sesame seeds

Directions

Add 1 cup of water to your pressure cooker. Then, place a steamer basket in the cooker. Lay the chicken wings in the steamer basket.

Close and lock the cooker's lid. Cook for 10 minutes at HIGH pressure.

Meanwhile, in a mixing bowl, combine the rest of the above ingredients. Coat the chicken wings with this honey mixture.

After that, place the wings under the broiler for about 5 minutes. Serve and enjoy!

Kale and Cheese Dipping Sauce

(Ready in about 10 minutes | Servings 16)

Ingredients

1 ½ cups kale leaves, torn

1 (14-ounce) can artichoke hearts, drained and coarsely chopped

1 cup light mayonnaise

1/2 cup Ricotta cheese

1 cup Mozzarella cheese, shredded

Sea salt and ground black pepper, to taste

1/2 teaspoon dried dill weed

1 teaspoon paprika

Directions

Pour 2 cups of water into your pressure cooker; place a rack in the bottom.

Mix all the above ingredients; transfer them to a baking dish that fits in your pressure cooking pot. Then, cover the baking dish with a foil. Place the baking dish onto the rack.

Lock the cooker's lid into place; cook on HIGH pressure for 10 minutes. After that, use a quick pressure release. Serve with pita wedges of choice. Enjoy!

Cheesy Rainbow Dip

(Ready in about 10 minutes | Servings 16)

Ingredients

1 (14-ounce) can artichoke hearts, drained and coarsely chopped

1 red bell pepper, chopped

1 yellow bell pepper, chopped

1 ½ cups Cottage cheese

1 cup Colby cheese, shredded

1/2 teaspoon dried basil

Sea salt and ground black pepper, to taste

1 teaspoon red pepper flakes, crushed

Directions

Add about 2 cups of water to a pressure cooker; lay a rack in the bottom of the cooker.

Combine together all the above ingredients in a baking dish. Then, cover the baking dish with an aluminum foil. Transfer the baking dish to the pressure cooker.

Cover and cook on HIGH pressure for about 10 minutes. Afterwards, use a quick pressure release. Serve.

LUNCH RECIPES

Meatball Soup with Noodles

(Ready in about 20 minutes | Servings 6)

Ingredients

2 tablespoons canola oil

1 onion, thinly sliced

1 cup carrot, sliced

6 cups vegetable broth

1 (16-ounce) bag frozen Italian meatballs

1 cup dried noodles

2 cups spinach, torn into pieces

1 tablespoon lemon juice

2 cloves garlic, minced

Salt and ground black pepper, to taste

Directions

First, heat the oil on HIGH until sizzling. Now sauté the onion and carrot for about 5 minutes.

Add the rest of the above ingredients. Securely lock the lid and set for 5 minutes on HIGH.

Taste and adjust the seasonings. Serve warm and enjoy!

Creamy Cauliflower and Cheese Soup

(Ready in about 10 minutes | Servings 6)

Ingredients

2 tablespoons butter

1 medium-sized leek, sliced

1 small-sized head cauliflower, chopped

2-3 baby carrots, trimmed and chopped

4 cups chicken broth

1 bay leaf

1/2 teaspoon cayenne pepper

1 teaspoon granulated garlic

1 cup heavy cream

1 cup sharp cheese, shredded

Salt and cracked black pepper, to taste

Directions

Warm the butter in your cooker until sizzling. Then, sauté the leeks until translucent, or for about 5 minutes.

Add the cauliflower, carrots, chicken broth, 1 bay leaf, cayenne pepper, and granulated garlic. Now lock the pressure cooker's lid; set for 4 minutes on HIGH. Then, release the cooker's pressure.

Stir in heavy cream and shredded sharp cheese; season with salt and black pepper. Serve.

Mom's Corn Chowder

(Ready in about 25 minutes | Servings 6)

Ingredients

1 tablespoon olive oil	3 cups vegetable broth
1 shallot, diced	3⁄4 teaspoon salt
2 cloves garlic, peeled and minced	1/4 teaspoon ground black pepper
1 carrot, chopped	1 (12-ounce) can evaporated milk
1 celery stalk, chopped	2 tablespoons cornstarch
5 cups fresh corn kernels, cut off the cob	3 tablespoons margarine

Directions

In your pressure cooker, heat olive oil over HIGH setting. Now, sauté the shallot and garlic for 4 to 5 minutes.

Add carrot, celery, corn kernels, vegetable broth, salt, and ground black pepper; securely lock the lid, and cook the soup for 6 minutes on HIGH.

In a small bowl, whisk together the milk and cornstarch; stir the mixture into your soup. Stir in the margarine. Let simmer for 2 to 3 minutes, or until the soup has thickened. Serve warm with the croutons if desired.

Chunky Butternut Bean Soup

(Ready in about 1 hour | Servings 6)

Ingredients

2 tablespoons olive oil

1 medium-sized leek, chopped

2 carrots, chopped medium

2 celery stalks, chopped

3 sprigs fresh thyme

16 ounces dried beans

9 cups vegetables broth

Sea salt and black pepper, to taste

1/2 teaspoon dried dill weed

1/2 teaspoon dried rosemary, chopped

2 cups butternut squash, diced

1/2 cup sour cream

Directions

Warm olive oil in your pressure cooker; sauté leek, carrot, and celery until they are softened.

Add the thyme, beans, broth, salt, and black pepper. Cook for 35 minutes on HIGH.

Using cold water method, open the cooker's lid; add dill, rosemary, and butternut squash. Cover and cook for 10 more minutes.

Serve with a dollop of sour cream. Enjoy!

Cheesy Potato and Spinach Soup

(Ready in about 20 minutes | Servings 6)

Ingredients

1/4 cup vegetable oil

6 white onions, white part only, sliced

1 red bell pepper, seeded and chopped

2 celery stalks, chopped

1/2 cup rice

3 potatoes, peeled and diced

5 cups vegetable stock

3/4 teaspoon sea salt

1/4 teaspoon ground black pepper

2 tablespoons white wine

3 tablespoons tomato paste

1 ½ cups fresh spinach, torn into large pieces

1/2 cup Monterey Jack cheese, grated

Directions

In a pressure cooker, warm vegetable oil. Add onions, bell pepper, and celery; sauté for about 2 minutes.

Stir in rice and potatoes. Continue cooking an additional minute.

Add vegetable stock, salt, black pepper, wine, and tomato paste. Stir well to combine.

Seal the lid and cook on high pressure. Now reduce the heat to maintain pressure, and cook for 4 minutes. Uncover and divide among soup bowls. Garnish with grated cheese and serve warm.

Creamed Sausage and Spinach Soup

(Ready in about 20 minutes | Servings 6)

Ingredients

2 tablespoons vegetable oil	1 teaspoon sugar
1 pound ground sausage	1 teaspoon dried basil
3 cloves garlic, peeled and minced	1 teaspoon dried oregano
1 onion, peeled and diced	1/4 teaspoon red pepper flakes, crushed
6 cups chicken broth	Salt and ground black pepper, to taste
1 (10-ounce) bag spinach leaves	1/2 cup heavy cream
4 carrots, thickly sliced	

Directions

First of all, heat vegetable oil until sizzling. Then, sauté the sausage, garlic and onion, until the sausage is browned, the onion is translucent, and the garlic is fragrant.

Add the rest of the ingredients, except for heavy cream.

Securely lock the lid and set on HIGH for 3 minutes. Then, release the cooker's pressure.

Add heavy cream before serving and enjoy!

Satisfying Chicken and Rice Soup

(Ready in about 30 minutes | Servings 6)

Ingredients

1 pound chicken thighs, boneless, skinless and cubed

3 tablespoons flour

Salt and ground black pepper, to taste

3 tablespoons butter

1 tablespoon canola oil

1 onion, diced

2 large carrots, chopped

2 large stalks celery, chopped

2 tablespoons tomato paste

1 rosemary sprig

1 thyme spring

1 ¼ cups wild rice

6 cups chicken broth

1 cup heavy cream

Directions

Coat the chicken thighs with sifted flour; season with salt and black pepper.

Now, heat butter and canola oil on HIGH until melted.

Lay the prepared chicken at the bottom of the pressure cooker; cook until they are lightly browned, about 5 minutes.

Add the rest of the ingredients, except for heavy cream; cook for 12 to 14 minutes on HIGH.

Let the pressure release naturally and gradually. Add heavy cream, and stir to combine. Serve warm.

Cheese and Onion Soup

(Ready in about 20 minutes | Servings 6)

Ingredients

3 tablespoons butter

2 onions, peeled and thinly sliced

2 teaspoons sugar

5 cups beef broth

2 tablespoons red wine

1 bay leaf

1 teaspoon dried thyme

Sea salt and freshly ground black pepper

6 slices Provolone cheese

Directions

In your pressure cooker, warm butter on HIGH until sizzling.

Cook the onions and sugar in the cooker, until they are caramelized, for about 10 minutes.

Add the beef broth, wine, bay leaf, dried thyme, salt, and ground black pepper; stir to combine. Now lock the pressure cooker's lid and cook for 8 to 10 minutes on HIGH.

Ladle into soup bowls and top with Provolone cheese. Serve and enjoy!

Rich Garbanzo Bean Soup

(Ready in about 1 hour | Servings 8)

Ingredients

2 ½ cups dried garbanzo beans, soaked overnight

1/2 cup dry lentils, brown (I have never tried red)

3 ripe tomatoes, diced

1 cup fresh cilantro, finely minced

3 cloves garlic, minced

1 onion, finely chopped

2 carrots, peeled and finely chopped

2 celery ribs, finely chopped

2 tablespoons vegetable oil

Sea salt and ground black pepper, to taste

1/4 teaspoon turmeric

1/2 cup flour

3 tablespoons tomato paste

1/2 cup rice noodles

Directions

Place garbanzo beans, lentils, tomatoes, and cilantro in your pressure cooker.

Add the garlic, onion, carrots, and celery. Pour in enough water to cover the vegetables.

Next, add the vegetable oil, salt, black pepper, and turmeric; cover with the lid. Cook for about 15 minutes.

In the meantime, combine the flour with 1 cup of warm water. Add this mixture to the cooker along with tomato paste. Cook an additional 10 minutes, stirring periodically.

Stir in rice noodles and cook for 10 more minutes. Ladle into eight soup bowls and serve warm.

Winter Hearty Chili

(Ready in about 1 hour | Servings 6)

Ingredients

1 ¼ cups pinto beans, soaked for 30 minutes

3 tablespoons canola oil

1 ½ pounds sirloin steaks, cubed

2 cloves garlic, minced

1 leek, chopped

1 tablespoon chili powder

1 bell pepper chopped

3 tomatoes, chopped

1 (28-ounce) can tomato sauce

5 cups beef broth

2 teaspoons sugar

Kosher salt and black pepper to taste

Directions

Drain and rinse the soaked pinto beans.

In the meantime, heat canola oil on HIGH until sizzling. Then, cook the steak, garlic, and leek for about 5 minutes.

Add remaining ingredients; seal the pressure cooker's lid, and set on HIGH for 24 minutes.

Open the lid naturally and adjust your chili for seasonings. Serve warm.

Chicken Soup with Farfalle

(Ready in about 25 minutes | Servings 6)

Ingredients

1 pound chicken breasts, boneless, skinless and cubed

2 tablespoons flour

Salt and ground black pepper, to taste

3 tablespoons butter

1 onion, diced

2 large-sized carrots, sliced

3 large-sized celery ribs, sliced

1 ½ cups uncooked farfalle pasta

6 cups chicken stock

3/4 teaspoon salt

1/2 teaspoon black pepper

1/2 teaspoon cayenne pepper

1 cup frozen corn kernels, thawed

Directions

Toss the chicken cubes with flour; generously season with salt and ground black pepper.

Then, warm the butter on HIGH until melted and sizzling.

Lay the coated chicken at the bottom of your pressure cooker; cook for about 5 minutes or until lightly browned, turning once.

Add the onion, carrots, and celery. Top with farfalle pasta and chicken stock; season with salt, black pepper, and cayenne pepper. Seal the lid and cook for 6 minutes on HIGH.

Now, release the cooker's pressure. Afterwards, stir in corn kernels and simmer for 1 to 2 minutes. Serve warm.

Creamed Tomato Soup

(Ready in about 20 minutes | Servings 6)

Ingredients

2 tablespoons butter

1 onion, diced

1 (28-ounce) can tomato sauce

4 cups chicken broth

8 tomatoes, finely chopped

2 cloves garlic, minced

1/2 teaspoon basil

1/2 teaspoon oregano

Sea salt and ground black pepper, to taste

1 cup heavy cream

Directions

Warm the butter on HIGH until melted.

Cook the onion in the pressure cooker for about 5 minutes.

Add the remaining ingredients, except for heavy cream. Seal the lid and cook for 8 minutes on HIGH.

Let the pressure release naturally for 5 to 10 minutes. Serve topped with heavy cream.

Soup with Cheese Tortellini

(Ready in about 15 minutes | Servings 6)

Ingredients

2 tablespoons canola oil

2 garlic cloves, minced

1 onion, diced

2 carrots, sliced

2 stalks celery, cut into 1/4 inch slices

1 cup dry cheese tortellini

4 cups vegetable stock

1 (24-ounce) jar spaghetti sauce

1 (14.5-ounce) can diced tomatoes

Sea salt and ground black pepper

Directions

Heat canola oil in your pressure cooker over HIGH heat.

Sauté the garlic, onion, carrots, and celery until tender.

Add the rest of the ingredients; stir to combine. Now lock the lid, set the pressure cooker to HIGH and cook for about 5 minutes.

Serve topped with grated Cheddar cheese if desired.

Jalapeño Chicken Soup with Corn

(Ready in about 30 minutes | Servings 6)

Ingredients

1 pound chicken breasts, boneless, skinless and cubed

2 tablespoons flour

Sea salt and ground black pepper

2 tablespoons canola oil

1 onion, diced

2 celery stalks, sliced

1 jalapeño pepper, seeded and diced

5 cups tomato soup

1/2 teaspoon ground cumin

Sea salt and black pepper, to taste

1 cup frozen corn kernels, thawed

4 corn tortillas, cut into strips

Directions

Dust the cubed chicken breasts with flour; season with salt and black pepper.

Then, heat oil on HIGH until sizzling. Lay the coated chicken in the cooker; sauté until they are lightly browned, or about 5 minutes.

Sauté the onion, celery, jalapeño pepper for about 1 minute. Add the tomato soup, cumin, salt, and black pepper.

Seal the pressure cooker's lid and set on HIGH for 7 minutes. Stir in corn and tortilla strips. Serve.

Lentil and Swiss Chard Soup

(Ready in about 35 minutes | Servings 4)

Ingredients

2 tablespoons olive oil

1 small-sized white onion, chopped

3 garlic cloves, minced

2 carrots, chopped

1 parsnip, chopped

1 celery rib, chopped

4 cups vegetable broth

1 cup dry lentils, rinsed and picked

1 cup Swiss chard leaves

Sea salt and freshly cracked black pepper

Directions

First, heat olive oil in your pressure cooker. Then, sweat the onion and garlic for a few minutes.

Add the carrots, parsnip, and celery; sauté for 1 to 2 minutes.

Add the vegetable broth and dry lentils, and cook for about 20 minutes.

Open the pressure cooker; add Swiss chard, and stir until it wilts. Season with salt and black pepper to taste. Serve.

Delicious Pea and Ham Soup

(Ready in about 30 minutes | Servings 8)

Ingredients

1 pound dried split peas

8 cups water

1 ham bone

1 cup scallions, chopped

2 carrots, diced

2 parsnips, diced

1 teaspoon mustard seed

1 teaspoon dried basil

2 tablespoons sherry wine

Directions

Fill the pressure cooker with all the above ingredients, except for sherry wine.

Put the lid on your pressure cooker, and bring to HIGH pressure. Cook for 20 minutes.

Add sherry and stir to combine. Serve and enjoy!

Easiest Adzuki Beans Ever

(Ready in about 10 minutes | Servings 4)

Ingredients

4 cups water

1 cup adzuki beans

2 tablespoons canola oil

1/2 teaspoon black pepper, ground

1 teaspoon salt

1 bay leaf

Directions

Fill the pressure cooker with all the above ingredients.

Seal the lid; bring to HIGH pressure and maintain for 8 minutes.

Then, allow pressure to release naturally. Ladle into soup bowls and serve hot.

Black Bean Salad

(Ready in about 10 minutes + chilling time | Servings 6)

Ingredients

4 cups water

2 cups black beans, soaked overnight

1 tablespoon canola oil

1 red onion, chopped

2 cloves garlic, peeled and smashed

2 tomatoes, chopped

1 cup corn kernels

3 teaspoons olive oil

1 teaspoon apple cider vinegar

3/4 teaspoon salt

1/2 teaspoon white pepper

1 sprig fresh thyme

Directions

Add water, beans, canola oil, red onion, and garlic to the pressure cooker. Now lock the lid.

Turn the heat to HIGH; cook approximately 8 minutes.

Next, wait for the pressure to come down.

Strain the beans and transfer them to a refrigerator in order to cool completely. Transfer to a serving bowl and add the rest of the ingredients. Enjoy!

Easiest Pinto Beans Ever

(Ready in about 1 hour 15 minutes | Servings 6)

Ingredients

8 cups water

1 cup dried pinto beans

2 tablespoons canola oil

2 bay leaves

1 teaspoon salt

3/4 teaspoon ground black pepper

Directions

Add 4 cups of water and pinto beans to your pressure cooker. Cover with the lid and bring to HIGH pressure for 1 minute. Then, quick-release the pressure.

Drain and rinse the beans; add the beans back to the pressure cooker. Let them soak for about 1 hour.

Add the rest of the ingredients; bring to HIGH pressure and maintain for about 11 minutes. Serve warm and enjoy!

Yellow Lentil with Kale

(Ready in about 25 minutes | Servings 4)

Ingredients

1 tablespoon canola oil

1 medium-sized leek, diced

1/4 teaspoon coriander

1/2 teaspoon thyme

1/4 teaspoon cumin

1 cup yellow dried lentils

2 tomatoes, chopped

1/2 cup water

2 cups kale, torn into small pieces

Directions

Heat canola oil in your pressure cooker over medium heat. Sauté the leeks together with coriander, thyme, and cumin for about 5 minutes. Then, add lentils, tomatoes, and water; stir well to combine. Close and lock the pressure cooker's lid.

Cook for about 12 minutes at HIGH pressure.

Afterwards, release the pressure according to manufacturer's instructions. Mix in the kale; stir until it is wilted; serve.

Delicious Red Lentil Curry

(Ready in about 20 minutes | Servings 8)

Ingredients

8 cups water

2 cups dried red lentils

3 tablespoons canola oil

3/4 teaspoon salt

1 cup scallions, diced

2 cloves garlic, minced

3 tablespoons curry powder

1 teaspoon cumin

1 teaspoon chili powder

1 (6-ounce) can tomato paste

Salt and ground black pepper, to taste

Directions

Add the water, lentils, 1 tablespoon of canola oil and salt to your pressure cooker.

Cover and bring to HIGH pressure for 8 minutes. Turn off the heat and allow pressure to release according to manufacturer's directions. Drain the lentils.

To prepare curry mixture: In a saucepan, warm the remaining 2 tablespoons of canola oil; sauté the scallions until they are caramelized.

Add the rest of the ingredients and cook for about 4 minutes, stirring frequently.

Add curry mixture to the prepared lentils; mix to combine. Serve warm and enjoy!

Lentil and Tomato Delight

(Ready in about 15 minutes | Servings 6)

Ingredients

1 tablespoon vegetable oil

1 parsnip, chopped

1 carrot, chopped

1 stalk celery, chopped

1 red bell pepper, chopped

1 green bell pepper, chopped

1 onion, chopped

1 cup dried lentils

1 (14.5-ounce) can tomatoes, chopped

2 cups water

1 teaspoon red pepper, flakes, crushed

Kosher salt and ground black pepper, to taste

Directions

Heat vegetable oil in a pressure cooker over medium heat. Add parsnip, carrot, celery, bell peppers, and onion. Sauté until the vegetables have softened.

Then add dried lentils, tomatoes, and water, and stir well. Seal the lid. Cook for 10 minutes at HIGH pressure.

Open the cooker according to manufacturer's directions. Season with red pepper, salt and black pepper. Enjoy!

Indian-Style Potato and Broccoli

(Ready in about 15 minutes | Servings 6)

Ingredients

2 cups potatoes, peeled and cubed

2 cups broccoli, broken into florets

2 tablespoons olive oil

2 cloves garlic, minced

1 teaspoon ginger, minced

1 teaspoon garam masala

1/2 teaspoon ground black pepper

1 teaspoon salt

Directions

Add the potatoes to your pressure cooker; cover with water. Seal the lid and cook under HIGH pressure for about 4 minutes. Then, remove the cooker from the heat; quick-release the pressure.

Add the broccoli. Bring to HIGH pressure; cook for 2 minutes. Drain and reserve. Clean the cooker.

Warm olive oil in the pressure cooker over LOW heat. Add the rest of the ingredients and cook for about 2 minutes.

Then, add the cooked potatoes and broccoli, along with 2 tablespoons of water. Let simmer over LOW heat for 10 minutes; stir periodically. Serve and enjoy!

Green Onion and Asparagus Salad

(Ready in about 10 minutes | Servings 4)

Ingredients

1 ½ pounds fresh asparagus, snap off the ends

1/2 cup water

1/2 cup green onions, minced

2 tablespoons lemon juice

3 tablespoons olive oil

1 teaspoon cayenne pepper

Salt and freshly ground white pepper, to taste

Directions

Place the asparagus flat in the pressure cooker; add the water.

Lock the lid and cook on HIGH for 3 minutes. Then, allow pressure to release naturally and gradually. Transfer the asparagus to a serving platter.

To make the dressing: In a measuring cup, whisk together the rest of the ingredients. Dress the asparagus and serve.

Easy Lemony Asparagus

(Ready in about 10 minutes | Servings 4)

Ingredients

1 cup water

Rind of 1 organic lemon

1 pound asparagus

Sea salt and ground black pepper, to taste

2 tablespoons olive oil

Directions

Place water and lemon rind in the pressure cooker; add a steamer basket.

Arrange the asparagus in the steamer basket. Close and lock the cooker's lid. Cook for 2 to 3 minutes at HIGH pressure. Next, open the cooker by releasing pressure.

Transfer to a serving platter. Sprinkle with salt and black pepper; drizzle with olive oil. Serve.

Sour Mushroom and Tofu Soup

(Ready in about 10 minutes | Servings 4)

Ingredients

2 tablespoons sesame oil

1 onion, thinly sliced

1 cup mushrooms, quartered

5 cups vegetable broth

1 (8-ounce) can sliced water chestnuts

3 tablespoons wine vinegar

3 tablespoons soy sauce

1/4 teaspoon white pepper

2 tablespoons cornstarch

1 (8-ounce) package tofu, cubed

1/2 scallions, thinly sliced

Directions

First, heat sesame oil in your cooker; next, sauté the onion until it's translucent or 3 to 4 minutes.

Add mushrooms, broth, water chestnuts, wine vinegar, soy sauce, and white pepper to the cooker.

Securely lock the lid and set for 5 minutes on HIGH. Then, release the cooker's pressure.

Next, mix the cornstarch with 2 tablespoons of water. Add the cornstarch mixture along with tofu; simmer for 2 minutes. Serve warm topped with scallions.

Basic Beef Broth

(Ready in about 1 hour 30 minutes | Servings 12)

Ingredients

1 tablespoon vegetable oil

1 ½ pounds bone-in chuck roast

1 pound beef bones, cracked

1 red onion, slice into rings

1 parsnip, peeled and chopped

1 carrot, peeled and chopped

1 celery stalk, cut and chopped

4 cups water

Directions

First of all, heat the vegetable oil over high heat. Then, add chuck roast and bones; brown on all sides for a few minutes, turning a few times.

Turn the heat to medium; add the onion, parsnip, carrot, and celery, and enough water to cover your ingredients. Close the cooker's lid.

Cook for about 1 hour 30 minutes at HIGH pressure. Open the cooker with the natural release method.

Next, remove the roast and beef bones with a slotted spoon. Discard the bones. Keep your broth 1 or 2 days in the refrigerator or 3 months in the freezer.

Easy Traditional Borscht

(Ready in about 25 minutes | Servings 6)

Ingredients

1 ½ tablespoons ghee

2 cloves garlic, peeled and minced

1/2 pound lamb, cut into bite-sized pieces

1 onion, peeled and diced

1 pound red beets, peeled, diced and rinsed

1 small-sized head cabbage, cored and chopped

1 (15-ounce) can tomatoes, diced

6 cups beef broth

1/4 cup wine vinegar

Sea salt and freshly ground black pepper, to taste

Sour cream, for garnish

Directions

Add the ghee, garlic, and lamb to your pressure cooker. Cook the lamb over medium heat, until it is browned. Add the onion and cook until translucent and fragrant.

Then, add the beets, cabbage, tomatoes, beef broth, wine vinegar to the pressure cooker.

Then, cook for 10 to 15 minutes at LOW pressure. Turn off the heat and quick-release the pressure.

Season with sea salt and black pepper according to your taste. Ladle your soup into serving dishes and garnish with sour cream. Enjoy!

Green Bean and Chicken Soup

(Ready in about 10 minutes | Servings 8)

Ingredients

6 carrots, peeled and grated

1 turnip, peeled and finely chopped

2 stalks celery, finely chopped

1 large-sized onion, peeled and diced

1 cup chicken breasts, boneless and cubed

2 tablespoons extra-virgin olive oil

2 teaspoons butter, melted

2 cloves garlic, peeled and minced

4 cups chicken stock

6 medium potatoes, peeled and diced

1 teaspoon dried rosemary

2 bay leaves

2 strips orange zest

Salt and freshly ground black pepper, to taste

8 chicken thighs, skin removed

2 (10-ounce) packages frozen green beans, thawed

Directions

Add the grated carrot, turnips, celery, onion, chicken meat, olive oil, and butter to your pressure cooker. Lock the lid into place. Bring to LOW pressure and maintain for 1 minute. Open the lid naturally.

Add the rest of the ingredients, except for green beans. Cover and bring to HIGH pressure. Then, allow pressure to release naturally and remove the lid.

Return the uncovered pressure cooker to MEDIUM heat and add the green beans. Now cook for 5 minutes. Taste for seasonings and serve warm.

Potato and Corn Chowder

(Ready in about 10 minutes | Servings 6)

Ingredients

2 tablespoons butter

2 white onions, chopped

6 cups vegetable stock

6 Idaho potatoes, peeled and diced

2 bay leaves

Salt and freshly ground black pepper, to taste

1 ½ cups corn

1/2 cup heavy cream

Directions

Melt the butter in your pressure cooker over medium heat. Then, sauté onions for 2 minutes. Pour in the vegetable stock. Add potatoes, bay leaves, salt, and black pepper.

Cover with the lid and bring to HIGH pressure; maintain pressure for 4 to 5 minutes. Discard the bay leaves.

Stir in the corn and heavy cream and serve warm.

Hearty Clam Chowder

(Ready in about 15 minutes | Servings 4)

Ingredients

4 thick strips bacon, diced

2 stalk celery, finely diced

1 carrot, finely diced

1 parsnip, finely diced

2 shallots, peeled and minced

1 pound potatoes, peeled and diced

3 (6 1/2-ounce) cans chopped clams, drained and liquid reserved

2 ½ cups vegetable broth

1 cup frozen corn

2 cups milk

1/2 teaspoon dried rosemary

1 teaspoon cayenne pepper

Sea salt and freshly ground black pepper, to taste

Directions

Fry the bacon over medium-high heat until it is just crisp. Add the celery, carrot, parsnip, and shallot; sauté for 3 to 5 minutes.

Stir in the potatoes and stir-fry for a few minutes longer. Stir in the clam liquid and vegetable broth.

Then, bring to HIGH pressure; maintain pressure for about 5 minutes. Allow pressure to drop naturally.

Stir in frozen corn, milk, rosemary, cayenne pepper, salt, black pepper, and reserved clams. Bring to a gentle simmer for 5 minutes. Serve.

Mushroom and Chicken Soup

(Ready in about 10 minutes | Servings 8)

Ingredients

1 parsnip, peeled and finely chopped

4 carrots, peeled and grated

2 stalks celery, finely chopped

1 large-sized onion, peeled and diced

2 cloves garlic, peeled and minced

1 cup mushrooms, thinly sliced

3 teaspoons butter, melted

4 cups chicken stock

1 teaspoon dried thyme

1 teaspoon dried rosemary

Salt and freshly ground black pepper, to taste

8 chicken thighs, skin removed

1 cup frozen whole kernel corn, thawed

1 cup frozen baby peas, thawed

Directions

Add the parsnip, carrot, celery, onion, garlic, mushroom, and butter to your pressure cooker. Seal the cooker's lid and bring to LOW pressure; maintain the pressure for 1 to 2 minutes. Then, open the lid naturally.

Add the remaining ingredients, except for corn and peas. Cover with the lid and bring to HIGH pressure. Then, remove the lid according to manufacturer's directions.

Add corn and peas and cook for 5 minutes. Ladle into soup bowls and serve with croutons if desired.

White Fish and Potato Chowder

(Ready in about 15 minutes | Servings 6)

Ingredients

2 tablespoons butter

2 leeks, thinly sliced

2 cups water

4 cups clam juice

6 russet potatoes, peeled and diced

2 bay leaves

Salt and freshly ground black pepper, to taste

1 pound white fish, cut into bite-sized pieces

1 teaspoon dried rosemary

1/2 teaspoon dried thyme

1/2 cup heavy cream

Directions

Melt the butter in your pressure cooker over medium heat. Then, sauté the leeks for 2 minutes. Stir in the water, clam juice, and potatoes. Add the bay leaves, salt, and black pepper.

Then, bring to HIGH pressure and maintain pressure for about 4 minutes. Remove the lid according to the manufacturer's instructions.

Add the fish to your pressure cooker. Simmer for about 3 minutes or until the fish is opaque. Stir in the rosemary, thyme, and heavy cream. Taste and adjust the seasonings. Serve warm.

Creamed Chestnuts Soup

(Ready in about 25 minutes | Servings 8)

Ingredients

1/2 pound dried chestnuts

2 tablespoons butter

1 medium-sized carrot, chopped

1 stalk celery, roughly chopped

1 leek, roughly sliced

1 teaspoon dried rosemary

1 teaspoon dried thyme

1 teaspoon dried sage

1/2 teaspoon ground black pepper

1 medium potato, peeled and roughly chopped

4 cups chicken broth

2 tablespoons dark rum

Kosher salt, to taste

Directions

First, soak chestnuts in the refrigerator overnight. Drain, rinse, and reserve.

Melt butter in your cooker over medium heat. Stir in the carrot, celery, leek, rosemary, thyme, sage, and ground black pepper; sauté until the vegetables are soft.

Now stir in the potatoes, chicken broth, and soaked chestnuts. Close and lock the cooker's lid. Turn the heat up to HIGH and cook for 15 to 20 minutes at HIGH pressure.

Afterwards, open the cooker with the natural release method. Lastly, add the rum and kosher salt to taste. Purée your mixture with an immersion blender. Serve warm.

Cream of Mushroom Soup

(Ready in about 20 minutes | Servings 4)

Ingredients

1/4 cup butter

1 onion, diced

2 cloves garlic, minced

2 cups mushrooms, sliced

2 carrots, diced

1/4 cup white wine

3 cups milk

1 teaspoon dried rosemary

1/2 teaspoon dried marjoram

1 cup béchamel sauce

Salt and black pepper, to taste

Directions

Warm the butter in your pressure cooker; sauté the onions until translucent and golden.

Add the garlic, mushrooms, carrots, and continue sautéing for 5 minutes longer. Stir in the wine, milk, rosemary, marjoram, and béchamel sauce. Season with salt and pepper.

Cover and bring to high pressure. Then, turn the heat to LOW and cook for about 8 minutes. Lastly, allow pressure to release naturally.

Purée the soup and serve warm.

Creamed Asparagus Soup

(Ready in about 20 minutes | Servings 6)

Ingredients

2 tablespoons butter

1 onion, diced

2 pounds asparagus, trimmed and cut into pieces

1 teaspoon garlic powder

1 teaspoon salt

1/2 teaspoon black pepper

1/4 teaspoon cayenne pepper

6 cups vegetable stock

1/4 cup milk

1 teaspoon lemon juice

Directions

Melt the butter in your pressure cooker; sauté the onion until tender and translucent. Add the asparagus, garlic powder, salt, black pepper, and cayenne pepper; sauté for 5 to 6 minutes.

Pour in the vegetable stock. Then, bring to HIGH pressure and cook for about 5 minutes.

Remove from the heat and allow pressure to release naturally. Add the milk and lemon juice, and purée your soup in a food processor. Serve warm.

Lima Bean Soup

(Ready in about 20 minutes | Servings 6)

Ingredients

2 cups dried lima beans

2 tablespoons olive oil

1/2 cup shallots, diced

2 cloves garlic, minced

1/2 cup water

2 cups vegetable broth

Sea salt and ground black pepper, to taste

Directions

Pour water into medium-sized dish. Then, add lima beans and soak them overnight.

Warm olive oil in your pressure cooker; sauté the shallots until they are tender and golden brown. Then, add the garlic and cook for 1 minute longer.

Add the water, vegetable broth, and soaked lima beans to the cooker. Seal the lid and continue to cook for 6 minutes. Remove from the heat and allow pressure to release gradually.

Purée the soup in a food processor; sprinkle with sea salt and ground black pepper. Serve warm.

Potato Cheese Soup

(Ready in about 15 minutes | Servings 6)

Ingredients

2 tablespoons butter

1/2 cup red onion, chopped

4 cups chicken broth

3/4 teaspoon sea salt

1/2 teaspoon black pepper

1/4 teaspoon red pepper flakes, crushed

6 cups potatoes, peeled and cubed

2 tablespoons water

2 tablespoons cornstarch

1/2 cup Ricotta cheese, cut into cubes

1 cup Cheddar cheese, shredded

2 cups half and half

1 cup frozen corn

Directions

Warm the butter in the pressure cooking pot. Sauté red onion for about 5 minutes. Add 2 cups chicken broth, salt, pepper, and red pepper flakes.

Put the steamer basket into the pressure cooker. Add the potatoes to the basket. Lock the lid in place, cook 4 minutes at HIGH pressure. Carefully remove the steamer basket from the pot.

In a small-sized bowl, dissolve cornstarch in water. Now add cornstarch mixture to the cooker, stirring often.

Add Ricotta cheese and Cheddar cheese. Stir until cheese is melted. Add remaining chicken broth, half and half, and corn. Cook for a few minutes longer until the soup is heated through. Serve.

Garlicky Bean Soup

(Ready in about 15 minutes | Servings 8)

Ingredients

2 cups dried white beans

3 tablespoons olive oil

1 medium-sized leek, sliced

4 cloves garlic, minced

2 cups water

4 cups vegetable stock

2 bay leaves

1 teaspoon apple cider vinegar

Sea salt and freshly cracked black pepper, to taste

Directions

Soak your white beans for 8 hours or overnight in enough water to cover them; drain and rinse.

In your pressure cooker, bring olive oil to temperature over medium heat. Now sauté the leek until it is golden brown. Add the garlic; continue sautéing for 1 minute more.

Pour in the water and vegetable stock; add bay leaves. Seal the lid and bring to HIGH pressure. Cook for about 10 minutes.

Remove the bay leaves; lastly, purée the soup and stir in the vinegar, salt, and black pepper. Ladle into individual dishes and serve warm.

Curried Chickpea Bisque

(Ready in about 25 minutes | Servings 8)

Ingredients

2 cups dried chickpeas

3 tablespoons canola oil

1 yellow onion, diced

2 cloves garlic, minced

1 teaspoon garam masala

2 teaspoons curry powder

2 cups vegetable broth

2 cups unsweetened soy milk

Salt and ground black pepper, to taste

Directions

Soak the chickpeas overnight.

Add canola oil to the cooker and sauté yellow onion until tender and translucent. Add the garlic, garam masala, and curry powder; then, sauté for 1 minute more.

Pour in vegetable broth and soy milk. Cover and bring to HIGH pressure. Maintain for 20 minutes.

Season with salt and pepper according to your taste. Add the soup to a food processor and purée until smooth; work in batches. Divide puréed soup among soup bowls and serve warm.

Vegetable Egg Soup

(Ready in about 15 minutes | Servings 6)

Ingredients

1/2 teaspoon star anise

1 teaspoon ginger

2-3 garlic cloves, minced

1 teaspoon celery seeds

1 teaspoon fennel seed

Salt to taste

1 teaspoon freshly ground black pepper

2 ripe tomatoes, chopped

4 cups water

2 cups vegetable broth

4 eggs, whisked

2 scallions, chopped

Directions

Put all the ingredients, except for eggs and scallions, into your pressure cooking pot.

Turn the heat up to HIGH. Cook for about 7 minutes at HIGH pressure.

Open the pressure cooker following manufacturer's instructions. Then, pour in the eggs and gently stir to combine.

Serve sprinkled with the scallions. Enjoy!

Nutty Vegetable Stew

(Ready in about 20 minutes | Servings 4)

Ingredients

1 tablespoon peanut oil

1 shallot, diced

2 green garlics, finely minced

1 yellow bell pepper, chopped

2 tablespoons fresh ginger, minced

1 sweet potato, peeled and cubed

2 cups canned tomatoes, diced and drained

1 (4-ounce) can chickpeas, drained

1 cup water

2 cups vegetable broth

1/2 cup peanut butter

Kosher salt and ground black pepper, to taste

1/2 cup nut milk of choice

Directions

Bring the peanut oil to MEDIUM heat in the pressure cooker. Then, sauté the shallot, green garlics, and bell pepper for about 3 minutes. Add the ginger, and sauté for 30 seconds more.

Add the remaining ingredients, except for the milk, to the pressure cooker.

Cover and bring to HIGH pressure; maintain for 10 minutes. After that, allow pressure to release naturally. Stir in the nut milk just before serving. Ladle into individual bowls and serve. Enjoy!

Beer and Beef Stew

(Ready in about 25 minutes | Servings 8)

Ingredients

2 teaspoons olive oil	2 tablespoons fresh rosemary, minced
1 onion, diced	2 pounds lean beef meat, cubed
2 carrots, diced	1 teaspoon sea salt
2 celery stalks, diced	1/2 teaspoon black pepper
1 parsnip, diced	1/2 teaspoon cayenne pepper
2 cloves garlic, minced	1 teaspoon cocoa powder
2 potatoes, peeled and diced	1 cup beer

Directions

Warm the oil in a pressure cooker over medium heat. Now sauté the onion, carrots, celery, parsnip, garlic, potatoes, rosemary, and meat for 5 to 6 minutes.

Add sea salt, black pepper, cayenne pepper, cocoa powder, and the beer. Close and lock the cooker's lid.

Turn the heat up to HIGH; then, lower the heat to the minimum needed to maintain pressure. Cook approximately 15 minutes at HIGH pressure. Serve warm.

Zesty Beef Stew

(Ready in about 25 minutes | Servings 8)

Ingredients

2 teaspoons vegetable oil

2 medium-sized sweet onions, diced

2 carrots, diced

1 celery stalk, diced

1 bell pepper, seeded and diced

2 potatoes, peeled and diced

2 tablespoons fresh thyme, minced

2 pounds lean beef meat, cubed

Sea salt and ground black pepper, to taste

1/2 teaspoon red pepper flakes, crushed

1 ½ cups water

Directions

Warm vegetable oil in a pressure cooker over medium heat. When the oil is hot enough, sauté sweet onions, carrots, celery, and bell pepper, until all the ingredients are browned.

Add the remaining ingredients. Close and lock the cooker's lid.

Cook this stew for about 15 minutes at HIGH pressure. Ladle into serving dishes and enjoy!

Vegan Brunswick Stew

(Ready in about 25 minutes | Servings 4)

Ingredients

2 tablespoons canola oil

1 leek, chopped

1 carrot, chopped

2 stalks celery, sliced

1 green bell pepper, diced

1 red bell pepper, diced

2 cups mushroom, chopped

1 (28-ounce) can crushed tomatoes

2 cups corn kernels

1 cup tomato paste

1/2 cup barbecue sauce

1 teaspoon salt

1/2 teaspoon black pepper

1 teaspoon cayenne pepper

Directions

Heat canola oil in the pressure cooker over medium heat; sauté the leek, carrot, celery, and bell peppers until all the vegetables are soft, or about 5 minutes.

Add all remaining ingredients. Cover, bring to HIGH pressure and maintain for 30 minutes. Remove from the heat, open the lid naturally, and serve right away.

Sausage and Pea Soup

(Ready in about 25 minutes | Servings 8)

Ingredients

1 pound ground sausage	28 ounces vegetable stock
2 tablespoons margarine	1 package (16-ounce) peas
1 medium-sized leek, finely chopped	1/2 cup half and half
2 cloves garlic, minced	1 teaspoon cayenne pepper
1 cup carrots, diced	Salt and fresh ground black pepper to taste
2 cups water	

Directions

In the preheated cooker, cook the sausage until browned.

Then, warm margarine in your pressure cooker pot. Sauté the leeks, garlic, and carrots until tender.

Stir in the remaining ingredients, except for half and half. Now choose 'HIGH' pressure and 10 minutes cook time. After that, wait 10 minutes, and open the lid naturally.

Puree the mixture with an immersion blender. Continue to simmer and add the reserved and browned sausage and half and half. Stir until it is heated through. Enjoy!

Chickpea and Navy Stew

(Ready in about 20 minutes | Servings 8)

Ingredients

1 ½ cups dried navy beans	1 cup dried chickpeas, soaked

2 cloves garlic, minced

2 tablespoons canola oil

4 cups water

Kosher salt and ground black pepper

1/4 cup sharp cheese, grated

Directions

Add all the above ingredients, except for cheese, to your pressure cooking pot. Close and lock the cooker's lid according to manufacturer's instructions.

Turn the heat up to HIGH; when the pot reaches pressure, lower the heat. Cook for 15 minutes at HIGH pressure.

Open the pressure cooker with the natural-release method.

Ladle the stew into serving dishes; top each serving with grated cheese. Serve.

Eggplant and Chickpea Stew

(Ready in about 30 minutes | Servings 4)

Ingredients

2 eggplants, cut into large cubes

1 large-sized carrot, diced

1 (14-ounce) can chickpeas, drained

2 cups water

4 cups vegetable stock

1 cup tomato paste

1 teaspoon cumin

1 teaspoon celery seeds

1/2 cup fresh parsley, chopped

1/4 teaspoon red pepper flakes, crushed

1/4 teaspoon ground black pepper

1 teaspoon salt

Directions

Add the ingredients to your pressure cooker; lock the cooker's lid into place.

Bring to LOW pressure and maintain for about 30 minutes. Turn off the heat and allow pressure to release according to manufacturer's directions.

Open the lid and ladle the stew into individual bowls. Serve warm.

Zucchini and Chickpea Stew

(Ready in about 30 minutes | Servings 4)

Ingredients

2 large-sized zucchinis, cut into bite-sized chunks

1 parsnip, chopped

1 large-sized carrot, diced

1 (14-ounce) can chickpeas, drained

4 cups chicken broth

3 cups water

2 tablespoons tomato ketchup

1 teaspoon dried thyme

1/2 cup fresh cilantro, chopped

1/4 teaspoon ground black pepper

1 teaspoon salt

Directions

Add all the above ingredients to a pressure cooker; cover with the lid.

Cook for about 30 minutes at LOW pressure. Turn off the heat; allow pressure to release according to manufacturer's instructions.

Turn off the heat and remove the cooker's lid. Taste and adjust the seasonings. Serve warm.

Vegan Sausage Stew

(Ready in about 15 minutes | Servings 6)

Ingredients

12 cups water
1 pound red potatoes, whole and unpeeled
6 ears corn on the cob, husked and halved
1 (14-ounce) package vegan sausage, sliced

Salt and black pepper, to taste
1 teaspoon cayenne pepper
1 teaspoon dried basil
2 heads garlic, peeled

Directions

Add the water and red potatoes to your pressure cooker. Now lock the cooker's lid into place; bring to HIGH pressure and maintain for 5 to 6 minutes. Then, quick-release the pressure.

Uncover the cooker and stir in all remaining ingredients. Cover and bring to HIGH pressure; maintain for 5 more minutes. Then, allow pressure to release naturally and gradually.

Remove the ingredients from the cooker with a slotted spoon. Serve and enjoy!

DINNER RECIPES

Yummy Vegan Gumbo

(Ready in about 2 hours | Servings 6)

Ingredients

1/2 cup canola oil

1/2 cup all-purpose flour

1 onion, diced

1 red bell pepper, diced

1 carrot, diced

1 stalk celery, diced

4 cloves garlic, minced

2 cups vegetable broth

4 cups water

1 tablespoon Vegan Worcestershire sauce

1 (16-ounce) package frozen chopped okra

2 bay leaves

Sea salt and black pepper, to taste

1 pound vegan chicken, chopped

1/2 cup parsley, chopped

6 cups hot cooked rice

Directions

Warm canola oil over medium heat in your pressure cooker. To make the roux: add the flour and cook, stirring frequently, until your roux gets a rich brown color, or for about 25 minutes.

Add the onion, bell pepper, carrot, celery, and garlic to the roux; continue to sauté for 5 minutes. Add the broth and water, bringing to a boil over HIGH heat for 20 minutes.

Add the rest of the above ingredients, except for rice. Cover, bring to LOW pressure and maintain for 1 hour 10 minutes. Afterwards, allow pressure to release naturally.

Serve over prepared rice and enjoy!

Barley and Chickpea Stew

(Ready in about 20 minutes | Servings 4)

Ingredients

1 cup barley

1 cup dry chickpeas, soaked

2 tablespoons olive oil, divided

2 cloves garlic, pressed

1 onion, diced

2 carrots, diced

1 parsnip, chopped

2 celery stalks, diced

1/2 head red cabbage, shredded

4 cups water

1 teaspoon sea salt

1/2 teaspoon ground black pepper

1/2 teaspoon cayenne pepper

Directions

Simply throw all of the above ingredients in the pressure cooker. Close and lock the lid.

Turn the heat to HIGH and cook your stew for 15 minutes at HIGH pressure.

Open with a natural release method. Release the rest of the pressure with the cooker's valve.

Season to taste and serve right away!

Asian-Style Tofu Stew

(Ready in about 15 minutes | Servings 4)

Ingredients

2 tablespoons sesame oil

1 small-sized onion, sliced

2 cloves garlic, minced

1 cup broccoli, chopped into florets

1 cup mushrooms, sliced

12 ounces soft silken tofu, drained and cubed

1 tablespoon red pepper, crushed

1 teaspoon tamari sauce

3 cups vegetable stock

Fresh chives, for garnish

Directions

Warm the sesame oil over medium heat in your pressure cooker. Then, sauté the onion and garlic for 3 to 4 minutes.

Add the rest of your ingredients, except for chives, to the pressure cooker. Cover with the lid; bring to LOW pressure and maintain for 5 minutes. Remove from heat and allow pressure to release naturally.

Remove the lid and serve in individual bowls. Sprinkle with chives. Enjoy!

Beef and Mushroom Stew

(Ready in about 35 minutes | Servings 8)

Ingredients

1 (3-pound) chuck roast, cut into bite-sized pieces

2 (4-ounce) cans mushrooms, drained and sliced

2 (10 3⁄4-ounce) cans cream of mushroom soup

2 cups water

1 tablespoon Worcestershire sauce

3 (24-ounce) bags frozen vegetables, thawed

Salt and freshly ground black pepper, to taste

1 teaspoon red pepper flakes, crushed

Directions

Add chuck roast, mushroom, mushroom soup, water, and Worcestershire sauce to the pressure cooker.

Then, bring to LOW pressure; maintain pressure for 30 minutes. Stir in frozen vegetables. Bring to a simmer and maintain pressure for 5 minutes.

Sprinkle with salt, black pepper, and red pepper. Taste for seasoning and serve warm.

Veggies in Lime-Butter Sauce

(Ready in about 10 minutes | Servings 6)

Ingredients

2 cups cauliflower florets

2 cups broccoli florets

1/2 teaspoon salt

1/2 teaspoon black pepper

1/2 teaspoon dried dill weed

1 cup water

4 tablespoons butter

1 tablespoon lime juice

1/2 teaspoon yellow mustard

Directions

Put the cauliflower, broccoli, salt, black pepper, dried dill, and water into your pressure cooker. Cover and bring to LOW pressure; maintain pressure for 2 to 3 minutes.

Turn off the heat; quick-release the pressure; remove the cooker's lid.

To make the sauce: whisk together the butter, lime juice, and yellow mustard. Drizzle the sauce over the cooked cauliflower and broccoli. Serve.

Delicious Braised Cauliflower

(Ready in about 10 minutes | Servings 6)

Ingredients

2 tablespoons sesame oil

1/2 cup sweet onion, chopped

2 cloves garlic, crushed

1/4 teaspoon pepper flakes, crushed

1 pound cauliflower, cut into florets

1/2 teaspoon salt

1/4 teaspoon ground black pepper

1/2 teaspoon dried basil

3/4 cups water

Directions

Heat sesame oil in your pressure cooker over medium heat. Add sweet onion, garlic, and red pepper flakes; cook, stirring continuously, for about 2 minutes. Add the cauliflower florets and continue cooking for about 5 minutes.

Sprinkle with salt, black pepper, and dried basil; add the water.

Cook for 2 to 3 minutes at HIGH pressure. Lastly, open the cooker by following the manufacturer's instructions. Serve over rice.

Seared Brussels Sprouts

(Ready in about 10 minutes | Servings 6)

Ingredients

2 tablespoons butter, at room temperature

1 pound Brussels sprouts, outer leaves

removed and halved

1/4 cup water

Salt and ground black pepper, to taste

1 teaspoon red pepper flakes, to taste

Directions

Add butter to your pressure cooker and melt it over medium-high heat. When the butter is melted, cook your Brussels sprouts for a few minutes or until tender.

Add the water, and lock on the lid. Bring to HIGH pressure, and maintain pressure for about 1 minute. Season with salt, black pepper, and red pepper to taste. Serve as a perfect light dinner.

Brussel Sprout Salad with Walnuts

(Ready in about 10 minutes | Servings 6)

Ingredients

1 cup water

1 pound Brussels sprouts, outer leaves removed and halved

2 tablespoons olive oil

1 teaspoon salt

1/4 teaspoon black pepper

1/2 cup walnuts, toasted and chopped

Dried cranberries, for garnish

Directions

Begin by pouring the water into your pressure cooker. Then, add the steamer basket to the cooker.

Throw Brussels sprouts in the steamer basket. Close and lock the cooker's lid according to manufacturer's instructions.

Turn the heat up to HIGH; when the pressure is reached, lower the heat to the minimum that is needed to maintain pressure. Cook for about 4 minutes at HIGH pressure.

Replace the sprouts to a serving dish. Drizzle your Brussels sprouts with olive oil; season with salt and black pepper. Sprinkle with walnuts and cranberries. Enjoy!

Aunt's Savoy Cabbage

(Ready in about 10 minutes | Servings 6)

Ingredients

2 tablespoons ghee or butter

1 yellow onion, sliced

1 clove garlic, minced

1 medium Savoy cabbage, cut into strips

3⁄4 cup beer

Salt and black pepper, to your taste

1/2 teaspoon smoked paprika

Directions

Begin by melting ghee (butter) in an uncovered cooker over medium heat. Then, sauté the onions and garlic, stirring occasionally, until they are fragrant and softened.

Stir in Savoy cabbage and beer. Cover and set the temperature to HIGH; cook for 5 minutes at HIGH pressure.

Afterwards, open the cooker by releasing pressure. Replace the cabbage to a nice serving platter; sprinkle with salt, black pepper, and smoked paprika; serve.

Tangy Red Cabbage

(Ready in about 10 minutes | Servings 4)

Ingredients

2 cloves garlic, minced

1 bunch scallions, sliced

1 chili pepper, finely minced

1⁄2 cup water

1⁄4 cup tamari sauce

4 cups red cabbage, cut into strips

2 carrots, julienned

Directions

Add the garlic, scallions, chili pepper, water, and tamari sauce to your pressure cooker; stir well. Stir in the cabbage and carrots.

Cover and bring to HIGH pressure; maintain pressure for 2 minutes.

Afterwards, remove the lid according to manufacturer's instructions. Transfer to a large platter and serve.

Red Cabbage with Pine Nuts

(Ready in about 10 minutes | Servings 8)

Ingredients

2 tablespoons olive oil

1 onion, diced

2 apples, peeled, cored, and sliced

1/2 cup white wine

1 head red cabbage, cut into strips

1 teaspoon kosher salt

1/2 teaspoon freshly ground black pepper

Pine nuts, for garnish

Directions

Heat olive oil in your pressure cooker over medium heat. Sauté the onion until translucent and soft.

Add the apples and wine.

Stir the cabbage into the pressure cooker. Cover and cook for 2 to 4 minutes at HIGH pressure.

When time is up, open the pressure cooker according to manufacturer's instructions. Season with salt and black pepper. Sprinkle with pine nuts and serve immediately.

Delicious Carrots in Milk Sauce

(Ready in about 10 minutes | Servings 4)

Ingredients

1 pound carrots, cut into 1-inch chunks

1/4 cup water

3/4 cup milk

Sea salt and white pepper, to taste

2 tablespoons olive oil

1 tablespoon flour

Directions

Fill your cooker with carrots, water, milk, salt, white pepper, and olive oil. Cover with the lid. Turn the heat up to HIGH. Cook approximately 4 minutes at HIGH pressure. Afterwards, open the pressure cooker by releasing pressure.

Next, remove carrots to serving dish using a slotted spoon.

To make the sauce: Place the pressure cooker over medium heat. Add flour and cook until the sauce has thickened, stirring continuously. Serve the sauce over prepared carrots and enjoy!

Flavorful Ginger Carrots

(Ready in about 5 minutes | Servings 4)

Ingredients

1 pound carrots, peeled and cut into matchsticks

2 tablespoons olive oil

1 teaspoon fresh ginger, minced

1 cup water

Kosher salt and ground black pepper, to your taste

1/2 teaspoon allspice

Directions

Add the carrot matchsticks, olive oil, ginger, and water to your cooker. Stir to combine well. Close and lock the cooker's lid.

Cook for 1 minute at HIGH pressure. Open the pressure cooker according to manufacturer's directions.

Season with salt, black pepper and allspice; serve right away!

Butter Corn Evening Treat

(Ready in about 10 minutes | Servings 4)

Ingredients

4 ears sweet corn, shucked

1/2 cup water

1 tablespoon butter

1/2 teaspoon cinnamon

Salt and white pepper, to taste

Directions

Place a rack in your pressure cooker; arrange the corn on the rack. Pour in the water.

Then, bring to LOW pressure; maintain pressure for about 3 minutes. Remove the lid according to manufacturer's directions.

Spread softened butter over each ear of corn; sprinkle with cinnamon, salt and white pepper. Serve.

Cilantro and Orange Sweet Corn

(Ready in about 10 minutes | Servings 4)

Ingredients

4 ears sweet corn, shucked

1/2 cup water

2 tablespoons butter

2 tablespoons fresh cilantro, chopped

2 teaspoons fresh orange juice

1/2 teaspoon orange rind, grated

Kosher salt and white pepper, to taste

1/2 teaspoon paprika

1/4 teaspoon grated nutmeg

Directions

Put a rack into your pressure cooking pot; lay the ears of corn on the rack. Pour the water into the cooker.

Cook for 3 minutes at LOW pressure.

In a small-sized bowl, combine the rest of the ingredients until they are well blended. Afterwards, spread this mixture on prepared ears of corn. Serve.

Tomato and Eggplant Salad

(Ready in about 15 minutes | Servings 6)

Ingredients

1 eggplant, peeled and diced

1/2 cup water

3 tablespoons vegetable oil

2 cloves garlic, minced

2 cups tomatoes, chopped

1 tablespoon white wine

1 teaspoon cayenne pepper

Sea salt and black pepper, to taste

2 tablespoons fresh parsley

Directions

Throw the eggplant and water in your pressure cooker. Cover and bring to HIGH pressure; maintain pressure for 4 minutes. Quick release the pressure, remove the lid and set aside.

Add the rest of the above ingredients, except for parsley. Bring to HIGH pressure and maintain pressure for about 2 minutes.

Sprinkle with fresh parsley and serve chilled.

Country Beef and Potato Stew

(Ready in about 55 minutes | Servings 4)

Ingredients

2 tablespoons olive oil

1 pound beef, cubed

1 small-sized onion, thinly sliced

3 cloves garlic, peeled and minced

4 potatoes, peeled and diced

1 teaspoon dried oregano

1/2 teaspoon dried basil

1 cup tomato sauce

1 cup water

3/4 cup white wine

Salt and black pepper, to taste

Directions

Warm olive oil in a cooking pot. Sauté the beef, onion, and garlic until the meat has browned and the onion becomes translucent.

Add the remaining ingredients; stir to combine ingredients well. Cover and cook for 45 minutes at LOW pressure. Serve over cooked rice and enjoy!

Creamed Beef with Quinoa

(Ready in about 25 minutes | Servings 6)

Ingredients

1 tablespoon olive oil

1 yellow onion, thinly sliced

2 cloves garlic, minced

1 pound top round, cut into strips

1/2 teaspoon cloves, ground

1 teaspoon ground coriander

3/4 teaspoon salt

1/2 teaspoon freshly ground black pepper

1 cup plain yogurt

1 (28-ounce) can whole stewed tomatoes

2 cups prepared quinoa

Directions

Heat olive oil in a cooking pot over medium heat. Sauté the onion until tender and translucent. Add the rest of the ingredients, except for quinoa, to your pressure cooker.

Turn the heat up to HIGH; when the cooker reaches pressure, lower the heat. Cook for about 15 minutes at HIGH pressure.

Afterwards, open the pressure cooker by releasing pressure. Serve over prepared quinoa.

Saucy Beef in Yogurt

(Ready in about 30 minutes | Servings 6)

Ingredients

1 tablespoon butter, at room temperature

1 red onion, diced

5 green garlics, minced

1 pound bottom round, cubed

1 tablespoon cumin

1 tablespoon coriander

1/2 teaspoon cardamom

1 teaspoon chili powder

Salt and black pepper, to taste

2 ripe tomatoes, chopped

1 cup whole milk yogurt

Directions

Start by melting the butter over medium heat in your cooker. Sauté the onion and green garlic until they are softened.

Add the remaining ingredients, except for the yogurt, to your pressure cooker.

Cook for 13 to 15 minutes at HIGH pressure. Lastly, open the cooker by releasing pressure.

Pour in the yogurt; simmer until it has thickened, or 10 to 12 minutes. Serve warm.

Corned Beef and Cabbage

(Ready in about 1 hour | Servings 6)

Ingredients

Non-stick cooking spray

2 onions, peeled and sliced

1 corned beef brisket

1 cup apple juice

2 teaspoons orange zest, finely grated

2 teaspoons yellow mustard

1/2 head cabbage, diced

Sea salt and ground black pepper, to taste

Directions

Treat the inside of the cooker with non-stick cooking spray. Arrange the onions on the bottom of your cooker.

Add the beef, apple juice, orange zest, and yellow mustard. Lock the lid into place; bring to LOW pressure; maintain for 45 minutes. Afterwards, remove the lid.

Place the cabbage on top of the ingredients. Then, bring to LOW pressure; maintain pressure for 8 minutes. Season with salt and black pepper to taste.

Carve the brisket and serve.

Old-Fashioned Beef Roast

(Ready in about 45 minutes | Servings 8)

Ingredients

1/2 pound carrots

2 parsnips, diced

2 stalks celery, diced

1 red bell pepper, seeded and thinly sliced

1 green bell pepper, seeded and thinly sliced

1 onion, peeled and sliced

2 cloves garlic, peeled and minced

1 boneless chuck roast, into serving-sized portions

1 envelope onion soup mix

Salt and ground black pepper, to taste

1 cup water

1 cup tomato juice

Directions

Arrange the vegetables in the bottom of your pressure cooker. Lay the chuck roast on the vegetable layer.

In a mixing bowl, combine the rest of the ingredients; mix well to combine; pour the mixture into the pressure cooker.

Then, bring to LOW pressure; maintain pressure for 45 minutes. Serve warm.

Burger and Cabbage

(Ready in about 20 minutes | Servings 6)

Ingredients

1 ½ pounds lean ground beef

1 leek, diced

1 1(5-ounce) can tomatoes, diced

1 cup tomato juice

3 cups cabbage, shredded

Salt and freshly ground black pepper, to taste

1 teaspoon cayenne pepper

Directions

Add the ground beef and leek to the pressure cooker. Cook over medium-high heat until your beef is lightly browned; drain off any rendered fat.

Stir in the rest of the ingredients.

Lock the lid into place; bring to LOW pressure and maintain pressure for about 8 minutes. Then, allow pressure to release gradually and naturally. Uncover, taste and adjust for seasonings. Serve.

Chicken in Orange Sauce with Walnuts

(Ready in about 20 minutes | Servings 8)

Ingredients

2 tablespoons margarine

3 pounds chicken thighs, boneless and skinless

1 teaspoon dried dill

1/2 teaspoon salt

1/4 teaspoon black pepper, ground

1/4 teaspoon fresh or dried ginger

1/2 cup white raisins

1/2 cup chopped walnuts

1 ½ cups orange juice

1 tablespoon cornstarch

1/4 cup cold water

Directions

Begin by melting margarine in the pressure cooker over MEDIUM heat. Then, fry the chicken thighs for 2 to 3 minutes, turning once. Add the remaining ingredients, except for cornstarch and water.

Lock the cooker's lid into place. Bring to LOW pressure; maintain pressure for about 10 minutes. Afterwards, remove the lid according to the manufacturer's instructions.

In a small-sized bowl, while whisking vigorously, combine the cornstarch with the water. Slowly stir into the cooker.

Continue to cook for 3 minutes or until the sauce has thickened and the mixture is thoroughly warmed. Serve.

Chicken and Baby Carrots in Tomato Sauce

(Ready in about 20 minutes | Servings 8)

Ingredients

2 tablespoons sesame oil

2 pounds chicken breasts, cubed

1 onion, peeled and finely chopped

1 pound baby carrots

Kosher salt ground black pepper, to taste

1/2 teaspoon curry powder

1 ½ cups tomato juice

1 tablespoon cornstarch

1/4 cup cold water

Directions

Heat sesame oil in the pressure cooker over MEDIUM heat. Sauté the chicken and onion for about 3 minutes, stirring periodically. Add the rest of the above ingredients, except for cornstarch and water.

Lock the cooker's lid into place. Bring to LOW pressure; maintain pressure for about 10 minutes. Uncover and quick-release the pressure.

In a small-sized bowl, combine together the cornstarch and the water. Gradually stir the cornstarch mixture into the pressure cooker.

Cook for 3 minutes or until everything is thoroughly heated. Serve right away.

Traditional Chicken Paprikash

(Ready in about 20 minutes | Servings 8)

Ingredients

2 tablespoons vegetable oil

1 medium-sized leek, peeled and diced

4 cloves garlic, finely minced

1 bell pepper, peeled and sliced

4 chicken breast halves

1/4 cup tomato sauce

2 tablespoons paprika

1 ½ cup chicken broth

1 tablespoon flour

3/4 cup sour cream

Salt and freshly ground black pepper, to taste

Directions

Bring the vegetable oil to temperature in the pressure cooker over medium-high heat. Add the leek, garlic, and bell pepper; then, sauté for about 3 minutes. Add the chicken and continue cooking until it is browned.

In a bowl, combine together the tomato sauce, paprika, and chicken broth. Pour this tomato mixture over the chicken in the cooker. Cover and bring to LOW pressure; maintain pressure approximately 10 minutes.

Remove the chicken from the pot by using a slotted spoon. Divide the chicken among serving plates. Combine together flour and sour cream.

Return the cooker to the heat; stir in the flour mixture. Simmer for 5 minutes, stirring continuously, or until the cooker juices have thickened. Salt and pepper to taste; spoon the sauce over the chicken.

Saucy Collard Greens

(Ready in about 20 minutes | Servings 6)

Ingredients

1 tablespoon canola oil

1 small-sized onion, diced

2 cloves garlic, minced

1 chipotle pepper, minced

4 cups vegetable broth

1 teaspoon liquid smoke

1 tablespoon tamari sauce

1 teaspoon white vinegar

Salt and black pepper, to taste

1 pound collard greens, tough stalks and stems removed, chopped

Directions

Warm the canola oil in your pressure cooker over MEDIUM heat. Add the onion, garlic, and chipotle pepper; sauté until the vegetables begin to soften, or 4 to 5 minutes.

Add all remaining ingredients, except for collard greens; stir well to combine. Lock the lid onto the pressure cooker. Bring the cooker up to HIGH pressure.

Then, maintain pressure for 10 minutes. Remove from the heat and quick-release the pressure. Carefully remove the lid. Add collard greens and simmer until they are completely wilted. Serve warm.

Herbed Fennel in Wine Sauce

(Ready in about 20 minutes | Servings 4)

Ingredients

2 tablespoons butter

1 large-sized sweet onion, diced

4 fennel bulbs, outer leaves removed, diced

1 cup white wine

1/2 teaspoon dried dill weed

1/2 teaspoon celery seeds

Salt and black pepper, to taste

Directions

Begin by bringing the butter to temperature in the pressure cooker over medium heat. Then, sauté sweet onion for about 3 minutes.

Stir in the fennel bulbs and continue sautéing for about 3 minutes. Stir in the wine, dill weed, and celery seeds. Lock the lid onto the pressure cooker, and bring to LOW pressure; maintain for 8 minutes.

Afterwards, remove the lid. Let it simmer until the fennel is thoroughly cooked. Salt and pepper; serve.

Green Beans with Sesame and Dill

(Ready in about 10 minutes | Servings 4)

Ingredients

2 cups water

1 pound green beans, trimmed

1/2 teaspoon cumin

1 teaspoon dill weed

1 tablespoon sesame oil

2 tablespoons sesame seeds, toasted

Salt and freshly cracked black pepper, to taste

Directions

Fill the bottom of your cooker with two cups of water. Place the steamer basket in the cooker.

Then, throw green beans in your steamer basket. Sprinkle the cumin and dill over green beans.

Secure the lid and allow to cook on HIGH; cook until the pressure indicator rises. Now decrease the heat and cook for 5 minutes.

Toss prepared green beans in the sesame oil. Sprinkle with sesame seeds, salt, and black pepper. Toss to combine and serve.

Easy and Yummy Fennel Purée

(Ready in about 20 minutes | Servings 4)

Ingredients

2 tablespoons butter

1 medium-sized leek, sliced

4 fennel bulbs, outer leaves removed, diced

1 cup vegetable broth

1 teaspoon red pepper flakes, crushed

Sea salt and black pepper, to taste

Directions

Melt the butter in the pressure cooker over medium heat. When the butter is melted, sauté the leeks for 3 to 4 minutes.

Add the fennel bulbs and continue sautéing for 3 to 4 minutes. Pour in the vegetable broth. Lock the lid onto the cooker, and bring to LOW pressure; maintain for 8 minutes.

Remove the lid. Then, simmer until the fennel bulbs are thoroughly cooked. Sprinkle with red pepper flakes.

To make a purée: transfer the cooked fennel to the food processor. Pulse until uniform and creamy; add some cooking liquid if necessary. Salt and pepper to your taste. Replace to the serving dish and serve.

Nutty Green Bean Salad

(Ready in about 10 minutes | Servings 4)

Ingredients

1 pound green beans, fresh or frozen

1 cup water

1/4 cup pine nuts, toasted

2 teaspoons lemon juice

1 tablespoon extra-virgin olive oil

Salt and black pepper, to taste

Directions

Arrange green beans in a steamer basket.

Pour the water into the pressure cooker; add the steamer basket. Cover with the lid.

Cook for about 7 minutes at HIGH pressure.

Afterwards, open the cooker by releasing pressure. Dress with pine nuts, lemon juice, and olive oil. Salt and pepper to taste. Serve.

Delicious Spicy Kale

(Ready in about 15 minutes | Servings 4)

Ingredients

2 cups water

1 teaspoon kosher salt

8 cups kale leaves, chopped

2 tablespoon sesame oil

2 cloves garlic, minced

1/2 teaspoon dried dill weed

1 teaspoon dried red pepper flakes

1/2 cup vegetable stock

1/2 teaspoon ground white pepper

Directions

Pour the water into a pressure cooker. Add salt and bring water to a boil. Blanch kale for 1 minute; drain and reserve.

Warm the sesame oil in your pressure cooker over MEDIUM heat. Add the garlic, dill weed, and red pepper flakes; cook for 30 seconds to 1 minute. Add the vegetable stock, white pepper, and reserved kale. Gently stir to combine well.

Cover the cooker, and bring to HIGH pressure; maintain pressure for about 6 minutes. Remove from the heat and carefully remove the lid by following the manufacturer's instructions; serve right now.

Parsnip and Carrot Purée

(Ready in about 20 minutes | Servings 4)

Ingredients

1/2 pound parsnips, peeled and diced

1/2 pound carrots, peeled and diced

3 tablespoons butter or ghee

1 heaping teaspoon salt

1/2 teaspoon freshly cracked black pepper

Fresh chopped parsley, as garnish

Directions

Place the parsnips and carrots in the pressure cooker; add enough water to cover them.

Lock on the cooker's lid. Bring to HIGH pressure; maintain pressure for 3 minutes. Remove the vegetables with a slotted spoon and reserve the cooking water.

Add the parsnips, carrots, and about 1/4 cup of cooking water to a food processor. Mix until it is uniform and smooth, adding more water as needed.

Add the purée back to the cleaned pressure cooker. Add the butter (ghee), salt, and black pepper; cook over LOW heat for 10 minutes, stirring continuously. Transfer to a serving dish and sprinkle with fresh parsley. Enjoy!

Apple Cider Pork

(Ready in about 1 hour 10 minutes | Servings 8)

Ingredients

2 tablespoons butter

1 pork roast

Salt and black pepper, to taste

3 cups apple cider

2 apples, cored and quartered

2 bay leaves

1/4 teaspoon allspice

Directions

Warm the butter on HIGH until melted.

Generously season the pork roast with salt and black pepper; lay pork roast in the cooker and cook until it is browned on each side.

Add the apple cider, apples, bay leaves, and allspice to the pressure cooker; securely lock the cooker's lid. Set to 1 hour on HIGH.

Allow the cooker's pressure to release naturally for about 10 minutes. Carve the pork roast and drizzle with the cooking liquid.

BBQ Back Ribs

(Ready in about 35 minutes | Servings 6)

Ingredients

1 teaspoon garlic powder

1 teaspoon salt

3/4 teaspoon ground black pepper

1 tablespoon cayenne pepper

2 ribs, cut to fit into cooker

1 onion, sliced into rings

1 ½ cups chicken broth

2 tablespoons tomato paste

1 (18-ounce) bottle BBQ sauce

Directions

In a small-sized mixing bowl, combine garlic powder, salt, black pepper, and cayenne pepper. Rub the mixture over the surface of your ribs.

Lay rubbed ribs at the bottom of your cooker; place the onion rings on the ribs; add chicken broth and tomato paste to the pressure cooker. Set the cooker to 15 minutes on HIGH.

Lastly, grill cooked ribs for about 15 minutes, turning once or twice, basting with BBQ sauce.

Creamed Shrimp with Pasta

(Ready in about 20 minutes | Servings 4)

Ingredients

2 tablespoons olive oil

2/3 cup red onion, diced

1 cup dried pasta of choice

12 ounces frozen shrimp

2 ½ cups chicken broth

2-3 cloves garlic, minced

1 teaspoon dried basil

1/2 teaspoon dried oregano

1/2 cup heavy cream

1 cup Parmesan cheese, grated

3/4 teaspoon salt

1/4 teaspoon ground black pepper

Directions

Warm olive oil over medium-high heat; sauté red onion for about 3 minutes, or until it is translucent.

Add pasta, shrimp, chicken broth, garlic, basil, and oregano to the pressure cooker. Securely lock the lid and set for 7 minutes on HIGH.

Use a quick release to release the pressure. Set the pressure cooker to HIGH; stir in heavy cream, Parmesan cheese, salt, and black pepper. Then, simmer for about 2 minutes. Serve right away.

Poached Salmon Fillets

(Ready in about 10 minutes | Servings 4)

Ingredients

3 tablespoons butter

2 pounds salmon fillets

1 cup chicken broth

1 cup scallions, chopped

2 cloves garlic, minced

Juice of 1 lime

1 tablespoon fresh tarragon, chopped

Kosher salt and ground black pepper, to taste

Directions

Simply throw all the above ingredients in your pressure cooker.

Securely lock the pressure cooker's lid; set to 6 minutes on HIGH.

Then, release the cooker's pressure. Serve right now.

Spiced Lemony Scallops

(Ready in about 10 minutes | Servings 4)

Ingredients

2 tablespoons olive oil

1 onion, thinly sliced

1 red bell pepper, seeded and sliced

1 jalapeño pepper, seeded and chopped

2 tomatoes, diced

1 tablespoon chopped fresh oregano

1 teaspoon granulated garlic

1/3 cup chicken stock

1 ½ pounds sea scallops

1 small-sized lemon, freshly squeezed

Salt and ground black pepper, to taste

Directions

Warm olive oil over medium-high heat. Then, sauté the onion, bell pepper, and jalapeño pepper until they are tender.

Add tomatoes, oregano, granulated garlic, and chicken stock to the cooker; stir to combine.

Top with the scallops. Drizzle with lemon juice; salt and pepper to taste.

Cover the cooker and set for 2 minutes on HIGH. Serve immediately.

Flaky Tilapia Fillets

(Ready in about 10 minutes | Servings 2)

Ingredients

2 tilapia fillets

Salt and black pepper, to taste

1 teaspoon garlic powder

2 sprigs thyme

1 sprig rosemary

2 slices lemon

2 tablespoons butter, softened

Directions

Prepare 2 squares of parchment paper.

Lay a fillet in the center of each square of parchment paper. Sprinkle with salt, black pepper, and garlic powder.

Sprinkle with thyme and rosemary. Drizzle with lemon and butter. Close up parchment paper around the tilapia fillets in order to form two packets.

Next, place a trivet at the bottom of the cooker. Pour 1 cup of water into the cooker. Lay the packets on the trivet.

Cover the cooker with the lid and set for 5 minutes on HIGH. Serve right away!

Tuna Steaks in Buttery Sauce

(Ready in about 10 minutes | Servings 4)

Ingredients

2 pounds tuna steaks

1/4 cup white wine

1/4 cup chicken broth

2 cloves garlic, minced

2 sprigs fresh rosemary	2 tablespoons capers
1 sprig fresh thyme	1 teaspoon cayenne pepper
6 tablespoons butter	Salt and black pepper, to taste

Directions

Add tuna steaks to your pressure cooker. Then, add white wine, chicken broth, garlic, rosemary, and thyme to the pressure cooker.

Cover and cook on HIGH for 4 minutes. Then, let the cooker's pressure release naturally.

Stir in butter, capers, cayenne pepper, salt and black pepper. Serve.

Pressure Cooker Mac and Cheese

(Ready in about 20 minutes | Servings 6)

Ingredients

3 cups macaroni of choice	Sea salt and ground white pepper, to taste
1 cup water	1 cup Ricotta cheese
2 cups vegetable broth	2 cups Cheddar cheese, shredded
2 tablespoons butter	

Directions

Add macaroni, water, vegetable broth, butter, salt, and white pepper to your pressure cooker.

Then, cook for 6 minutes on HIGH. Perform a quick release to release the pressure.

Stir in Ricotta cheese and Cheddar cheese. Stir to combine and let stand for 5 to 10 minutes to thicken. Serve.

Sausage and Veggie Risotto

(Ready in about 10 minutes | Servings 4)

Ingredients

| 2 tablespoons canola oil | 2 garlic cloves, minced |
| 8 ounces ground pork sausage | 1 onion, diced |

1 green bell pepper, diced

1 carrot, chopped

2 stalks celery, diced

2 cups white rice

1 teaspoon chili powder

1 teaspoon cayenne pepper

1/4 teaspoon black pepper

Sea salt to taste

2 ¼ cups chicken stock

Directions

Heat canola oil until sizzling.

Then, cook the sausage, garlic, onion, bell pepper, carrot, and celery in the pressure cooker, for about 6 minutes.

Stir in the rest of the above ingredients. Cook for 4 minutes on HIGH.

Let the pressure release naturally for a few minutes. Serve warm and enjoy!

Mushroom and Sausage Risotto

(Ready in about 10 minutes | Servings 4)

Ingredients

2 tablespoons vegetable oil

8 ounces chicken sausage

2 garlic cloves, minced

1 onion, diced

1 cup mushrooms, chopped

2 carrots, trimmed and chopped

2 cups rice

1 teaspoon paprika

Sea salt and ground black pepper, to taste

2 ¼ cups chicken stock

Directions

In your pressure cooker, heat vegetable oil until sizzling.

Then, sauté the sausage, garlic, onion, mushrooms, and carrot, until the sausage is lightly browned and the mushrooms are tender and fragrant.

Stir in the remaining ingredients. Cook on HIGH for 4 minutes.

Let the pressure release gradually and naturally for a few minutes. Serve right away.

Pea Risotto with Cream Cheese

(Ready in about 15 minutes | Servings 8)

Ingredients

2 tablespoons olive oil

1 leek, finely chopped

2 cloves garlic, minced

2 cups Arborio rice

5 cups vegetable stock

1/4 cup dry white wine

1 bay leaf

2 cups frozen peas, thawed

Salt and ground black pepper, to taste

1 cup cream cheese

Directions

First, heat olive oil in your pressure cooker over medium heat. Sauté the leek and garlic until tender, or about 5 minutes.

Add rice, and sauté for 1 minute more.

Add the remaining ingredients, except for cream cheese. Securely lock the lid; cook for 6 minutes on HIGH.

Stir the peas into the prepared risotto; taste and adjust the seasonings. Divide the risotto among serving dishes and top with a dollop of the cream cheese. Enjoy!

Collard Greens with Bacon

(Ready in about 20 minutes | Servings 4)

Ingredients

4 strips bacon, diced

1 small-sized onion, peeled and chopped

2-3 cloves garlic, minced

2 bunches collard greens, coarsely chopped

2 cups vegetable broth

2 teaspoons minced

Sea salt and ground black pepper, to taste

Directions

In your pressure cooker, fry the bacon strips until they are nearly crisp, or about 5 minutes. Add remaining ingredients and lock the lid. Set for 15 minutes on HIGH.

Let the pressure release naturally for 5 to 10 minutes. Serve warm and enjoy!

Sugar Snap Peas with Corn and Ricotta

(Ready in about 10 minutes | Servings 6)

Ingredients

2 tablespoons olive oil

1 white onion, diced

4 cups corn kernels

3 cups sugar snap peas

1/2 cup vegetable broth

1 teaspoon dried thyme

1/2 teaspoon onion powder

1/2 teaspoon garlic powder

Sea salt and ground black pepper

3/4 cup Ricotta cheese, cubed

Directions

Heat olive oil over medium-high heat. Then, sauté white onion until it is tender, fragrant, and translucent, or for 3 to 4 minutes.

Add the remaining ingredients, except for Ricotta cheese. Securely lock the cooker's lid; cook for about 3 minutes on HIGH.

Stir in Ricotta cheese just before serving. Enjoy!

Penne Pasta with Smoked Salmon

(Ready in about 10 minutes | Servings 6)

Ingredients

1/4 cup vegetable oil

2 cups penne pasta

2 cups water

2 cups chicken stock

Sea salt and freshly ground black pepper, to taste

1 teaspoon dried thyme

1/2 teaspoon dried rosemary

3 tablespoons butter

1/2 cup Ricotta cheese

2 green garlics, finely minced

1 pound smoked salmon, cut into bite-sized pieces

1/3 cup Parmesan cheese, grated

Directions

Heat the oil over medium heat. Stir in the pasta, water, stock, salt, black pepper, thyme, and rosemary. Cook at HIGH pressure for 8 minutes.

Quick-release the pressure; remove the lid according to manufacturer's directions.

Cut in the butter. Add Ricotta cheese, green garlic, and smoked salmon; toss to combine well. Top with Parmesan cheese and serve immediately.

Fettuccine with Bacon and Cheese

(Ready in about 10 minutes | Servings 6)

Ingredients

2 tablespoons canola oil

2 cups fettuccine pasta

3 cups beef broth

1 cup water

Salt and freshly ground black pepper, to taste

1/2 teaspoon dried rosemary

1 teaspoon mustard seeds

3 tablespoons butter

1/2 cup cream cheese

1/2 cup scallions, finely chopped

2 garlic cloves, finely minced

1/2 pound crisp fried bacon, crushed

1/3 cup Parmigiano-Reggiano cheese, grated

Directions

In your pressure cooker, warm the oil over medium heat. When the oil is warm enough, stir in the fettuccine, broth, water, salt, black pepper, rosemary, and mustard seeds. Cook at HIGH pressure approximately 8 minutes.

Next, remove the lid according to manufacturer's directions.

Add the remaining ingredients; gently toss until everything is well incorporated. Serve and enjoy.

Saucy Bulgur with Mushrooms

(Ready in about 20 minutes | Servings 4)

Ingredients

1 cup bulgur

3 cups chicken broth

2 tablespoons butter

1 yellow onion, sliced

2 carrots, peeled and chopped

2 celery ribs, peeled and chopped

1/2 cup mushrooms, chopped

1/2 teaspoon dried sage

1/2 teaspoon salt

1/2 teaspoon ground black pepper

Directions

Add the bulgur and broth to your pressure cooker.

Lock the lid into place; cook under HIGH pressure for 9 minutes. Then, allow pressure to release gradually and naturally. Reserve cooked bulgur.

In a large-sized sauté pan, over medium heat, warm the butter; when the butter is melted, sauté the onion, carrot, and celery for 6 to 7 minutes.

Add the remaining ingredients; sauté for an additional 2 minutes.

Combine the vegetable mixture with the cooked bulgur. Serve right away.

Couscous-Stuffed Peppers with Walnuts

(Ready in about 25 minutes | Servings 4)

Ingredients

2 cups water

1 cup couscous

2 tablespoons toasted walnuts, chopped

4 ounces feta cheese, crumbled

1/2 teaspoon dried dill weed

1/2 teaspoon dried basil

1 teaspoon dried oregano

1 teaspoon salt

1/2 teaspoon ground black pepper

4 large-sized red bell peppers, seeded and stemmed

Directions

Preheat your oven to 350 degrees F. Add the water and couscous to your pressure cooker.

Cover with the lid and bring to HIGH pressure, and maintain for 2 minutes. Turn off the heat, and allow pressure to release.

Next, remove the lid and fluff your couscous; add the walnuts, feta cheese, dill, basil, oregano, salt, and black pepper. Stir to combine well.

Stuff the peppers with prepared couscous mixture; place the stuffed peppers in a baking dish. Bake in the preheated oven for 15 minutes. Serve warm and enjoy!

Couscous with Kalamata Olives and Peppers

(Ready in about 10 minutes + chilling time | Servings 4)

Ingredients

2 cups water

1 cup couscous

1/2 cup Kalamata olives, pitted and chopped

1/2 cup scallions, chopped

1 red bell pepper, seeded and diced

1 yellow bell pepper, seeded and diced

2 cloves garlic, minced

2 teaspoons extra-virgin olive oil

1 teaspoon wine vinegar

1/4 teaspoon ground white pepper

1 teaspoon salt

Directions

Stir the water and couscous into a pressure cooker. Lock the lid into place; cook on HIGH pressure for 2 minutes.

Remove from the heat and allow pressure to release according to manufacturer's directions. Carefully remove the cooker's lid.

Fluff the couscous and stir in all remaining ingredients. Taste and adjust the seasonings. Refrigerate at least 2 hours before serving. Enjoy!

INSTANT POT

BREAKFAST RECIPES

Rice Pudding with Zante Currants

(Ready in about 30 minutes | Servings 6)

Ingredients

1 ½ cups rice

1/2 cup sugar

1 tablespoon honey

A pinch of sea salt

5 cups milk

2 whole eggs

1 cup half and half

1 cup Zante currants

1/2 teaspoon freshly grated nutmeg

Directions

In the inner pot, combine together the rice, sugar, honey, salt, and milk. Choose the "Sauté" button; bring to a boil. Stir in order to dissolve the sugar.

Cover your instant pot. Turn to the stream release to "SEALING" position. Press the "Rice" button. After about 15 minutes perform the quick pressure release

In the meantime, whisk the eggs and half and half in a mixing bowl.

Remove the lid from the pot. Stir in the egg mixture. Now add Zante currants and grated nutmeg. Press the "Sauté". Cook, uncovered, until it starts to boil. Then, turn off the cooker.

Serve right away. If you want to serve chilled, it is good to know that the pudding will thicken as it cools. Enjoy!

Cinnamon Fig Bread Pudding

(Ready in about 45 minutes | Servings 4)

Ingredients

6 slices of cinnamon bread, torn into pieces

3 whole eggs

3 cups milk

1/2 teaspoon vanilla paste

1/4 teaspoon kosher salt

1/2 cup sugar

1 tablespoon honey

1 cup dried figs, chopped

1/2 teaspoon cinnamon powder

Directions

Coat a 5 cup bowl with non-stick cooking spray (butter flavor). Simply throw cinnamon bread pieces into the bowl.

In a separate bowl, mix all the remaining ingredients, except for figs. Pour this custard mixture over bread pieces. Scatter chopped dried figs over the top. Allow to sit for about 15 minutes to let bread pieces absorb the custard mixture.

Cover bowl tightly with a piece of buttered foil.

Put a steaming rack into the inner pot; pour in two cups of water.

Lock the cooker's lid. Use "Manual" setting on HIGH; cook for 25 minutes. Lastly, use a natural release for about 15 minutes.

Vegan Summer Oatmeal

(Ready in about 15 minutes | Servings 2)

Ingredients

2 peaches, pitted and diced

1 teaspoon vanilla paste

2 apricots, pitted and halved

1/2 teaspoon cinnamon powder

1 cup steel-cut oats

2 cups water

1 cup almond milk

Directions

Simply throw everything in the inner pot.

Now press "Manual"/ "Adjust"; set for 3 minutes.

Use 10 minutes natural release. Eat warm.

Apricot Oats with Currants

(Ready in about 15 minutes | Servings 2)

Ingredients

1 cup steel-cut oats

1 cup soy milk

2 cups water

1 tablespoon raw almond butter

1 teaspoon ground flax seeds

1/2 teaspoon cinnamon

1/2 cup fresh apricot, chopped

1/4 cup dried currants

Directions

Add all the above ingredients to the inner pot of your Instant Pot.

Now press "Manual"/ "Adjust". Set for 3 minutes.

Lastly, perform natural release method.

Easy Hard Boiled Eggs

(Ready in about 10 minutes | Servings 2)

Ingredients

1 cup water

4 eggs

Salt and freshly cracked black pepper, to taste

Directions

Pour the water into the pot; now position a steamer basket atop the rack.

Place the eggs in the steamer basket, using canning lids to hold the eggs.

Close the lid. Press "STEAM" setting; adjust time to 5 minutes. Lastly, quick release the steam valve. Then, transfer the eggs to a cold water for about 2 minutes.

Peel your eggs and season with salt and black pepper. Enjoy!

Creamy Quick Oats

(Ready in about 10 minutes | Servings 4)

Ingredients

1 cup water

1 cup oats

1 2/3 cups water

2 cups water

A pinch of salt

A dash of cinnamon

Cream, for garnish

Directions

Pour 1 cup of water into your Instant Pot; now place the trivet in the pot.

Put oats together with 1 2/3 cups of water into a heat-proof bowl; place the bowl on the trivet.

Press "Manual" and cook for about 7 minutes. Next, quick release steam.

Divide among serving bowls and top with cream. Enjoy!

White Wheat Berries with Potatoes

(Ready in about 15 minutes | Servings 4)

Ingredients

2 cups white wheat berries, soaked overnight in lots of water

2 tablespoons olive oil

2 medium onions, peeled and sliced

3 cloves garlic, smashed

1/2 teaspoon dried rosemary

1/2 teaspoon dried thyme

4 medium potatoes, cubed

Directions

Combine white wheat berries and 6 ½ cups water in your Instant Pot.

In a sauté pan, warm olive oil over medium-high heat. Then, sauté the onions and garlic until tender. Add rosemary and thyme and cook for 1 more minute, stirring frequently.

Choose "Multi-grain" setting and cook wheat together with potatoes. When the mixture is cooked, add sautéed onions and garlic. Sprinkle with seasoned salt and ground black pepper. Serve.

Oats with Honey and Walnuts

(Ready in about 10 minutes | Servings 4)

Ingredients

1 cup steel-cut oats

2 cups water

1/8 teaspoon kosher salt

1 tablespoon honey

1/2 teaspoon walnuts, chopped

Directions

Add 1 cup of water to your Instant Pot. Place trivet in the pot.

Throw steel-cut oats with two cups of water and salt in a heat-proof bowl; place the bowl on the trivet. Lock in cooker's lid. Use "Manual", and cook for about 6 minutes.

While oats are cooking, toast the walnuts in a clean cast-iron skillet.

When your oats are ready, add honey and stir to combine. Serve sprinkled with some chopped walnuts.

Wheat Berry with Veggies and Greek Yogurt

(Ready in about 15 minutes | Servings 4)

Ingredients

2 cups white wheat berries, soaked overnight in lots of water

2 tablespoons butter

2 sweet onions, peeled and sliced

Salt and black pepper, to taste

2 medium carrots, thinly sliced

2 celery stalks, chopped

Greek yogurt, for garnish

Directions

In your Instant Pot, combine white wheat berries with 6 ½ cups water.

In a pan, melt the butter over medium heat. Then, sauté sweet onions until tender and translucent. Add salt and ground black pepper.

Press "Multi-grain" setting; cook wheat together with carrots and celery until they are tender. Now add sautéed sweet onions. Serve topped with Greek yogurt.

Congee with Seeds

(Ready in about 45 minutes | Servings 6)

Ingredients

1/2 cup brown rice

1/8 cup peanut, coarsely chopped

1/4 cup walnut, minced

2 tablespoons sesame seeds

1 teaspoon hemp seeds

1/4 cup dates, pitted and chopped

7 cups of water

Directions

Simply put all the above ingredients into your Instant Pot.

Now press "Congee" button. To serve: divide among six serving bowls; dot with soy sauce if desired. Enjoy!

Creamed Congee with Strawberries

(Ready in about 45 minutes | Servings 6)

Ingredients

1/2 cup brown rice

1 tablespoon butter

1 teaspoon vanilla extract

1 teaspoon cinnamon powder

1/4 cup dried strawberries, chopped

1 tablespoon honey

7 cups of water

Directions

Throw all the above ingredients into your Instant Pot.

Choose "Congee" button. Serve at room temperature.

Steamed Eggs with Scallions

(Ready in about 15 minutes | Servings 2)

Ingredients

2 eggs

2/3 cup cold water

1/4 cup scallions, chopped

1 clove garlic, minced

Salt and white pepper, to taste

Directions

Whisk together the eggs and water in a small-sized mixing bowl. Transfer the mixture to a heat-proof bowl. Add the remaining ingredients; mix to combine and set aside.

Pour 1 cup of water into the inner pot of your Instant Pot. Place the trivet in the cooker. Place the bowl in the steamer basket.

Close the lid and close the vent valve. Press "Manual" setting on HIGH; cook for 5 minutes. Now manually release pressure by turning the valve to 'open'. Serve with your favorite bread and enjoy.

Eggs with Bacon and Cheese

(Ready in about 25 minutes | Servings 6)

Ingredients

6 medium-sized eggs

1/2 cup heavy cream

1 small-sized leek, finely chopped

1 cup bacon, chopped

1 cup spinach leaves, chopped

1 cup Monterey Jack cheese, shredded

Sea salt and ground black pepper, to taste

1/2 teaspoon dried thyme

1/2 teaspoon dried basil

1/4 teaspoon dried oregano

Fresh chopped chives, for garnish

Directions

In a bowl, whisk the eggs with heavy cream. Add the remaining ingredients, except for chives; mix well to combine.

Pour the egg mixture into a heat-proof dish; cover with a foil.

Pour 1 cup of water into your cooker. Place the trivet inside. Set the bowl on the trivet. Close the lid tightly.

Press "Manual" and HIGH pressure; cook for 20 minutes. Allow the pressure to release naturally. Serve topped with fresh chives.

Ham and Cheese Omelet

(Ready in about 25 minutes | Servings 6)

Ingredients

1/2 cup whole milk

6 medium-sized eggs

1 small-sized yellow onion, finely chopped

2 cloves garlic, peeled and minced

1 cup cooked ham, chopped

1 red bell pepper, seeded and thinly sliced

1 handful Cheddar cheese, grated

Salt and black pepper, to taste

A dash of grated nutmeg

1/2 teaspoon dried basil

Directions

Start by whisking the milk and eggs. Add the rest of the above ingredients; stir until everything is well incorporated.

Pour this mixture into a heat-resistant dish and cover.

Pour 1 cup of water into the base of Instant Pot. Lay the trivet inside. Lay the dish on the trivet.

Close the lid. Press "Manual"; cook for 20 minutes under HIGH pressure. Serve right away.

Spicy Jalapeño Eggs

(Ready in about 30 minutes | Servings 6)

Ingredients

6 tablespoons water

6 eggs, beaten

1 green garlic, minced

1/2 cup green onions, finely chopped

1 fresh medium jalapeño pepper, minced

1 red bell pepper, seeded and thinly sliced

1 handful Cheddar cheese, grated

A few drops of Tabasco

Salt and freshly ground black pepper, to taste

1/2 teaspoon ground allspice

Directions

In a large-sized dish, combine together the water and eggs. Stir in the remaining ingredients; stir until everything is well mixed.

Pour this egg mixture into a heat-resistant dish; cover.

Pour 1 cup of water into the Instant Pot. Place a rack in the cooker. Lay the dish on the rack.

Cover and choose "Manual" button; cook 20 minutes under HIGH pressure. Serve warm.

Quick and Easy Quinoa

(Ready in about 10 minutes | Servings 6)

Ingredients

1 cup quinoa, rinsed well

1/2 teaspoon seasoned salt

1/4 teaspoon ground black pepper

1 ½ cups water

1 orange, zested and squeezed

Directions

In your cooker, place all the ingredients, except for orange juice.

Close and lock the lid. Press "Manual" key and cook for 1 minute. Next, open the cooker using Natural Pressure Release

Add orange juice and stir to combine. Taste and adjust for seasonings. Serve.

Mediterranean Wheat Berry Salad

(Ready in about 40 minutes | Servings 6)

Ingredients

1 ½ cups dry wheat berries

2 tablespoons olive oil

4 cups water

1/4 teaspoon sea salt

1 tablespoon olive oil

1 tablespoon apple cider vinegar

1 cup tomatoes, chopped

1/4 cup scallions, chopped

2 ounces feta cheese

1 teaspoon rosemary

Directions

Start by toasting the wheat berries.

Stir the olive oil into your cooker. Now press the "Sauté" button. Then, add the toasted wheat berries and cook for 5 minutes, stirring continuously. Press "Cancel".

Next, add the water and sea salt; cook under HIGH pressure for 30 minutes.

Drain the wheat berries and rinse them with cold water. Place the wheat berries in a salad bowl. Toss with the remaining ingredients. Serve chilled.

Bean and Mint Salad

(Ready in about 10 minutes | Servings 4)

Ingredients

1 cup dry beans, soaked

4 cups water

1 garlic clove, smashed

1 bay leaf

1 sprig fresh mint

2 tablespoons olive oil

Sea salt and black pepper, to taste

Directions

Add the soaked beans, water, garlic clove, and bay leaf to the cooker.

Close and lock the lid. Use "Manual"; choose 8 minutes pressure cooking time.

Use Natural Pressure Release to open the cooker. Strain the beans and transfer to a salad bowl. Toss with the remaining ingredients. Serve chilled.

Cauliflower and Anchovy Salad

(Ready in about 15 minutes | Servings 6)

Ingredients

For the Salad:

1 head cauliflower, cut into florets

1 cup water

2 oranges, peeled and sliced thinly

For the Vinaigrette:

1 lemon, zested and squeezed

4 anchovies

1 hot pepper, finely chopped

1 tablespoon capers

4 tablespoons extra-virgin olive oil

Salt and black pepper, to taste

Directions

Add cauliflower and water to the cooker. Close and lock the lid. Press "Manual" and choose 7 minutes pressure cooking time.

Meanwhile, make your vinaigrette by combining all ingredients.

When time is up, open the cooker according to manufacturer's instructions. Dress the cauliflower with the vinaigrette; garnish with orange slices and serve chilled.

Broccoli and Pineapple Salad

(Ready in about 15 minutes | Servings 6)

Ingredients

For the Salad:

2 carrots, thinly sliced

1 head broccoli, broken into florets

1 cup water

1/4 pineapple, peeled and sliced thinly

For the Vinaigrette:

1 orange, zested and squeezed

4 tablespoons extra-virgin olive oil

Salt and white pepper, to taste

1/2 teaspoon cayenne pepper

1 tablespoon fresh basil, roughly chopped

1 tablespoon fresh cilantro, roughly chopped

Directions

In your Instant Pot, place carrots, broccoli, and water. Then, lock the cooker's lid. Choose "Manual" and 7 minutes pressure cooking time.

To make the Vinaigrette: thoroughly mix all the vinaigrette components.

Afterwards, open your cooker according to manufacturer's instructions. Dress the salad and garnish with pineapple slices; serve chilled.

Two-Mushroom Pâté

(Ready in about 20 minutes | Servings 16)

Ingredients

3/4 cup dry mushrooms, rinsed

1 cup boiling water

2 tablespoons butter

1 onion, peeled and sliced

1 pound fresh mushrooms, thinly sliced

1/4 cup dry white wine

1 teaspoon kosher salt

1/2 teaspoon black pepper, freshly cracked

Directions

In a heat-proof measuring cup, combine dry mushroom and boiling water. Cover and set aside. The mushrooms will soak up the water.

Press "Sauté" button. When the cooker is hot, warm the butter. Now sauté the onion until it is softened. Then, stir in the fresh mushrooms; sauté until fragrant and golden brown.

Pour in white wine; allow the wine to evaporate completely. Add soaked mushrooms and stir to combine. Season with salt and pepper.

Close and lock the cooker's lid. Press "Manual" and choose 12 minutes pressure cooking time. To make the Pâté: mix the ingredients with an immersion blender. Transfer to a refrigerated in order to chill completely before serving.

Chicken Liver Pâté Spread

(Ready in about 10 minutes | Servings 16)

Ingredients

1 teaspoon olive oil

1 medium-sized leek, roughly chopped

3/4 pound chicken livers

1/4 cup rum

2 anchovies in oil

1 tablespoon butter

1 teaspoon dried thyme

1 teaspoon dried sage

1/2 teaspoon dried basil

Salt and ground black pepper, to taste

Directions

Put the olive oil into a cooker; sauté the leeks. Then, add the chicken livers and cook until the livers are seared.

Pour in rum. Close and lock the lid of your cooker. Cook for 5 minutes at HIGH pressure.

Add the remaining ingredients and stir to combine. Serve well chilled with your favorite rustic bread.

Yam Barley Congee

(Ready in about 45 minutes | Servings 12)

Ingredients

6 tablespoons pot barley

3 tablespoons buckwheat

3 tablespoons brown rice

6 tablespoons black glutinous rice

10 tablespoons black eye beans

1/2 pound purple yam, cubed

Salt and black pepper, to taste

Directions

Add the ingredients to the inner pot. Pour in the water to the 8 mark.

Close the lid. Select "Congee"; cook for 45 minutes.

Sweeten with honey if desired. Enjoy!

Quick Turmeric Quinoa

(Ready in about 10 minutes | Servings 6)

Ingredients

2 tablespoons butter

1 white onion, chopped

2 garlic cloves, finely minced

2 cups quinoa, well rinsed

2 teaspoons turmeric

1/2 teaspoon white pepper

1 teaspoon salt

2 tablespoons fresh parsley leaves, coarsely chopped

Directions

In the pre-heated cooker, warm the butter; sauté onion and garlic for 30 seconds.

Then, tap the quinoa from the strainer into the cooker. Then add turmeric, white pepper, and salt.

Close and lock the lid. Cook for 1 minute at HIGH pressure. Fluff your quinoa with a fork and garnish with fresh parsley. Serve.

Oats with Prunes and Raisins

(Ready in about 10 minutes | Servings 4)

Ingredients

2 cups water

1 cup nondairy milk

A pinch of salt

1 cup steel-cut oats

1/2 vanilla paste

2 cinnamon sticks

1/4 cup prunes, chopped

1/4 cup walnuts, chopped

1/4 cup golden raisins

2 tablespoons honey

Directions

Add the water, nondairy milk, salt, oats, vanilla paste, 2 cinnamon sticks, and prunes to the cooker. Use "Manual" and cook 3 minutes.

Then, let the pressure come down and carefully open the pot.

Discard cinnamon sticks, and set your oats aside. Stir in the walnuts, raisins, and honey. Serve right away.

Easiest Cream Cheese Ever

(Ready in about 40 minutes | Servings 8)

Ingredients

4 cups whole milk

1/4 cup white vinegar

1 teaspoon sea salt

Directions

Add the milk to the cooker. Then, hit the "Yogurt" setting, and bring it to a boil. Cook for 20 to 30 minutes.

Add vinegar and sea salt. Let set until clumps begin to form. Pour into the yogurt drainer.

Transfer to your refrigerator to chill. Use as a light spread for your breakfast. Enjoy!

Hazelnut Bread Pudding

(Ready in about 55 minutes | Servings 6)

Ingredients

Butter, for bowl

6 slices bread of choice, torn into bite-sized pieces

3 eggs

3 cups whole milk

1/4 teaspoon grated nutmeg

1/2 teaspoon cinnamon powder

1/4 teaspoon cardamom

1 teaspoon hazelnut extract

1/4 teaspoon kosher salt

1/2 honey

1/2 cup hazelnuts, chopped

Directions

Butter bowl that will fit easily into your pot. Add the bread pieces to the buttered bowl.

To make the custard: Combine the remaining ingredients, except for hazelnuts. Mix to combine well.

Pour custard mixture over bread piece in the bowl. Scatter chopped hazelnuts over the top. Allow to soak for about 15 minutes.

Cover bowl tightly with a buttered foil. Put a steaming rack into the inner pot; pour in 2 cups water.

Lock the lid and choose "Manual"; cook on HIGH for 25 minutes. Afterwards, perform natural release for 15 minutes. Serve and enjoy!

Quinoa with Zucchini and Swiss Chard

(Ready in about 20 minutes | Servings 4)

Ingredients

1 cup quinoa, rinsed

1 ½ cups water

2 tablespoons apple cider vinegar

1 teaspoon thyme

1 teaspoon mustard

1 tablespoon agave syrup

Sea salt and freshly ground black pepper, to taste

1 onion, sliced thin

2 cloves garlic, minced

1/4 cup chicken stock

1/2 zucchini, thinly sliced

6 Swiss chard leaves, stems removed and chopped

Directions

Add the quinoa, water, and apple cider vinegar to the Instant Pot; set for 1 minute. Allow it to rest for about 10 minutes. Open the lid and fluff the quinoa.

Meanwhile, whisk together the thyme, mustard, agave syrup, salt, and black pepper.

Then, place a saucepan over medium-high heat. Add onion, garlic, chicken stock, and zucchini. Then, sauté for about 5 minutes.

Add Swiss chard and cook for another 2 minutes. Serve this vegetable mixture over prepared quinoa.

Morning Quinoa and Spinach Salad

(Ready in about 20 minutes | Servings 4)

Ingredients

1 ½ cups water

1 cup quinoa, rinsed

2 tablespoons white wine

1 tablespoon olive oil

1 onion, sliced thin

2 cloves garlic, minced

1/4 cup chicken stock

1/2 cup spinach, chopped

1/2 teaspoon dried rosemary

1 teaspoon dried thyme

2 tablespoons wine vinegar

2 tablespoons extra-virgin olive oil

Sea salt and freshly ground black pepper, to taste

Directions

Stir the water, quinoa, and white wine into the inner pot of the Instant Pot; cook for 1 minute. Open the lid according to manufacturer's instructions. Rinse your quinoa and reserve.

Then, place sauté pan over medium-high heat and warm the olive oil. Sauté the onion and garlic until tender.

Now add chicken stock, spinach, rosemary, and thyme; cook for 5 to 6 minutes or until the greens are wilted and the mixture is thoroughly heated. Add the sautéed mixture to the rinsed quinoa and transfer to a refrigerator in order to cool completely

Dress the salad with vinegar, olive oil, salt, and black pepper. Enjoy!

Summer Quinoa Salad

(Ready in about 10 minutes + chilling time | Servings 4)

Ingredients

1 cup white quinoa, well-rinsed

1 teaspoon lemon zest

1/4 teaspoon kosher salt

1 ½ cups water

1 cup cherry tomatoes, quartered

2 cucumbers, thinly sliced

1 cup green onions, sliced

1 tablespoon apple cider vinegar

1/2 cup Feta cheese, crumbled

Directions

In the pressure cooker, place the quinoa, lemon zest, salt, and water.

Then, lock the lid of your cooker. Press "Manual" and 1 minute pressure cooking time. Then, open the cooker naturally.

Rinse and fluff the quinoa and transfer to a bowl. Let it cool completely.

Add the rest of the ingredients to the chilled quinoa. Gently stir to combine and serve.

Italian-Style Rice Salad

(Ready in about 20 minutes + chilling time | Servings 6)

Ingredients

2 cups basmati rice, soaked and well rinsed

1/2 teaspoon salt

3 cups water

1/2 red onion, chopped

1 green bell pepper, seeded and chopped

1 red bell pepper, seeded and chopped

Sea salt and coarse black pepper, to taste

1 tablespoon extra-virgin olive oil

2 tablespoons fat-free Italian-style dressing

1/4 cup olives, pitted and sliced

Directions

First, add basmati rice to the Instant Pot. Add salt and water. Cover and use "Manual" button and 4 minutes pressure cooking time.

Then, open the Instant Pot using the 10-minute Natural pressure release.

Add the remaining ingredients. Stir to combine and serve well chilled.

Homemade Yogurt

(Ready in about 12 hours | Servings 6)

Ingredients

1 ½ cups whole milk

1 tablespoon sugar

1 tablespoon powdered milk

1 tablespoon yogurt

Directions

Add milk to the jars and cook for 2 minutes in your Instant Pot. Cool milk to 90 degrees F.

Stir in the rest of the ingredients; stir to combine well.

Press "Yogurt" button; set for 12 hours. Serve chilled.

Basic Apple Sauce

(Ready in about 15 minutes | Servings 16)

Ingredients

12 apples, cored and diced

1/2 teaspoon cinnamon powder

1/2 cup water

Directions

Arrange diced apples in the inner pot of your Instant Pot.

Add cinnamon and water. Place a circle of parchment paper over the apples. Cover and use "Manual" setting; then, set cooking time to 10 minutes.

Afterwards, release the pressure naturally. Mix with an immersion blender until smooth and creamy. Enjoy!

Cannellini Salad with Pepper and Carrot

(Ready in about 15 minutes | Servings 4)

Ingredients

1 cup dry cannellini beans, soaked

4 cups water

1/2 cup green onions, chopped

2 garlic cloves, smashed

1 sprig thyme

1 teaspoon sage

1 red bell pepper, thinly sliced

2 carrots, thinly sliced

2 tablespoons olive oil

1 tablespoon sherry vinegar

Sea salt and ground black pepper, to taste

1 tablespoon fresh cilantro

Directions

Add the soaked beans, water, green onions, and smashed garlic to the cooker.

Close and lock the lid. Press "Manual" and choose 8 minutes pressure cooking time.

Then, open the cooker using natural pressure release. Strain the beans and add the rest of the ingredients. Serve and enjoy!

Kidney Bean Salad

(Ready in about 15 minutes | Servings 4)

Ingredients

4 cups water

1 cup dry kidney beans, soaked

1 cup shallots, chopped

1 sprig thyme

1 sprig rosemary

1 green bell pepper, thinly sliced

1 red bell pepper, thinly sliced

2 tablespoons olive oil

1 tablespoon apple cider vinegar

1 tablespoon sunflower seeds

Sea salt and ground black pepper, to taste

Directions

Add the water, soaked kidney beans, shallots, thyme, and rosemary to the inner pot of your cooker.

Cover and use "Manual" and 8 minutes pressure cooking time.

Then, open your Instant Pot by using natural pressure release. Drain kidney beans and add the remaining ingredients. Serve well chilled.

Bacon and Vegetable Breakfast

(Ready in about 10 minutes | Servings 4)

Ingredients

2 tablespoons canola oil

3 slices bacon, chopped

1 cup cabbage, shredded

1 red bell pepper, thinly sliced

Salt and black pepper, to taste

Directions

Press "Sauté" and add the canola oil to melt. Add the rest of the ingredients.

Seal the lid and choose "Manual" for 5 minutes. Serve over bread or cooked quinoa.

Breakfast Bean Casserole

(Ready in about 30 minutes | Servings 8)

Ingredients

1 pound lima beans

1/2 teaspoon sea salt

1 bay leaf

3/4 cup butter

1/4 cup sugar

1 teaspoon granulated garlic

1 teaspoon mustard

1 teaspoon sea salt

1 cup sour cream

Fresh chopped chives, for garnish

Directions

First, soak lima beans with 10 cups of water. Then, add salt and bay leaf, and press "Manual". Cook for 4 minutes under HIGH pressure.

Press "Keep Warm" button and leave it for 10 minutes; next, quick release pressure.

Drain lima beans; add them back to the pot. Next, add the remaining ingredients, except for chives.

Cook for 10 minutes on "Manual" under HIGH pressure. Serve garnished with fresh chives. Enjoy!

Bean and Apple Salad

(Ready in about 45 minutes | Servings 8)

Ingredients

10 ounces red kidney beans

3 cloves garlic, finely minced

1 onion, chopped fine

1 crisp apple, cored and diced

1/4 cup brown sugar

1 teaspoon sea salt

1 tablespoon fresh basil

1 tablespoon dry oregano

1 teaspoon red pepper flakes, crushed

Black pepper, to taste

Directions

Soak kidney beans overnight.

Then, transfer soaked beans to the inner pot along with the remaining ingredients. Add water (2 inches above the top of beans).

Cook for 45 minutes. Serve chilled.

Rice Pudding with Prunes and Dates

(Ready in about 20 minutes | Servings 6)

Ingredients

1 ½ cups Arborio rice

1/2 cup sugar

1 tablespoon maple syrup

A pinch of kosher salt

5 cups whole milk

2 eggs

1 cup evaporated milk

1/2 cup prunes, chopped

1/2 cup dates, pitted and chopped

Cinnamon powder to taste

Anise seeds, to taste

Directions

In the inner pot, combine Arborio rice, sugar, maple syrup, kosher salt, and 5 cups of whole milk.

Now choose the "Sauté" button; bring to a boil, stirring continuously to dissolve the sugar. Then, lock the lid in place. Press the "Rice" button.

Meanwhile, whisk the eggs and evaporated milk. Afterwards, perform the quick-pressure release. Stir in the egg-milk mixture, prunes, dates, cinnamon, and anise.

Press the "Sauté". Cook uncovered until the pudding starts to boil. Serve at room temperature.

Wheat Berry Salad with Cranberries

(Ready in about 20 minutes + chilling time | Servings 6)

Ingredients

1 cup wheat berries	3/4 teaspoon white pepper
2 cups water	3 tablespoons extra-virgin olive oil
1/4 cup apple cider vinegar	1 cup shallot, chopped
1 teaspoon yellow mustard	1 cup dried cranberries
1 teaspoon sea salt	1/2 cup hazelnuts, chopped

Directions

The night before, soak wheat berries in cold water. Rinse them and drain.

Transfer the soaked wheat berries to the Instant Pot; add 2 cups of water. Now pressure cook for about 20 minutes. Drain and transfer to a salad bowl. Add the rest of above ingredients.

Lastly, refrigerate the salad overnight or at least 3 hours. Enjoy!

Almond Banana Bread

(Ready in about 40 minutes | Servings 8)

Ingredients

1/3 cup butter, softened	1/2 cup sugar

1 large-sized egg

1 teaspoon vanilla paste

1/2 teaspoon almond extract

2 ripe bananas, mashed

1 ½ cups cassava flour

1 ½ teaspoons baking powder

A pinch of salt

1/2 teaspoon cinnamon powder

1/2 teaspoon ground cloves

1/3 cup almond milk

1 tablespoon cream of tartar

Directions

First, beat together the butter and sugar. Add egg, vanilla paste, and almond extract; beat well until the mixture is very creamy. Add bananas; mix again.

In another mixing bowl, mix flour, baking powder, salt, cinnamon, and cloves. Gradually add this dry mixture to the prepared wet mixture, while whisking with a large spoon.

In a small bowl, to make 'buttermilk', whisk together the almond milk and cream of tartar. Add 'buttermilk' to the dough mixture. Cover with a foil.

Spoon the dough mixture into a cake pan. Add 2 cups of water to the bottom of your instant pot. Set metal trivet in the bottom. Lower the cake pan onto the trivet.

Close the lid. Choose "MANUAL" for 30 minutes. Allow the cake to cool slightly on a wire rack before serving.

Muffins with Bacon and Scallions

(Ready in about 15 minutes | Servings 4)

Ingredients

4 large-sized eggs, beaten

1/4 teaspoon seasoned salt

4 tablespoons Cheddar cheese, shredded

1/2 cup scallions, diced

Freshly cracked black pepper, to taste

4 slices cooked ham, crumbled

Directions

Pour the water into your Instant Pot. Put the steamer basket into the bottom of the pot.

Mix together all the above ingredients. Pour the mixture into silicon muffin cups. Place muffin cups on steamer basket in the pot.

Cover and choose HIGH Pressure and 8 minutes cook time. Then, perform a quick pressure release.

Open the lid according to manufacturer's directions. Serve right now.

Easy Morning Pudding with Pears

(Ready in about 20 minutes | Servings 4)

Ingredients

2 tablespoons butter

1 ½ cups white rice

2 large pears, cored and diced

1/4 teaspoon salt

1 teaspoon cinnamon powder

1/4 teaspoon ground cloves

1/4 teaspoon freshly grated nutmeg

1/4 cup brown sugar

1 cup apple juice

3 cups whole milk

1/2 cup golden raisins

Directions

Warm the butter in your cooker for about 3 minutes or until it's melted. Stir in white rice; cook, stirring constantly, for 4 minutes more.

Add the remaining ingredients, except for golden raisins. Select HIGH and 6 minutes cook time. Next, use a quick pressure release. Stir in golden raisins.

Serve topped with a splash of milk.

Bacon and Spinach Muffins

(Ready in about 20 minutes | Servings 4)

Ingredients

4 large-sized eggs, beaten

1/4 teaspoon salt

1/4 teaspoon black pepper, ground

4 tablespoons sharp cheese, shredded

1 cup spinach leaves, chopped

1 teaspoon garlic powder

4 slices bacon, crumbled

Directions

Pour the water into the base of your Instant Pot. Put the steamer basket into the cooker.

In a bowl, combine together all the above ingredients; stir to combine well. Pour the muffin batter into silicon muffin cups. Place muffin cups on prepared steamer basket.

Cover and press "HIGH"; cook for 8 minutes. Then, use a quick pressure release.

Open the cooker according to manufacturer's instructions. Serve right now or at room temperature. Enjoy!

Morning Quinoa Pilaf

(Ready in about 15 minutes | Servings 6)

Ingredients

2 tablespoons butter

1 white onion, diced

1 cup cabbage, shredded

1 carrot, chopped

1 celery stalk, chopped

2-3 cloves garlic, minced

3 cups quinoa

1 quart vegetable stock

1 sprig rosemary

1 sprig thyme

Kosher salt and ground black pepper, to taste

Directions

Place the butter in the inner pot of your cooker. Press "RICE" button; sauté the onion, cabbage, carrot, celery, and garlic for 2 to 3 minutes.

Add the rest of your ingredients. Place the lid on the cooker and lock the lid.

Choose the "RICE" function. Carefully remove the lid. Serve warm.

French Bread Pudding with Orange and Cherries

(Ready in about 20 minutes | Servings 4)

Ingredients

4 egg yolks

2 cups half & half

1 medium-sized orange, zested and juiced

1/2 cup caster sugar

1 tablespoon acacia honey

2 tablespoons butter

1/2 teaspoon cinnamon powder

1/2 teaspoon anise seeds

1/2 teaspoon cardamom

3 cups French yeast bread, torn into pieces

3/4 cup dried cherries

Directions

In a medium bowl, whisk the eggs yolks; add half & half, orange, sugar, honey, butter, cinnamon, anise, and cardamom; beat everything well.

Soak the bread pieces and cherries in the creamed egg mixture for about 10 minutes.

Pour the prepared mixture into a baking dish; cover with a foil. Set the rack in the inner pot. Pour 2 cups of warm water. Now lay the baking dish on the rack in the cooker.

Then, lock the lid; switch the pressure release valve to closed. Press the "MEAT" button. Adjust time to 15 minutes. When the steam is released, carefully open the lid and discard the foil. Serve at room temperature.

Lemon and Blackberry Jam

(Ready in about 20 minutes | Servings 16)

Ingredients

4 liquid pints fresh blackberries

3 tablespoons pectin powder

2 cinnamon sticks

1 vanilla bean

5 cups caster sugar

1 small-sized lemon, juiced

Directions

Put the blackberries into your cooker along with the pectin powder. Use the "MEAT" button. Now add cinnamon sticks, vanilla bean, and 2 cups of sugar; cook until the sugar dissolves.

Once the sugar has dissolved, allow the mixture to a boil for about 3 minutes. Add remaining sugar and lemon juice. Then, ladle the jam into the 5 liquid pint jars.

Using a flexible spatula gently press the jam to release any excess air bubbles. Seal prepared jars.

Place the jars in the inner pot; add water. Put the lid on and choose the "STEAM" and 8 minutes.

Open your cooker and carefully remove the jars with the canning tongs. Enjoy with peanut butter and your favorite bread.

Sweet Potato Casserole with Marshmallows

(Ready in about 25 minutes | Servings 6)

Ingredients

3 pound sweet potatoes, peeled and cut into quarters

1 ½ cups water

1 teaspoon sea salt

1/2 teaspoon cayenne pepper

1/2 teaspoon freshly ground black pepper

For marshmallow-pecan topping:

1/3 cup all-purpose flour

2/3 cup brown sugar

1/2 teaspoon freshly grated nutmeg

2 tablespoons butter, melted

1/2 cup walnuts, chopped

2 cups mini marshmallows

Directions

Add sweet potatoes, water, sea salt, cayenne pepper, and black pepper to the inner pot.

Lock the lid. Press the "SOUP" function; adjust the timer to 10 minutes.

When the steam is released, open the cooker. Mash cooked sweet potatoes; taste and adjust seasoning if needed. Transfer sweet potato puree to an oven-safe casserole dish.

In a bowl, add flour, brown sugar, nutmeg, and butter. Fold in walnuts. Spread topping mixture over sweet potato puree. Top with mini marshmallows.

Bake at 400 degrees F in the preheated oven for 10 minutes. Enjoy!

Sunday Pumpkin Risotto

(Ready in about 15 minutes | Servings 4)

Ingredients

2 ounces butter, melted

1 small-sized onion, diced

2 cloves garlic, minced

12 ounces rice

4 cups vegetable stock

6 ounces pumpkin puree

1 teaspoon dried basil

1 teaspoon dried thyme

1/2 teaspoon cinnamon powder

1/4 teaspoon ground allspice

1/2 cup heavy cream

Directions

Press the "SOUP" button. Warm butter. Sauté the onion and garlic until tender. Add rice and cook for 10 minutes, stirring often. Add the rest of the above ingredients, except heavy cream.

Secure and lock the lid. Once the timer reaches 0, press "CANCEL". Carefully remove the lid. Fold in heavy cream. Serve and enjoy!

Coffee Can Bread

(Ready in about 25 minutes | Servings 6)

Ingredients

1 bread recipe

Butter, for inside the can

1 coffee can

3 tablespoons flour

Directions

Make the dough according to recipe directions.

Butter the inside of the coffee can. Then, flour the inside of the can. Roll up the bread and put into the can.

Add a piece of oil to the top of the can. Let your bread raise until it's 1-inch from the top. Add 8 cups of water to the cooker.

Put the lid on and use "Manually" function; cook for 15 minutes to 20 minutes.

Allow prepared bread to cool down for several minutes. Serve.

LUNCH RECIPES

Tomato Cabbage Rolls

(Ready in about 1 hour | Servings 6)

Ingredients

3 cloves garlic, minced

1/2 cup onions chopped

1 pound ground beef

1 ½ cups rice

2 (6.5-ounce) cans tomato sauce

1 teaspoon cayenne pepper

Sea salt, to taste

8 large cabbage leaves, blanched

Black peppercorns, to taste

2 (10-ounce) cans diced tomatoes

Directions

Combine the garlic, onion, beef, rice, tomato sauce, cayenne pepper, and salt in a mixing bowl; mix until everything is well combined.

Divide the meat mixture among softened cabbage leaves. Roll the cabbage leaves up to form logs.

Place the rolls in a cooker. Add peppercorns and diced tomatoes.

Then, seal the lid of the cooker. Now cook for 1 hour under LOW pressure. Use the quick-release function. Serve warm.

Juicy BBQ Pork

(Ready in about 1 hour | Servings 8)

Ingredients

8 pounds pork butt roast

1 teaspoon garlic powder

1 teaspoon cayenne pepper

Sea salt and freshly ground black pepper, to taste

2 (12-ounce) bottles BBQ sauce

Directions

Generously season the pork with garlic powder, cayenne pepper, salt, and black pepper; place seasoned pork roast in your Instant Pot. Fill with enough water to cover the meat.

Close the lid and bring up to 15 pounds of pressure. Cook on HIGH pressure for 1 hour. Reserve about 2 cups of pot juices. Shred the pork with two forks and mix with BBQ sauce, adding reserved juice. Serve warm over mashed potatoes.

Herbed Pot Roast

(Ready in about 35 minutes | Servings 8)

Ingredients

3 pounds chuck roast

Salt and ground black pepper, to taste

2 tablespoons canola oil

1 onion, thinly sliced

1 parsnip, peeled and thinly sliced

1 carrot, peeled and thinly sliced

1 celery stalk, thinly sliced

8 red potatoes

1 tablespoon tomato paste

1 1/3 cups beef stock

1 sprig thyme

1 sprig rosemary

4 cloves garlic, peeled and minced

1/4 cup red wine

Directions

Season the chuck roast with salt and ground black pepper.

Place the inner pot in your cooker. Place canola oil in the inner pot. Press the "MEAT" button. Sear the beef on all sides. Reserve the beef.

Add the vegetables to the inner pot and cook for about 3 minutes. Add the beef back to the pot, along with the rest of the ingredients.

Place the lid on. Press the "WARM" button. Cook for 25 minutes. Carefully remove the lid. Serve.

Chicken Curry Soup

(Ready in about 20 minutes | Servings 4)

Ingredients

1 can coconut milk

3 cups water

1 teaspoon ground ginger

1 teaspoon curry powder

6 ounces frozen carrots

6 ounces sugar snap peas

6 ounces frozen okra

1 medium-sized chicken breast, chopped

Directions

Throw all ingredients into your Instant Pot.
Choose "Soup" setting. Serve hot and enjoy!

Red Cabbage with Apples

(Ready in about 35 minutes | Servings 4)

Ingredients

2 tablespoons bacon fat

1 onion, diced

2 tart apples, peeled, cored and diced

1 head red cabbage, shredded and stems removed

1/4 red apple cider vinegar

1 cup dry red wine

1 cup beef stock

1/2 teaspoon ground black pepper

1/2 teaspoon dried thyme

1 teaspoon sea salt

1/2 teaspoon ground cloves

3 tablespoons brown sugar, light or dark

2 tablespoons all-purpose flour

1 tablespoon cornstarch dissolved in 3 tablespoons dry red wine

Directions

Set Instant Pot to "SAUTE". Warm bacon fat until it is completely melted. Then, sauté the onion and apples until soft, or approximately 10 minutes. Hit "Cancel" function.

Add the cabbage, apple cider vinegar, red wine, stock, ground black pepper, thyme, sea salt, ground cloves, and brown sugar.

Dust with flour; gently stir to combine. Select "Manual" and cook 8 to 10 minutes. Perform a quick-release for 10 minutes.

Next, push "Sauté" and set to More. Bring to a boil; add prepared cornstarch slurry. Allow it to boil for about 5 minutes, or until cooking liquids are thickened. Serve warm.

Rigatoni with Sausage and Bacon

(Ready in about 15 minutes | Servings 4)

Ingredients

1 tablespoon olive oil

1 cup bacon

1 pound sausage meat

1 medium-sized leek, chopped

2 cloves garlic, peeled and minced

2 cups tomato purée

Salt and ground black pepper, to taste

1 teaspoon red pepper flakes crushed

1 pound dry rigatoni pasta

1 tablespoon fresh sage

1 tablespoon fresh basil, chopped

1/4 cup Parmigiano-Reggiano, grated

Directions

Press "Sauté" button. Then, warm olive oil. Cook the bacon for about 4 minutes. Now, add sausage meat and cook until it is browned and thoroughly cooked.

Add the leeks and garlic; sauté them for a few minutes. Now add tomato purée, salt, black pepper, and red pepper flakes. Add rigatoni pasta and water to cover your pasta.

Close and lock the lid. Choose "MANUAL" and LOW pressure for 5 minutes.

Afterwards, release the pressure by using the quick pressure release. Stir in sage, basil and Parmigiano-Reggiano. Enjoy!

Old-Fashioned Minestrone Soup

(Ready in about 25 minutes | Servings 4)

Ingredients

1 pound ground beef

1 cup cooked beans

1 large-sized potato, diced

2 carrots, trimmed and thinly sliced

2 celery stalks, chopped

1 onion, chopped

3 cloves garlic, minced

32 ounces beef broth

28 ounces canned tomatoes, crushed

1 teaspoon sea salt

1/2 teaspoon ground black pepper

Directions

Add the ingredients to your Instant Pot and stir to combine.

Put the lid on; choose "MANUAL" and high pressure for 20 minutes. Serve warm and enjoy.

Delicious Short Ribs with Vegetables

(Ready in about 50 minutes | Servings 8)

Ingredients

8 short ribs, excess fat trimmed

Sea salt and freshly ground black pepper, to taste

2 tablespoons vegetable oil

1 parsnip, chopped

3 carrots, peeled and thinly sliced

3 cloves garlic, peeled and finely minced

1 red onion, chopped

1 cup vegetable broth

1 cup water

2 tablespoons tomato paste

8 potatoes, small

1 sprig rosemary

1 bay leaf

Directions

Generously season the short ribs with sea salt and black pepper. Warm vegetable oil in the inner pot. Push the "MEAT" button. Now brown the ribs on all sides. Reserve the ribs.

Add the parsnip, carrots, garlic, and onion; sauté for 4 minutes.

Add the reserved browned ribs back to the pot; stir in the rest of the ingredients. Press the "STEW"; then, cook for 40 minutes.

Afterwards, remove the lid according to manufacturer's instructions. Serve.

Creamy Potato Soup

(Ready in about 30 minutes | Servings 6)

Ingredients

8 medium potatoes, peeled and diced

1 celery stalk, thinly sliced

3 carrots, sliced

1/2 cup celery, chopped

1/2 cup spinach leaves, chopped

1 yellow onion, chopped

3 cups broth

Salt and ground black pepper, to taste

1 tablespoon fresh basil leaves, finely chopped

1/2 teaspoon red pepper flakes, crushed

1 tablespoon ground f chia seeds

Sharp Cheddar cheese, grated

Directions

Simply throw all ingredients, except for the cheese, into your Instant Pot. Now press the "Soup" button and adjust the timer to 30 minutes.

Process the soup with an immersion blender. Ladle the soup into bowls; top with grated cheese. Serve with cornbread if desired.

Mushroom and Bean Soup

(Ready in about 25 minutes | Servings 4)

Ingredients

1 pound mushrooms, thinly sliced

1 cup canned cannellini beans

2 carrots, trimmed and thinly sliced

1 large-sized parsnip, chopped

2 celery stalks, chopped

3 cloves garlic, minced

1 onion, chopped

4 cups vegetable stock, preferably homemade

3 cups canned tomatoes, crushed

1/2 teaspoon dried basil

1/2 teaspoon dried dill weed

1 teaspoon sea salt

1/2 teaspoon ground black pepper

Directions

Simply throw all ingredients into your Instant Pot; stir to combine well.

Cover with the lid and choose "MANUAL" function and "HIGH" pressure for 20 minutes. Serve right now.

Short Ribs with Mushrooms

(Ready in about 50 minutes | Servings 8)

Ingredients

10 short ribs, excess fat trimmed

1 teaspoon salt

3/4 teaspoon ground black pepper

2 tablespoons olive oil

1 cup mushrooms, quartered

1 yellow onion, peeled and chopped

2 carrots, peeled and thinly sliced

2 cloves garlic, peeled and finely minced

2 cups vegetable stock

2 tablespoons tomato ketchup

1 sprig rosemary

Directions

First, season the short ribs with salt and ground black pepper. Then, heat olive oil in the inner pot. Choose the "MEAT" function and brown your short ribs on all sides. Set the ribs aside.

Add the mushrooms, onion, carrots, and garlic to the pot; then, sauté for 4 minutes.

Next, add the ribs back to the pot along with the rest of the ingredients. Now choose the "STEW" function; cook approximately 40 minutes.

Transfer to a serving platter and enjoy!

Hot Jalapeño Vegetable Soup

(Ready in about 35 minutes | Servings 6)

Ingredients

2 tablespoons butter, softened

1 teaspoon coriander seeds

1 celery, chopped

2 carrots, chopped

1 medium onion

1 pickled jalapeño, chopped

4 cups water

3 potatoes, cubed

3 quarts chicken broth

1 teaspoon dried thyme

1 teaspoon ground cumin

Cornbread, for garnish

Directions

Press "Sauté" and melt the butter for a minute or so. Drop in coriander seeds, celery, carrots, onion and jalapeño. Sauté for about 5 minutes.

Add the remaining ingredients, except for cornbread. Press "Soup" setting and set the timer to 30 minutes. Serve warm with cornbread. Enjoy!

Comforting Potato and Bacon Soup

(Ready in about 20 minutes | Servings 6)

Ingredients

1 yellow onion, peeled and diced

3 slices bacon

1 teaspoon olive oil

2 cups vegetable broth

2 ½ pounds potatoes, peeled and cubed

2 carrots, diced

1 teaspoon cayenne pepper

1 teaspoon dried basil

1/2 teaspoon dried oregano

1/2 teaspoon dried dill weed

1 teaspoon garlic powder

1 cup water

1 ½ cups canned evaporated milk

1 tablespoon salt

3/4 teaspoon ground black pepper

Directions

Press "Sauté" function and stir in the onion, bacon, and olive oil. Sauté for about 4 minutes, stirring continuously.

Add vegetable broth, potatoes, carrots, and seasonings. Stir to combine. Cover with the lid, press "Steam" button and adjust the timer to 10 minutes.

When beeps, perform a quick pressure release. Remove bacon and reserve. Add water, evaporated milk, salt, and black pepper.

Mix with your immersion blender, but leave chunks of potatoes. Taste and adjust the seasonings. Serve with reserved bacon.

Chili Bean Soup

(Ready in about 45 minutes | Servings 6)

Ingredients

1 cup dry beans, soaked in water overnight

1 ham bone

1 bay leaf

1 red onion chopped

1 (15-ounce) can tomatoes, diced

1 celery rib, diced

3 carrots, diced

1 teaspoon chili powder

1 teaspoon cumin powder

1 teaspoon garlic powder

Kosher salt and ground black pepper, to taste

Directions

Drain and rinse your beans.

Put the beans along with ham bone and bay leaf into your cooker; now add just enough water to cover. Seal Instant Pot and cook on "Bean/Chili" setting.

Discard the ham bone and bay leaf; now add remaining ingredients and stir to combine well.

Choose "Soup" setting, adjusted down to 20 minutes. Open your pot according to manufacturer's directions. Serve and enjoy!

Country Chicken and Vegetable Soup

(Ready in about 35 minutes | Servings 6)

Ingredients

2 frozen chicken breasts, boneless and skinless

3 carrots, trimmed and chopped

4 potatoes, diced

1 onion, peeled and diced

4 cups chicken stock

Salt and cracked black pepper, to taste

Directions

Simply throw all the above ingredients in your Instant Pot.

Turn "Manual" setting on your Instant Pot; set the timer for 35 minutes. Serve right away!

Rainbow Lentil Soup

(Ready in about 20 minutes | Servings 6)

Ingredients

2 cloves garlic, minced

1 red onion, chopped

1 teaspoon smoked paprika

Sea salt and ground black pepper, to taste

2 carrots, thinly sliced

1 pound Yukon Gold potatoes, diced

1 cup red lentils, rinsed

1 cup green lentils, rinsed

2 bay leaves

8 cups water

Directions

First, choose "Sauté" function. Sauté the garlic, onions, paprika, salt, black pepper, carrots, and potatoes for about 5 minutes, stirring continuously.

Stir in the lentils, bay leaves, and water.

Cover the pot and bring to HIGH pressure. Afterwards, use the quick-release method to release the pressure.

Taste and adjust the seasonings. Serve warm.

Butternut Squash and Lentil Soup

(Ready in about 20 minutes | Servings 6)

Ingredients

2 tablespoons olive oil

1 onion, diced

3 cloves garlic, minced

1 ½ pounds butternut squash, roughly chopped

1 teaspoon cumin powder

1 teaspoon Garam masala

Salt and cayenne pepper to taste

4 cups vegetable stock

1 cup lentils, rinsed

1 can tomatoes, diced

Fresh chopped parsley leaves, chopped

Directions

Choose the "Sauté" function; warm olive oil. Sauté the onion and garlic for 4 to 5 minutes.

Add the butternut squash, cumin, Garam masala, salt, and cayenne pepper. Continue to cook for about 3 minutes.

Add the stock and lentils. Secure the lid closed. Press the "Manual" button, and adjust the timer to 6 minutes under HIGH pressure. Stir in the tomatoes.

Mix the soup with your immersion blender. Serve topped with fresh parsley. Enjoy!

Chipotle Pumpkin Soup with Pecans

(Ready in about 25 minutes | Servings 6)

Ingredients

2 cloves garlic, smashed

1 onion, chopped

1 teaspoon ground allspice

1 teaspoon salt

1 teaspoon cayenne pepper

1 teaspoon black pepper

1 chipotle pepper, seeded and finely minced

2 medium-sized potatoes, peeled and diced

2 large apples, peeled, cored and diced

2 (15-ounce) cans pumpkin puree

1/4 cup pecans, pulsed

2 cups water

2 cups vegetable stock

Toasted pumpkin seeds, for garnish

Directions

Using the "Sauté" function, cook the garlic and onion until they are browned, or about 4 minutes.

Add allspice, salt, cayenne pepper, black pepper, and chipotle. Add the potatoes, apples, pumpkin puree, ground pecans, water, and stock.

Click the "Manual" button; adjust cooking time to 4 minutes under HIGH pressure. Afterwards, let the pressure release naturally for about 10 minutes.

Carefully open the lid; transfer the soup to your food processor; pulse until completely smooth and creamy, working in batches. Serve warm sprinkled with toasted pumpkin seeds.

Black Bean Soup

(Ready in about 20 minutes | Servings 4)

Ingredients

1 ½ cups dry black beans, soaked overnight

2 tablespoons vegetable oil

1 large-sized onion, chopped

4 cloves garlic, minced

1/2 teaspoon chipotle powder

6 cups vegetable stock

2 large bay leaves

2 teaspoons dried basil leaves

1 teaspoon sea salt

1/4 teaspoon ground black pepper

Cayenne pepper to taste

Fresh chopped cilantro, for garnish

Directions

Drain black beans and reserve.

Push "Sauté" button; warm vegetable oil. Then, sauté the onion and garlic for 2 to 4 minutes.

Add the chipotle powder, reserved beans, vegetable stock, bay leaves, and basil; season with salt, black pepper, and cayenne pepper; stir well.

Next, lock the lid in place, and click the "Manual"; cook for 7 minutes. Allow the pressure to come down gradually and naturally; carefully remove the lid.

Garnish with cilantro and serve.

Creamy Curry Lentil Soup

(Ready in about 15 minutes | Servings 6)

Ingredients

1 red onion, diced

3 cloves garlic, peeled and minced

2 tablespoons red curry paste

1 (15-ounce) can coconut milk

2 cups vegetable stock

1 ½ cups lentils

2 ripe tomatoes, chopped

Salt and ground black pepper, to taste

Directions

Choose the "Sauté" function on your cooker. Sauté the onion and garlic until beginning to brown. You can add a splash of stock to prevent the mixture from sticking.

Then, choose the "Cancel". Add the curry paste, and stir well. Pour in the coconut milk and stock. Now add lentils and tomatoes. Season with salt and black pepper. Stir again to combine well.

Close the lid and choose "Manual"; set the time to 6 minutes. Serve warm and enjoy!

Sweet Potato and Lentil Soup

(Ready in about 15 minutes | Servings 6)

Ingredients

1 tablespoon olive oil

1 onion, diced

2-3 cloves garlic, peeled and minced

1 ½ pounds sweet potatoes, diced

1 teaspoon cumin powder

2 tablespoons chili powder

1 teaspoon celery seeds

1 cup dried lentils

1 teaspoon sea salt

1/4 teaspoon ground black pepper

4 cups vegetable broth

2 (15-ounce) cans kidney beans, drained and rinsed

1 tablespoon curry paste

1 (15-ounce) can coconut milk

28 ounces tomatoes, diced

1 tablespoon parsley, roughly chopped

1/2 cup fresh cilantro, roughly chopped

1 tablespoon apple cider vinegar

Directions

Click the "Sauté" function. Then, warm olive oil; add onion and garlic and sauté until tender.

Add the sweet potatoes and cook for 1 to 2 more minutes. Click "Cancel" button. Add all of the remaining ingredients to your cooker.

Close the lid and put the steam valve to 'sealed'. Choose "Manual" and adjust the time to 10 minutes.

After the pressure has released, open the lid. Ladle the soup into individual bowls and serve hot!

Winter Sweet Potato Soup

(Ready in about 15 minutes | Servings 6)

Ingredients

1 tablespoon canola oil

2 cloves garlic, finely chopped

1 onion, roughly chopped

3 large-sized sweet potatoes, cubed

2 ripe tomatoes, peeled, seeded and chopped

1 (14-ounce) can coconut milk

1/2 teaspoon freshly grated nutmeg

1/4 teaspoon cinnamon powder

1 tablespoon lemon juice

2 cups vegetable stock

1/2 cup peanut butter

Sea salt and black pepper, to taste

Directions

Choose the "Sauté" setting. Then, heat canola oil, and stir in the garlic and onion, stirring frequently, until they are softened. Press "Cancel".

Stir in all of the other ingredients; stir to combine well.

Close the lid and choose "Manual". Let it cook for about 4 minutes. Remove the lid according to manufacturer's instructions.

Puree the soup to your desired consistency, using an immersion blender.

The Best Vegan Chili

(Ready in about 25 minutes | Servings 8)

Ingredients

1 1/3 cup dried black beans, soaked

2/3 cup dried red beans, soaked

2 cups onion, chopped

2 cloves garlic, minced

3 ½ cups boiling water

1 celery stalk, chopped

2 carrots, chopped into sticks

1 bell pepper, de-seeded and thinly sliced

2 tablespoons chili powder

1 teaspoon cumin powder

1 teaspoon cayenne pepper

1 teaspoon coriander

Salt and black pepper, to taste

2 (14.5-ounce) cans diced tomatoes

Directions

Drain and rinse soaked beans.

In your cooker, sauté the onion and garlic for about 5 minutes, adding boiling water to prevent burning as needed.

Add the remaining ingredients, except for tomatoes. Set to "Manual" and HIGH pressure for 12 minutes.

Stir in the canned tomatoes. Serve hot topped with roasted red peppers if desired.

Three-Bean Vegan Chili

(Ready in about 25 minutes | Servings 8)

Ingredients

2 cloves garlic, minced

1 medium-sized leek, thinly sliced

3 ½ cups hot vegetable stock

2/3 cup dried cannellini beans, soaked, drained and rinsed

2/3 cup dried pinto beans, soaked, drained and rinsed

2/3 cup dried kidney beans, soaked, drained and rinsed

2 carrots, chopped into sticks

1 parsnip, chopped

1 green bell pepper, de-seeded and thinly sliced

1 chili pepper, finely minced

1 teaspoon red pepper flakes, crushed

1 teaspoon coriander

1 teaspoon sea salt, to taste

5-6 black peppercorns

2 (14.5-ounce) cans diced tomatoes

Directions

In your cooker, sauté the garlic and leek for about 4 to 5 minutes, adding vegetable stock to prevent it from burning.

Now stir in the rest of above ingredients, except for canned tomatoes. Choose 'Manual' setting and HIGH pressure for 12 minutes.

Add the tomatoes and stir to combine well. Serve immediately topped with shredded vegan cheese or nutritional yeast if desired. Enjoy!

Delicious Country Stew

(Ready in about 45 minutes | Servings 8)

Ingredients

16 ounces stew meat

1 onion, finely chopped

2 garlic cloves, minced

4 potatoes, chopped

2 celery stalks, chopped

2 carrots, chopped

2 cups beef bone broth

1 tablespoon lard

1 tablespoon sea salt

1 teaspoon red pepper flakes, crushed

1 teaspoon black pepper, ground

1 bay leaf

1 teaspoon cumin powder

1 teaspoon celery seeds

2 tablespoons tomato paste

2 tablespoons arrowroot flour

Directions

Choose "Sauté" on your Instant Pot. Sauté meat, onion and garlic until the meat is no longer pink.

Add the remaining ingredients, except for arrowroot flour. Now place the lid on your Instant Pot and press "Meat/ Stew".

Cook for 35 minutes under HIGH pressure.

To make the slurry, combine 1/4 of the cooking liquid with the arrowroot flour. Add the slurry back to the pot. Serve warm.

Pork and Lotus Root Soup

(Ready in about 45 minutes | Servings 6)

Ingredients

1 pound pork side rib

8 ounces fresh lotus root, peeled and sliced

1/2 teaspoon black pepper, ground

1 teaspoon paprika

1 tablespoon sea salt

6 cups of water

Directions

Simply throw all ingredients into Instant Pot Electric Pressure Cooker.

Choose "Soup" button. Cook approximately 40 minutes. Serve warm.

Spiced Lentil Stew

(Ready in about 25 minutes | Servings 8)

Ingredients

1 large-sized yellow onion, chopped

3 cloves garlic, minced

1 teaspoon smoked paprika

1 teaspoon turmeric

1 teaspoon cumin

1/2 teaspoon black pepper

1/4 teaspoon chili flakes

1 sweet potato, peeled and cubed

1 stalk celery, chopped

2 carrots, peeled and diced

1 ½ cup green lentils

2 cups vegetable stock

1/4 cup raisins

1 can tomatoes, diced

Directions

Sauté onions and garlic for about 3 minutes, adding stock as needed, so they do not stick.

Add the remaining ingredients, except for canned tomatoes. Cover and set to "Manual", and 10 minutes pressure. Afterwards, allow pressure to come down naturally.

Next, stir in tomatoes. Cook for 5 minutes, stirring continuously. Taste and adjust the seasonings. Serve.

Root Vegetable Soup with Pork Ribs

(Ready in about 45 minutes | Servings 6)

Ingredients

1 pound pork side rib

2 carrots, peeled and sliced

1 turnip, peeled and sliced

1 tablespoon sea salt

1/2 teaspoon black pepper, ground

1 teaspoon paprika

6 cups vegetables stock

1 cup greens, diced

Directions

Simply throw all ingredients, except for greens, into Instant Pot Electric Pressure Cooker.

Choose "Soup" button. Cook approximately 40 minutes. Add greens and stir until they're wilted. Serve warm.

Beans with Mushrooms and Farro

(Ready in about 35 minutes | Servings 4)

Ingredients

1 cup dried navy beans

1/2 cup farro

3 cups mushrooms, thinly sliced

1 cup green onion, chopped

5 cloves garlic, finely chopped

1 small-sized jalapeno pepper, finely chopped

1 tablespoon shallot powder

2 tomatoes, diced

Directions

Throw all of the ingredients, except the tomatoes, into the Instant Pot. Press "Soup" button and cook 30 minutes.

Add the diced tomatoes. Stir to combine well. Serve hot and enjoy!

Family Beef Stew

(Ready in about 45 minutes | Servings 6)

Ingredients

3 pounds beef chuck roast, cubed

2 tablespoons vegetable oil

4 cloves garlic, minced

1 large-sized onion, slice into rings

3 carrots, chopped

6 medium-sized potatoes, diced

1 green bell pepper, sliced

1 red bell pepper, sliced

2 cups vegetable stock

1 cup water

1 (8-ounce) can tomato sauce

1 tablespoon Worcestershire sauce

2 tablespoons cornstarch

1/2 teaspoon dried dill weed

1 teaspoon dried thyme

Sea salt and ground black pepper, to taste

Directions

Sear the meat in vegetable oil using 'Sauté' function. Deglaze the pot with some broth. Add the garlic and onion, and continue sautéing for 1 to 2 more minutes. Turn off your cooker.

Add all remaining ingredients. Close and lock the lid on the cooker. Cook under HIGH pressure for 35 minutes.

Next, perform 10 minutes natural pressure release. Serve warm dolloped with sour cream if desired.

Turkey and Bean Chili

(Ready in about 25 minutes | Servings 8)

Ingredients

2 tablespoons vegetable oil

1 medium-sized leek, chopped

1 ½ pounds ground turkey

2 cups chicken stock

2 (14-ounce) cans diced tomatoes with green chilies

2 (14-ounce) cans beans, drained and rinsed well

1 tablespoon chili powder

1 ½ cups water

Sharp Cheddar cheese, shredded

Directions

First, heat the oil in your cooker. Add the leek and sauté for 7 to 8 minutes. Add the ground turkey and cook until the meat has browned.

Add the rest of the above ingredients, except for Cheddar cheese. Cover and cook under HIGH pressure for 5 minutes.

Ladle into soup bowls and serve topped with shredded Cheddar cheese. Enjoy!

Summer Chicken Chili

(Ready in about 25 minutes | Servings 8)

Ingredients

2 tablespoons olive oil

1 medium-sized onion, chopped

2-3 cloves garlic, minced

1 red bell pepper, chopped

1 ½ pounds ground chicken

1 ½ cups water

2 cups chicken broth

2 (14-ounce) cans kidney beans, drained and rinsed well

2 (14-ounce) cans diced tomatoes with green chilies

Fresh chopped chives, for garnish

Directions

Choose "Sauté" function and warm olive oil; then cook onion, garlic, and bell pepper for about 8 minutes or until they are tender and fragrant. Stir in the ground chicken and cook until it has browned.

Add the remaining ingredients, except for chives. Put the lid on, and cook under HIGH pressure for 5 to 7 minutes.

Ladle into soup bowls and garnish with fresh chives. Enjoy!

Hamburger Cabbage and Barley Soup

(Ready in about 30 minutes | Servings 6)

Ingredients

1 pound hamburger

2 garlic cloves, minced

1 red onion, finely chopped

6 cups beef stock

2 ripe Roma tomatoes, seeded and chopped

1 cup quick barley

1 celery stalk, chopped

3 carrots, peeled and sliced

2 parsnips, sliced

5 cups cabbage, chopped

1 teaspoon dried thyme

1 teaspoon dried marjoram

Sea salt and freshly cracked black pepper to your taste

Directions

Press "Sauté" button and cook hamburger for several minutes. Drain off the excess fat; stir in the garlic and onion; continue sautéing a few more minute.

Next, add beef stock, tomatoes, and barley. Choose "Soup" function and let it cook under HIGH pressure for about 10 minutes.

Perform a quick pressure release; add the rest of the ingredients. Put the cooker's lid back on and press "Soup" button; bring to HIGH pressure. Serve warm.

Broccoli Chowder with Velveeta Cheese

(Ready in about 15 minutes | Servings 8)

Ingredients

8 cups broccoli florets

4 cups chicken stock, homemade

1/2 cup leek, chopped

Sea salt and ground black pepper, to your liking

1 teaspoon mustard powder

1 cup Velveeta cheese

Directions

Put all the ingredients, except Velveeta cheese, into the Instant Pot.

Now place the lid on, and press "MANUAL" button for 6 minutes. After that, remove the lid according to manufacturer's directions.

Use your immersion blender to blend the soup. Add Velveeta cheese and push "Sauté" button; stir until Velveeta is completely melted. Enjoy!

Delicious Spring Chili

(Ready in about 30 minutes | Servings 8)

Ingredients

2 pounds coarse ground chicken

1 (14.5-ounce) can beef broth

2 cups dry pinto beans

1 tablespoon cumin powder

1 teaspoon celery seeds

2 can green chilies, diced

1 ½ cups water

1 can tomato, diced

1 cup green onions, chopped

2 green garlics, chopped

Directions

In your Instant Pot, brown ground chicken; deglaze a pan with beef broth.

Add the rest of the above ingredients. Choose "Bean/Chili" function. Remove the lid according to manufacturer's instructions. Serve right now topped with fresh chives if desired.

Potato Leek Soup with Cremini Mushrooms

(Ready in about 20 minutes | Servings 10)

Ingredients

2 small-sized leeks, trimmed and sliced

2 cloves garlic, minced

8 cups water, boiling

2 pounds potatoes, peeled and cubed

2 parsnips, peeled and diced

3 medium-sized carrots, peeled and diced

1 cup cremini mushrooms, roughly chopped

1 teaspoon marjoram

1/2 teaspoon fennel seeds

Salt and black pepper, to your liking

2 cups unsweetened coconut milk

Directions

Choose "Sauté" function; now sauté the leeks and garlic approximately 5 minutes, adding boiling water as needed.

Add the rest of the ingredients, except for coconut milk. Lock the cooker's lid in place; cook under HIGH pressure for about 6 minutes.

After that, allow the cooker's pressure to come down gradually and naturally. Pour in the coconut milk.

Mix your soup with an immersion blender. Adjust the seasonings, and serve warm topped with nutritional yeast if desired.

Creamy and Cheesy Cauliflower Soup

(Ready in about 15 minutes | Servings 8)

Ingredients

8 cups cauliflower florets

1 cup boiling water

3 cups vegetable broth

2 garlic cloves, minced

1/2 cup shallots, chopped

Sea salt and ground black pepper, to your liking

1 teaspoon paprika

1 teaspoon marjoram

1 teaspoon cumin powder

1 cup Cheddar cheese, shredded

Directions

Simply throw all the ingredients, except for Cheddar cheese, into your cooker.

Next, place the lid on, and choose "MANUAL"; set time to 6 minutes. Open the cooker.

Process the soup in a blender or a food processor, working in batches. Ladle into individual bowls and serve topped with shredded Cheddar cheese. Enjoy!

Zucchini and Summer Squash Soup

(Ready in about 25 minutes | Servings 8)

Ingredients

1 onion, peeled and chopped

4 zucchinis, shredded

4 yellow summer squashes, shredded

2 serrano peppers, diced

1 orange bell pepper, diced

1 (12-ounce) package silken tofu, pressed

1 cup boiling water

1 cup vegetable stock

1 tablespoon chili powder

1 teaspoon cumin powder

1 teaspoon smoked paprika

Directions

Add the onion to your cooker. Press "Sauté" button; then, sauté the onions until tender and translucent.

Add the rest of the ingredients and press "Soup" button.

Remove the lid according to manufacturer's directions. Allow to cool slightly; mix with an immersion blender.

Serve in individual bowls topped with fresh chopped cilantro. Enjoy!

Beef and Kale Stew with Noodles

(Ready in about 25 minutes | Servings 8)

Ingredients

2 tablespoons butter

1/2 pound ground beef

1 teaspoon dried basil leaves

1/2 teaspoon dried thyme

1/2 teaspoon marjoram

1/2 teaspoon cayenne pepper

Salt and black pepper, to taste

1 onion, diced

3 carrots, diced

1/2 cup white wine

2 Roma tomatoes, seeded and chopped

8 cups bone broth

2 large handfuls kale, chopped

8 ounces noodles

Directions

Set your cooker to "Sauté". Now melt butter; then, add the ground beef and all of the seasonings. Cook till the meat has browned.

Add the onion and carrot, and cook for about 7 minutes. Pour in the wine to deglaze the pan.

Add the rest of the ingredients, and stir to combine. Serve topped with fresh cilantro if desired.

Potato and Porcini Mushroom Soup

(Ready in about 20 minutes | Servings 10)

Ingredients

2 small-sized yellow onions, sliced into rings

2 cloves garlic, minced

8 cups water, boiling

1 pound potatoes, peeled and cubed

3 medium-sized carrots, peeled and diced

1 celery stalk, chopped

1 cup Porcini mushrooms, roughly chopped

1/2 teaspoon dried dill weed

1 teaspoon marjoram

Salt and black pepper, to your liking

2 cups non-dairy milk, unsweetened

Directions

Click "Sauté" button; sauté yellow onions and garlic for 4 to 5 minutes, adding water as needed.

Stir in the remaining ingredients, except for milk. Cover and cook under HIGH pressure for 6 minutes.

Open the lid following the manufacturer's directions. Pour in non-dairy milk.

Blend the soup in a food processor or use your hand blender. Serve your soup topped with croutons if desired.

Easiest Beef Stroganoff

(Ready in about 15 minutes | Servings 6)

Ingredients

3 tablespoons olive oil

2 pounds beef sirloin, sliced

1 red onion, peeled and finely chopped

1 pound mushrooms, sliced

1 bay leaf

2 cups beef stock

1 teaspoon dried thyme

1/2 teaspoon dried rosemary

1/4 cup sour cream

Directions

Press the "MEAT" button. Warm olive oil and sear the meat for several minutes.

Add the remaining ingredients, except the sour cream.

Place the lid on your pot, lock the lid. Push the "STEW" button. Lastly, when the steam is completely released, open the lid.

Serve dolloped with sour cream. Enjoy!

Festive Chicken with Beans

(Ready in about 35 minutes | Servings 6)

Ingredients

2 tablespoons canola oil

1 whole chicken, cut into pieces

1 red onion, diced

2 cloves garlic, peeled and minced

1 serrano pepper, seeded and diced

1 pound dried beans

2 large-sized tomatoes, diced

2 tablespoons white wine

1 tablespoon smoked paprika

4 cups chicken broth

Sea salt and freshly ground pepper, to your liking

2 tablespoons fresh cilantro, chopped

Directions

Press "Sauté" button and heat the oil. Then, sear the chicken on all sides, stirring periodically. In the pan drippings, sauté the onions, garlic, and serrano pepper.

Add the remaining ingredients; add the chicken back to the cooker. Place the lid on the cooker. Press the "BEAN" button and cook for 30 minutes.

Next, remove the lid according to manufacturer's directions. Serve warm and enjoy!

Sausage and Seafood Delight

(Ready in about 20 minutes | Servings 6)

Ingredients

2 pounds smoked sausage, sliced

3 pounds shrimp

1 pound potatoes, peeled and diced

3 corn on the cobs, quartered

20 clams

3 cups water

1 cup vegetable stock

2 bay leaves

Salt and ground black pepper, to taste

Fresh chopped chives, as garnish

Directions

Simply throw all the ingredients, except for chives, into the inner pot of your cooker.

Press the "BEANS" button; cook for about 15 minutes. Serve sprinkled with chopped chives. Enjoy!

Sausage and Garbanzo Bean Stew

(Ready in about 30 minutes | Servings 6)

Ingredients

2 teaspoons canola oil

4 Italian turkey sausage links, casings removed

3 cloves garlic, minced

1 onion, diced

1 cup pearl barley

1 bone-in chicken breast half, skinless

3 cups chicken stock

1 (15-ounce) can garbanzo beans, drained

1 cup kale leaves, chopped

1 cup mild salsa

Salt and ground black pepper, to your liking

Directions

Press "Sauté" button. Heat canola oil. Stir in turkey sausage and cook until browned.

Reserve sausage. Now cook garlic and onion in pan drippings until they are tender. Add barley and cook 1 more minute, stirring frequently.

Add reserved sausage back to your cooker. Add chicken and chicken stock to the cooker.

Close the lid securely; place pressure regulator on vent pipe. Choose "Soup" function. Then, allow pressure to drop on its own.

Next, remove chicken from the pot; shred meat and add it back to your soup. Add garbanzo beans, kale, salsa, salt, and black pepper to your liking. Serve warm and enjoy!

Lentil and Split Pea Soup

(Ready in about 30 minutes | Servings 6)

Ingredients

1 cup red lentils

1 cup split peas

3 cloves garlic, minced

1 onion, coarsely chopped

1 parsnip, coarsely chopped

2 carrots, coarsely chopped

8 cups chicken broth

1 teaspoon paprika

1/2 teaspoon dried dill weed

Sea salt and ground black pepper, to your liking

1 teaspoon wine vinegar

Directions

Simply throw all the above ingredients in your pot. Seal the lid.

Use "Soup" function and cook 30 minutes.

Turn off the heat; allow pressure to subside. Taste and adjust seasonings. Serve warm and enjoy!

Lentil and Mushroom Soup with Kale

(Ready in about 30 minutes | Servings 8)

Ingredients

5 medium-sized Bella mushrooms, thinly sliced

1 cup red lentils

1 cup split peas

3 cloves garlic, minced

1 shallot, coarsely chopped

2 carrots, coarsely chopped

8 cups chicken broth

1 teaspoon cayenne pepper

1/2 teaspoon red pepper flakes, crushed

1/2 teaspoon dried dill weed

1 teaspoon dried basil

Sea salt and ground black pepper, to your liking

1 teaspoon wine vinegar

1 cup kale leaves, shredded

Directions

Clean and prepare your ingredients. Then, put the ingredients, except kale, into your cooker. Cover with the lid.

Choose "Soup" setting; adjust cook time to 30 minutes.

Carefully open the cooker. Add shredded kale leaves and stir until they are thoroughly heated and wilted. Garnish with green onions if desired. Serve right now!

Old-Fashioned Cheese-Onion Soup

(Ready in about 20 minutes | Servings 6)

Ingredients

3 tablespoons margarine

4 onions, peeled and sliced

4 cups beef stock

1 sprig rosemary

2 sprigs thyme

1/2 cup sherry

Sea salt and freshly ground black pepper, to your liking

Cayenne pepper, to your liking

1 bay leaf

6 slices sharp cheese

6 slices bread, toasted

Directions

Press the "MEAT" button. Then, warm margarine; now sauté the onions until they are caramelized.

Add the rest of the ingredients, except for cheese and toasted bread. Cook for 1 more minute.

Next, lock the lid. Press the "SOUP" button; press the time adjustment button until you reach 12 minutes.

Ladle into soup bowls and serve topped with cheese and toasted bread slices. Enjoy!

Coconut Pork Curry

(Ready in about 25 minutes | Servings 4)

Ingredients

1 tablespoon green curry paste

1 cup pork, cut into pieces

1 cup vegetable stock

3 cloves garlic, minced

1 lemon grass stalk

1 parsnip, chopped

1 carrot, chopped

1 onion

2 medium-sized potatoes

1 bell pepper, chopped

Salt and black pepper, to your liking

1 teaspoon sweet paprika

1 can coconut milk

Directions

Place all ingredients, except coconut milk, in your Instant Pot. Stir to combine.

Close and lock the lid; use "Meat" option and cook approximately 20 minutes.

While your curry is still hot, add 1 can of coconut milk. Stir again to combine well. Garnish with the fresh coriander if desired and serve warm. Good luck!

Beef and Yogurt Curry

(Ready in about 25 minutes | Servings 4)

Ingredients

1 cup beef, cut into pieces

1 tablespoon red curry paste

1 cup beef stock

4 cloves garlic, peeled and minced

1 turnip, peeled and chopped

1 parsnip, chopped

1 carrot, chopped

1 onion, chopped

1 tablespoon vinegar

1 medium-sized zucchini, peeled and diced

Salt and black pepper, to your liking

1/4 teaspoon cinnamon powder

1 teaspoon ground allspice

1 can natural yogurt

Directions

Simply throw the ingredients, except for yogurt, in your cooker.

Cover with the lid and press "Meat" button; cook for 15 to 20 minutes.

While the curry is still hot, pour in natural yogurt. Stir until everything is well combined. Serve over rice. Enjoy!

Chicken and Navy Bean Soup

(Ready in about 30 minutes | Servings 6)

Ingredients

1 (15.5-ounce) can navy beans, rinsed and drained

1 (14.5-ounce) can stewed tomatoes

1 ½ cups chicken stock

1/2 pound cooked chicken breast, chopped

2 tablespoons olive oil

1/2 cup sour cream

1 teaspoon cayenne pepper

Salt and ground black pepper, chopped

1/4 cup fresh cilantro, chopped

Directions

Place the ingredients, except for cilantro, in the inner pot of cooker.

Next, lock the lid. Choose the "SOUP" function; press the time adjustment button until you reach 20 minutes.

Serve warm garnished with fresh cilantro.

DINNER RECIPES

Rice with Pineapple and Cauliflower

(Ready in about 30 minutes | Servings 6)

Ingredients

2 cups rice

1/2 pineapple, cut into chunks

1 broccoli, minced

2 teaspoons olive oil

1 teaspoon salt

1/4 teaspoon white pepper

Directions

Pour the water to the level 2 mark on the inner pot of your cooker.

Put the ingredients into the cooker. Choose the "Rice" button.

Serve warm, sprinkled with fresh parsley.

Penne with Sausage and Tomato Sauce

(Ready in about 20 minutes | Servings 6)

Ingredients

1 cup bacon

1 pound sausage meat

1 shallot, finely chopped

2 cloves garlic, minced

2 cups tomato purée

Salt to taste

1 pound pasta penne pasta

1 teaspoon dried basil

1 teaspoon dried oregano

1/4 cup Parmesan cheese, grated

Directions

Set the cooker on "Sauté". Cook the bacon for about 4 minutes. Now brown sausage until it's thoroughly cooked.

Add the shallot and garlic; sauté them for 4 minutes or until tender. Add the rest of the ingredients, except for Parmesan cheese.

Choose "Manual", and LOW pressure for 5 minutes. Stir in Parmesan cheese and serve right away. Bon appétit!

Instant Pot Slow Cooker Meatloaf

(Ready in about 8 hours | Servings 10)

Ingredients

For the Meatloaf:

Non-stick cooking spray

1 pounds ground meat

1 onion, finely chopped

1 large-sized egg

1 cup rice, cooked

1 can drained mushrooms

1 teaspoon onion powder

1 teaspoon garlic powder

1 cup milk

Salt and ground black pepper, to taste

1 teaspoon dried thyme

For the Topping:

1 tablespoon brown sugar

3/4 cup ketchup

Directions

Lightly oil an inner pot with non-stick cooking spray. Mix all ingredients for the meatloaf.

Shape the mixture into a round loaf; transfer it to the pot. Then, mix the ingredients for the topping. Place the topping over the meatloaf.

Close and lock the cooker's lid. Choose the "Slow Cook" key and cook on LOW for 6 to 8 hours. Enjoy!

Old-Fashioned Pork Belly

(Ready in about 35 minutes | Servings 6)

Ingredients

2 pounds pork belly, sliced

1/2 cup soy sauce

1 tablespoon sugar

3 tablespoons cooking wine

4-star anise

2 cups water

4 slices fresh ginger

1 sweet onion, peeled and chopped

6 cloves garlic, sliced

Directions

Heat "Sauté"; then, sear pork belly on both sides. Add the remaining ingredients.

Press "Meat" key and cook for 30 minutes or so, until your meat are almost falling apart. Serve right away!

Friday Night Lasagna

(Ready in about 30 minutes | Servings 6)

Ingredients

Non-stick cooking spray

1 package dry lasagna noodles

1 jar pasta sauce of choice

1 ½ cups cream cheese

1 cup mushrooms, thinly sliced

1 teaspoon sea salt

1/4 teaspoon ground black pepper

1/4 teaspoon cayenne pepper

1/2 teaspoon red pepper flakes

1 teaspoon dried basil

1/2 teaspoon dried rosemary

1 teaspoon dried oregano

Directions

Coat a spring-form pan with cooking spray.

Arrange lasagna noodles in the bottom of the pan. Then, spread the pasta sauce. Lay your cream cheese.

Top with sliced fresh mushrooms. Sprinkle with some spices and herbs. Repeat the layers until you run out of ingredients. Cover with a piece of an aluminum foil.

Next, place the trivet in the bottom of Instant Pot. Pour in 1 ½ cups water. Cook for 20 minutes under HIGH pressure.

Allow your lasagna to rest for about 10 minutes before removing from the pan.

Peanut and Vegetable Salad

(Ready in about 25 minutes | Servings 4)

Ingredients

1 pound raw peanuts, shelled

2 cups water

1 bay leaf

2 tomatoes, chopped

1 cup sweet onion, diced

1/4 cup hot peppers, finely minced

1/4 cup celery, diced

2 tablespoons fresh lime juice

2 tablespoons olive oil

3/4 teaspoon salt

1/2 teaspoon freshly ground black pepper

Directions

First, blanch raw peanuts in boiling salted water for about 1 minute; drain. Then, discard the skins.

Next, cook peanuts, along with two cups of water and the bay leaf; let peanuts cook about 20 minutes under pressure.

Transfer cooked peanuts to a large-sized salad bowl. Add the remaining ingredients and toss to combine.

Pulled BBQ Beef

(Ready in about 1 hour 10 minutes | Servings 6)

Ingredients

Non-stick cooking spray

1 1/3 pounds frozen beef roast

1 beef stock

For the BBQ sauce:

1/2 cup ketchup

2 teaspoons honey

1 teaspoon paprika

1 teaspoon kosher salt

1/2 teaspoon ground black pepper

1/4 cup water

Directions

Oil your Instant Pot with cooking spray. Put beef roast and stock into the pot. Put the lid on, choose the "Meat" key and set to 70 minutes.

Meanwhile, combine together the BBQ sauce ingredients in a mixing bowl.

Turn the pot off. Next, use a quick pressure release. Now pull the cooked meat apart into chunks.

Add the beef back to the Instant Pot; pour the BBQ sauce over it. Assemble the sandwiches and serve.

Tuna with Noodles and Feta

(Ready in about 20 minutes | Servings 6)

Ingredients

1 tablespoon vegetable oil	1 ½ teaspoons garlic powder
1 red onion, chopped	1/2 teaspoon sea salt
8 ounces dry egg noodles	1/4 teaspoon black pepper
1 can (14-ounce) tomatoes, diced	1 can tuna fish in water, drained
1 ¼ cups water	Feta cheese, crumbled
1 dried basil	

Directions

Warm the oil and sauté the onion for about 2 minutes.

Stir in the noodles, tomatoes, water; click "Soup" button and set time to 10 minutes. Turn the pot off.

Add the remaining ingredients, except for feta; cook for 4 more minutes until it is warmed through. Serve garnished with feta cheese.

Party Barbecue Pork

(Ready in about 1 hour | Servings 16)

Ingredients

8 pounds pork butt roast

1 teaspoon cumin powder

1 teaspoon onion powder

1 teaspoon garlic powder

Sea salt and black pepper, to your liking

2 (12-ounce) bottles barbecue sauce

Directions

Season the pork with cumin powder, onion powder, garlic powder, salt and black pepper; now fill the cooker with enough water to cover.

Close the lid and press "Meat" button. Cook for 1 hour.

Reserve 2 cups of cooking juice. Shred your pork and drizzle with barbecue sauce. Serve right now.

Pasta with Beef and Tomato Sauce

(Ready in about 10 minutes | Servings 6)

Ingredients

1 pound lean ground beef

2 pounds tomato paste

1 onion

2 garlic cloves, minced

1 pound fresh mushrooms, chopped

Sea salt and ground black pepper, to taste

1/2 teaspoon dried dill weed

1/2 teaspoon dried basil

1 pound dried egg noodles

Directions

Press "Sauté" button and brown the beef.

Add the rest of the ingredients. Pressure cook for 7 minutes. Serve warm.

Saucy Salmon Fillets

(Ready in about 10 minutes | Servings 16)

Ingredients

4 salmon filets

Salt and ground black pepper, to taste

1 tablespoon lemon juice

3 tablespoons mayonnaise

1 tablespoon brown sugar

2 tablespoons olive oil

1 tablespoon fresh parsley

Directions

Season salmon filets with salt and black pepper. Press "Sauté" and brown your filets on both sides.

Add about 3/4 cup water to pot. Lay browned salmon on a rack. Seal the cooker's lid and choose "Steam" for about 5 minutes.

In the meantime, mix remaining ingredients in a bowl or a measuring cup. Then, pour the sauce over the filets.

Pork Ribs with Vegetables

(Ready in about 40 minutes | Servings 4)

Ingredients

2 pork ribs

2 cups BBQ sauce

1 cup water

2 onions, slice into rings

2 parsnips, thinly sliced

2 carrots, thinly sliced

Directions

Lay the ribs in your Instant Pot. Pour in 1 cup of BBQ sauce and 1 cup of water. Close the cooker's lid.

Then, press "Meat" key. Add the onions, parsnips, and carrots. Cover with the lid and choose "Manual" button, and set to 2 minutes. Drizzle with remaining BBQ sauce and serve right now.

Grandma's Juicy Spareribs

(Ready in about 45 minutes | Servings 6)

Ingredients

1 tablespoon olive oil

1 onion, sliced

1/4 cup tomato paste

1/4 tamari sauce

2 tablespoons brown sugar

1/3 cup rice wine vinegar

1 (20-ounce) can of pineapple

1 teaspoon ginger, finely chopped

1 teaspoon granulated garlic

1 teaspoon coriander, ground

Salt and black pepper, to taste

4 pounds ribs, cut for serving.

Cornstarch slurry

Directions

Heat the oil, and sauté the onions until just tender.

Stir in the rest of the ingredients, except for cornstarch slurry.

Next, choose "Stew" function for 12 minutes. Then, release pressure. Add cornstarch slurry and stir until the juice has thickened. Serve warm and enjoy!

Summer Brown Rice Salad

(Ready in about 30 minutes | Servings 4)

Ingredients

2 cups brown rice

2 ½ cups water

8 grape tomatoes, halved

1 cucumber, cored and diced

2 bell peppers, sliced

1 cup scallions, chopped

1 teaspoon red pepper flakes

Salt and white pepper, to your liking

Directions

Add rice and water to your Instant Pot. Close and lock the lid. Press "Manual"; choose 22 minutes pressure cooking time.

Next, open the cooker using Natural Pressure Release. Transfer to a bowl in order to cool completely.

Add the rest of the ingredients. Afterwards, gently stir to combine and serve.

Black Bean and Mint Salad

(Ready in about 15 minutes | Servings 4)

Ingredients

1 cup black beans, soaked overnight

4 cups water

3 garlic cloves, smashed

1 sprig fresh mint

1 tablespoon extra-virgin olive oil

1 tablespoon red wine vinegar

Salt and freshly cracked black pepper, to your liking

Directions

Add black beans, water, and garlic to the inner pot of your Instant Pot. Press "Manual" and choose 8 minutes pressure cooking time.

Drain your beans and add the remaining ingredients. Gently stir until everything is well mixed. Serve chilled and enjoy!

Black Bean and Mango Salad

(Ready in about 15 minutes | Servings 4)

Ingredients

4 cups water

1 cup black beans, soaked overnight

2 bay leaves

1 small-sized mango, diced

1 zucchini, peeled and thinly sliced

1/4 cup cilantro, coarsely chopped

2 tablespoons coconut oil, softened

2 tablespoons lime juice

Salt and white pepper, to your liking

Directions

Simply put the water, black beans, bay leaves into the inner pot. Choose "Manual" function and 8 minutes pressure cooking time.

Drain your beans, discard bay leaves, and allow them to cool completely. Now add the remaining ingredients and stir to combine. Serve right now.

Rice and Tuna Salad

(Ready in about 30 minutes | Servings 4)

Ingredients

2 ½ cups water

2 cups brown rice

2 cups tuna in spring water

1 onion, thinly sliced

1 cup frozen petits pois, defrosted

2 tablespoons extra-virgin olive oil

1 teaspoon red pepper flakes

1/2 teaspoon dried dill weed

Salt and ground black pepper, to your liking

1 bunch flat-leaf parsley, roughly chopped

Directions

Add lightly salted water and rice to your cooker. Close and lock the lid. Choose "Manual" function and 22 minutes pressure cooking time.

Then, open the cooker using natural pressure release. Allow rice to cool completely.

Add the rest of the ingredients. Stir and serve well chilled.

Peppery Jasmine Rice Salad

(Ready in about 30 minutes | Servings 4)

Ingredients

3 cups Jasmine rice, rinsed

3 cups water

1 green bell pepper, cut into thin strips or chopped

1 red bell pepper, cut into thin strips or chopped

1 orange bell pepper, cut into thin strips or chopped

1 cup scallions, chopped (white and green parts)

1 tablespoon lemon zest, grated

3 tablespoons extra-virgin olive oil

1/3 cup mixed mint and cilantro, roughly chopped

Directions

Throw rinsed rice in your Instant Pot. Add water and lock the lid.

Press "Manual" key; use the [+ -] button to choose 4 minutes.

Next, open the cooker and allow rice to cool completely. Transfer your rice to a salad bowl. Add remaining ingredients. Now stir to combine. Serve and enjoy!

Cilantro Bean Purée

(Ready in about 20 minutes | Servings 6)

Ingredients

2 tablespoons vegetable oil

1 red onion, peeled and chopped

1 bunch cilantro, roughly chopped

1 teaspoon garlic powder

1/2 teaspoon chipotle powder

2 cups dry pinto beans, soaked

2 cups water

1/2 teaspoon black pepper

1 teaspoon red pepper flakes, crushed

1 teaspoon sea salt

Directions

Press "Sauté" in order to pre-heat the Instant Pot. Now warm the oil and sauté the onion, cilantro, garlic powder, and chipotle powder.

Stir in the beans and water. Close and lock the lid of your cooker. Choose "Manual" and 10 minutes pressure cooking time.

Next, reserve 2 spoonfuls of beans. Puree the remaining beans using a potato masher. Season with black pepper, red pepper, and salt. Garnish with reserved whole beans.

Apple and Ginger Risotto with Pecans

(Ready in about 20 minutes | Servings 4)

Ingredients

4 cups soy milk

1 ¾ cups risotto rice

4 apples, cored and diced

1/4 teaspoon grated nutmeg

1/4 teaspoon ground cinnamon

1/4 cup candied ginger, diced

1/2 cup pecans, toasted and roughly chopped

Directions

Put all of the above items, except for pecans, into your Instant Pot.

Choose the "Manual" key and adjust the timer to 12 minutes. Serve sprinkled with pecans. Enjoy!

Cauliflower and Broccoli Salad

(Ready in about 20 minutes | Servings 6)

Ingredients

For the Salad:

2 medium-sized carrots, thinly sliced

1 small head cauliflower, broken into florets

1 head broccoli, broken into florets

1 cup water

For the Vinaigrette:

3 tablespoons extra-virgin olive oil

2 tablespoons fresh orange juice

1 tablespoon capers

Salt and ground black pepper, to your liking

Directions

Add carrots, cauliflower, broccoli and water to the Instant Pot. Cover with the lid and press "Manual"; use the [+ -] button to choose 7 minutes pressure cooking time.

Meanwhile, mix all the items for vinaigrette. Strain out the vegetables and dress with the vinaigrette.

Colorful Vegetable Dinner

(Ready in about 15 minutes | Servings 4)

Ingredients

1 eggplant, peeled and cubed

1 teaspoon sea salt

1/4 cup olive oil

2 zucchinis, cut into rounds

1 shallot, sliced

2 potatoes, cubed

3 ripe tomatoes, diced

1 bunch basil, chopped

2 tablespoons pine nuts, toasted

Directions

Put the eggplant cubes into a strainer; sprinkle with sea salt and let stand for 30 minutes.

Push "Sauté" button; warm the olive oil; sauté the eggplant, zucchini, shallots, and potatoes until they are tender and fragrant.

Stir in the tomatoes and basil. Close the cooker's lid and choose "Manual"; use 6 minutes cooking time. Serve sprinkled with toasted pine nuts.

Classic Italian Caponata

(Ready in about 15 minutes | Servings 4)

Ingredients

1 eggplant, unpeeled and cubed

1 teaspoon salt

1/4 cup olive oil

4 large garlic cloves, chopped

1 red onion, sliced

3 tablespoons red wine vinegar

1 bunch fresh basil, chopped

Directions

First, generously sprinkle the eggplant cubes with salt; let them stand in a colander at least 35 minutes. Rinse the eggplant in water; squeeze them and reserve.

Choose "Sauté" function; heat the oil and sauté the eggplant, garlic, and onion until they are tender.

Stir in red wine. Cover and choose "Manual"; choose 6 minutes cooking time.

Serve sprinkled with fresh basil leaves and olives if desired.

Bean and Leek Mash

(Ready in about 20 minutes | Servings 6)

Ingredients

2 tablespoons vegetable oil

1 medium-sized leek, finely chopped

3 cloves garlic, peeled and minced

1 teaspoon cumin seeds

2 cups water

2 cups canned beans, soaked

1/2 teaspoon black pepper

1 teaspoon sea salt

Fresh chopped chives, for garnish

Directions

Choose "Sauté" function in order to pre-heat your cooker. Heat vegetable oil; sauté the leek, garlic, and cumin seeds.

Add the water and beans. Cover the cooker with the lid and press "Manual" key; cook for about 10 minutes.

Puree the bean mixture using a potato masher. Salt and pepper it. Garnish with fresh chopped chives. Enjoy!

Mashed Garbanzo Beans

(Ready in about 40 minutes | Servings 6)

Ingredients

2 cups dried garbanzo beans

2 bay leaves

4 garlic cloves, finely minced

1/4 cup cilantro

1 tablespoon stone ground mustard

Toasted pumpkin seeds, for garnish

Directions

Place garbanzo beans and bay leaves in your cooker. Add water to cover the beans (2-inch). Cook under HIGH pressure for 35 minutes. Next, let the pressure go down on its own.

Drain and rinse garbanzo beans, and discard bay leaves. Then, mash them with a potato masher, fork or pastry blender.

Add minced garlic, cilantro, and mustard, salt and pepper to your liking. Adjust the seasonings. Serve sprinkled with toasted pumpkin seeds. Enjoy!

Super Creamy Mashed Potatoes

(Ready in about 30 minutes | Servings 4)

Ingredients

2 cups water

6 medium-sized potatoes

1 cup cream

1 teaspoon kosher salt

1/4 teaspoon ground black pepper

1/2 teaspoon cayenne pepper

Directions

Place the salted water and washed potatoes in your cooker.

Cook on "Manual" setting for 20 minutes. Then, perform a quick pressure release. Now remove the skins from your potatoes. Reserve cooking liquid.

Mash cooked potatoes together with cream, adding small quantities of the reserved liquid. Season with salt, black pepper, and cayenne pepper. Taste and adjust the seasonings. Serve.

Mashed Cauliflower and Potatoes

(Ready in about 30 minutes | Servings 4)

Ingredients

3 cups water

1 head cauliflower

6 medium-sized potatoes

1/2 cup milk

1 tablespoon butter, softened

1 teaspoon garlic powder

1 teaspoon kosher salt

1/2 teaspoon cayenne pepper

1/4 teaspoon ground black pepper

Directions

Add lightly salted water, cauliflower, and potatoes to your cooker.

Press "Manual" key and cook for 20 minutes. Then, remove the skins from your potatoes. Reserve cooking liquid.

Mash the cauliflower and potatoes together with the rest of the ingredients, adding reserved liquid as needed. Serve warm.

Creamy Fish Curry

(Ready in about 20 minutes | Servings 6)

Ingredients

1 tablespoon olive oil

1 shallot, chopped

3 garlic cloves, finely minced

1/4 teaspoon ginger powder

1 teaspoon chili powder

1 teaspoon ground cumin

1/2 teaspoon ground turmeric

2 bay leaves

1 ½ pounds white fish fillets, cut into bite-size pieces

1 small-sized can unsweetened coconut milk

Salt to your liking

1 tablespoon fresh lemon juice

Directions

Choose "Sauté" function. Warm olive oil and sauté the shallot, garlic and ginger until they are softened. Add chili powder, cumin, and turmeric.

Cook for 1 to 2 more minutes and add the rest of the ingredients, except for lemon juice.

Cover and press "Manual"; choose 3 minutes pressure cooking time. Drizzle with lemon juice and serve immediately.

Classic Chicken Curry

(Ready in about 25 minutes | Servings 6)

Ingredients

1 tablespoon canola oil

1 leek, chopped

2 garlic cloves, finely minced

1 carrot, chopped

1 tablespoon ginger, freshly grated

1 teaspoon fennel seeds

1 teaspoon celery seeds

1 teaspoon ground cumin

1/2 teaspoon ground turmeric

1 ½ pounds chicken breasts, cut into bite-size chunks

2 cups coconut milk

Salt and ground black pepper, to your liking

1/4 cup fresh parsley leaves, roughly chopped

Directions

Press "Sauté" key. Now heat the oil; sauté the leek, garlic, carrot and ginger in hot oil; cook until they're just tender. Add fennel seeds, celery seeds, cumin, and turmeric, and cook for an additional 2 minutes.

Stir in the remaining ingredients, except for parsley.

Lock the cooker's lid and choose "Manual" and 7 minutes pressure cooking time. Serve warm garnished with fresh parsley leaves.

Chicken in Herbed Lemon Sauce

(Ready in about 35 minutes | Servings 6)

Ingredients

Juice of 3 lemons

3 garlic cloves, minced

1 sprigs fresh sage, chopped

1 sprig fresh thyme, chopped

2 sprigs fresh rosemary, chopped

4 tablespoons extra-virgin olive oil

Sea salt and ground black pepper, to your liking

1 whole chicken, cut into pieces

1/2 cup white wine

1 cup water

Directions

To make the marinade: in a mixing bowl, place lemon juice, garlic, sage, thyme, rosemary, olive oil, salt, and black pepper. Mix to combine well.

Place the chicken pieces in the marinade. Then, leave to marinate, covered, at least 3 hours in the refrigerator

Press "Sauté" key to pre-heat the cooker. Cook the chicken pieces for about 5 minutes, turning periodically.

Deglaze your pot with white wine and cook until it has evaporated. Add the chicken back to the pot along with marinade. Pour in water.

Press "Manual" and cook for 12 more minutes. Next, take the chicken out of the Instant Pot.

Press "Sauté" and cook for several minutes in order to thicken the sauce. Garnish with fresh lemon slices if desired and enjoy!

Delicious Cauliflower Salad

(Ready in about 15 minutes + chilling time | Servings 6)

Ingredients

For the Salad:

2 heads cauliflower, broken into florets

1 ½ cups water

For the Dressing:

3 tablespoons coconut oil, softened

2 tablespoons fresh lemon juice

Salt and ground black pepper, to your liking

1/4 teaspoon fresh cilantro, roughly chopped

Directions

Put the cauliflower and water into your Instant Pot. Then, press "Manual"; and choose 8 minutes pressure cooking time. Transfer the cauliflower to a salad bowl.

In the meantime, mix all the dressing ingredients. Lastly, drizzle the dressing over the cauliflower. Serve well chilled.

Maple Beans with Bacon

(Ready in about 35 minutes | Servings 6)

Ingredients

3 cups navy beans

3 cups chicken stock

2 cups water

1 onion, diced

1/2 cup bacon bits

2 tablespoons tomato paste

Sea salt and ground black pepper, to taste

1 teaspoon molasses

Directions

Soak the beans overnight. Then, transfer them to your Instant Pot.

Add the rest of the ingredients. Stir to combine and choose "Bean" function. Serve right now.

Lentil and Black Rice with Vegetables

(Ready in about 25 minutes | Servings 4)

Ingredients

1/2 cup black lentils

1/2 cup black rice

2 cloves garlic, pressed/minced

1 small-sized onion, finely chopped

1 cup mushrooms, thinly sliced

1 carrot, chopped

1 stalk celery, chopped

1/2 teaspoon seasoned salt

1 teaspoon fennel seeds

1 teaspoon dried coriander

1/2 teaspoon ground black pepper

2 cups vegetable broth

Directions

Place the lentils and rice in a bowl; now cover with water. Let them soak approximately 30 minutes.

Click "Sauté" and cook the vegetables for 3 to 5 minutes, adding small amounts of water or wine to prevent burning.

Add the soaked lentils and rice along with the rest of the ingredients. Lock the lid in place and cook for 9 minutes. Lastly, let the pressure come down naturally.

Chili Grits with Scallions

(Ready in about 20 minutes | Servings 4)

Ingredients

1 cup scallions, chopped

2 cloves garlic, minced

2 cups boiling water

2 cups vegetable stock

1 cup grits

1 teaspoon chili powder

1 teaspoon dried basil

1 teaspoon dried oregano

1/2 teaspoon cayenne pepper

Directions

Press "Sauté" and add the scallions and garlic; cook, until fragrant, stirring occasionally.

Add boiling water, vegetable stock, grits, and seasonings. Stir to combine well. Lock the cooker's lid in place. Now click "Manual", and cook for 5 minutes under high pressure.

Quick release the pressure and serve right away.

Easy Peasant Polenta

(Ready in about 20 minutes | Servings 4)

Ingredients

1 tablespoon canola oil

2 cloves garlic, minced

1 cup sweet onions, finely chopped

4 cups vegetable stock

1 cup cornmeal

1 teaspoon cumin powder

1/2 teaspoon dried dill weed

1 teaspoon dried basil

1/2 teaspoon red pepper flakes

Directions

Choose "Sauté" function; Warm canola oil, and sauté the garlic and sweet onions; cook for about 5 minutes or until they're tender.

Add the remaining ingredients. Now stir to combine. Now choose "Manual", and cook for 5 minutes on HIGH pressure.

Spoon your cornmeal into individual bowls and serve with butter if desired.

Mushroom and Veggie Delight

(Ready in about 15 minutes | Servings 4)

Ingredients

2 tablespoons olive oil

1 onion, chopped

2 stalks celery, finely chopped

1 parsnip, finely chopped

2 carrots, finely chopped

1 green bell pepper, finely chopped

2 cloves garlic, minced

1 cup mushrooms. sliced

2 cups vegetable stock

1 (27-ounce) can tomatoes, chopped

1 squash

Salt and ground black pepper, to your liking

Directions

Press "Sauté" button, and heat olive oil. Then, sauté the onions, celery, parsnip, carrots, bell pepper, and garlic. Cook for about 5 minutes.

Stir in the remaining ingredients. Press "Manual" and set the time to 7 minutes. Serve warm with a piece of bread.

Family Baked Chicken

(Ready in about 35 minutes | Servings 6)

Ingredients

2 tablespoons sugar

2 teaspoons salt

1 medium-sized chicken

1/2 teaspoon ground black pepper

1 piece of ginger, minced

1 tablespoon soy sauce

1 tablespoon wine

1 shallot, minced

Directions

Sprinkle the chicken with sugar and 1 teaspoon of salt. Cover the bottom of the inner pot with remaining 1 teaspoon of salt.

Lay the chicken in the inner pot. Now add black pepper, ginger, soy sauce, and wine.

Choose the "Poultry" mode. Serve with shallot and enjoy!

Old-Fashioned Beans

(Ready in about 35 minutes | Servings 8)

Ingredients

3 tablespoons olive oil

1 onion, chopped

4 cloves garlic, minced

4 thin bacon slices, chopped

1 onion soup mix

1 cup water

1 pound pinto beans, soaked overnight

1 teaspoon mustard

1 tablespoon brown sugar

Directions

Click "Sauté" button; warm olive oil; then, cook the onion, garlic, and bacon for 4 to 5 minutes.

Add soup mix and 1 cup of water; stir to combine; click "Sauté" and cook for 5 minutes. Now add the beans and 4 cups of water.

Stir in the mustard and brown sugar. Choose "Bean/Chili" setting and close the cooker's lid. Serve immediately.

Holiday Ham with Pineapple

(Ready in about 20 minutes | Servings 8)

Ingredients

1 tablespoon vegetable oil

1 ham, cubed

1/2 cup water

3 baby potatoes, and cubed

1 can crushed pineapple

1/4 cup brown sugar

Salt to your liking

5-6 black peppercorns

Directions

Choose "Sauté" function, and heat the oil. Add the ham cubes and water. Now use "Manual" mode, and cook for 5 minutes.

Next, stir in the sweet potatoes, crushed pineapple, and brown sugar. Season with salt to your liking and add black peppercorns.

Click "Manual" and pressure cook for 7 minutes. Serve warm and enjoy!

Orange Short Ribs

(Ready in about 45 minutes | Servings 4)

Ingredients

1 cup water

3/4 cup soy sauce

1/4 cup sweetener

1 blood orange, squeezed

1 head of garlic, peeled and crushed

1 cup scallions, chopped

Salt and ground black pepper, to taste

4 beef short ribs

2 tablespoons sesame oil

Directions

Combine together the water, soy sauce, sweetener, and orange juice in a mixing bowl.

Add the garlic, scallions, salt, and ground black pepper; mix thoroughly. Place the ribs in the bowl and marinate at least 4 hours.

Heat sesame oil in a large skillet. Sear your ribs for about 3 minutes on each side. Transfer seared short ribs to the Instant Pot.

Next, choose the "Meat\Stew" mode, and cook for 30 minutes. To release pressure, use natural release method. Serve warm.

Bean and Rice Dinner

(Ready in about 45 minutes | Servings 6)

Ingredients

1/2 cup brown rice

1/4 cup peanut

1/8 cup red bean

1/4 cup sesame seeds

1/8 cup golden raisins

14 cup brown sugar

8 cups of water

Directions

Put all items into the Instant Pot.

Now press the "Porridge" button. Serve warm.

Fried Rice with Chicken

(Ready in about 30 minutes | Servings 6)

Ingredients

3 cups multi-grain rice

3 cups water

1 cup chicken, cut into chunks

1/4 cup green onions, chopped

1 cup carrots, thinly sliced

2 tablespoons butter, softened

1 tablespoon apple cider vinegar

Salt and ground black pepper, to taste

1/2 teaspoon dried dill weed

1/2 teaspoon dried basil

Directions

Add all the above ingredients to your Instant Pot.

Use the "Multigrain" mode. Serve right now.

Rice with Mushrooms and Pork

(Ready in about 30 minutes | Servings 6)

Ingredients

3 cups water

3 cups brown rice

1/2 cup pork, cut into chunks

1 cup mushrooms, sliced

1 yellow onion, chopped

1 celery stalk, thinly sliced

2 tablespoons vegetable soil

1 teaspoon mustard seeds

1/2 teaspoon cayenne pepper

1 teaspoon fennel seeds

Salt and ground black pepper, to taste

Directions

Simply throw the ingredients in the Instant Pot.

Choose the "Multigrain" mode. Serve warm and enjoy!

Pasta with Italian Sausage

(Ready in about 20 minutes | Servings 4)

Ingredients

1 pound Italian sausage

2 cloves garlic, minced

1 onion, diced

1 cup Porcini mushrooms, thinly sliced

1 box pasta of choice

1 jar pasta sauce

2 cups water

3/4 cup Mozzarella cheese, shredded

Directions

Using the "Sauté" function, brown Italian sausage along with the garlic, onions, and mushrooms. Cook until the vegetables are tender.

Add the pasta, pasta sauce, and water. Use "Meat" setting and cook for 6 minutes on HIGH. When it beeps, do a quick release. Stir in mozzarella cheese.

Seasoned Chicken with Cheese

(Ready in about 30 minutes | Servings 6)

Ingredients

Skinless and boneless chicken, cut into bite-sized chunks

1 teaspoon kosher salt

1/2 teaspoon ground black pepper

2 tablespoons oil

1 onion, finely chopped

2 cloves garlic, minced

1 (10-ounce) can tomato sauce

1 teaspoon molasses

1 teaspoon dried oregano

1 teaspoon dried basil

1 teaspoon bouillon granules

1 cup Cheddar cheese, grated

1 tablespoon flour

1 tablespoon butter, at room temperature

1 cup olives, pitted and halved

Directions

Generously season your chicken with salt and black pepper. Heat oil and sauté chicken chunks until they start to brown.

Add onion and garlic and sauté until they are tender. Now add tomato sauce, molasses, oregano, basil, and bouillon granules. Stir to combine.

Secure the lid and select the "Manual" mode. Cook for 10 minutes. Carefully remove the lid and add cheese; stir to combine.

Combine flour and butter in a mixing bowl. Add this mixture to the Instant Pot to thicken the sauce. Serve warm garnished with olives.

Pasta with Beef and Mushrooms

(Ready in about 20 minutes | Servings 4)

Ingredients

1 tablespoon olive oil

1 pound lean ground beef

1 onion

2 garlic cloves, minced

2 pounds tomato puree

1 ½ cups mushrooms, chopped

1 teaspoon dried basil leaves

1/2 teaspoon dried oregano

Salt and black pepper, ground

1 cup dried egg noodles

Directions

Cook ground beef in olive oil using the "Sauté" function on your cooker. Then, add the onions and garlic; sauté until they're tender.

Add the rest of the ingredients. Pressure cook for 7 minutes. Serve and enjoy!

Easiest Chicken Risotto

(Ready in about 20 minutes | Servings 4)

Ingredients

1 stick butter, at room temperature

1 red onion, chopped

3 garlic cloves, chopped

1 pound chicken, diced

2 cups rice

1 cup white wine

4 cups chicken stock

1 teaspoon rosemary

Salt and freshly ground black pepper, to your liking

Chopped fresh parsley, for garnish

Directions

Use "Sauté" function to preheat your cooker. Now warm the butter, and cook the onion, garlic, and chicken for about 2 minutes.

Stir in rice and wine. Add chicken stock, rosemary, salt, and black pepper. Use "Manual" mode, and adjust the time to 12 minutes. Give it another good stir. Now seal the lid.

Serve topped with fresh parsley. Enjoy!

Pancetta Risotto with Feta Cheese

(Ready in about 20 minutes | Servings 4)

Ingredients

1 tablespoon olive oil

1 leek, chopped

2 garlic cloves, chopped

1 ½ cups pancetta, diced

2 cups rice

5 cups chicken stock

1 tablespoon apple cider vinegar

1 teaspoon dried thyme

1/2 teaspoon dried basil

1/2 teaspoon dried dill weed

1 teaspoon mustard powder

Salt and freshly ground black pepper, to your liking

Feta cheese, crumbled

Directions

Press "Sauté" button and heat the oil; sauté the leek and garlic until they are tender.

Stir in the pancetta, rice, and chicken stock. Add apple cider vinegar, thyme, basil, dill weed, and mustard powder.

Next, press "Manual" button; set the time to 12 minutes. Season with salt and black pepper; stir to combine well and cover with the lid.

Serve topped with crumbled Feta cheese. Serve right away.

Herby Pasta with Meat and Mushrooms

(Ready in about 30 minutes | Servings 4)

Ingredients

2 tablespoons canola oil

2 cloves garlic, minced

1 large-sized onion, chopped fine

1 pound ground pork

1 pound ground beef

1 teaspoon sea salt

1/2 teaspoon ground black pepper

1/2 teaspoon red pepper flakes

1/2 teaspoon dried dill weed

1/2 teaspoon dried basil

1 teaspoon dried sage

2 small cans mushrooms, sliced

1 jar pasta sauce

1 pound uncooked pasta

3 cups chicken broth

1 cup dry wine

Directions

Press "Sauté" button and warm canola oil. Sauté the garlic, onion, pork, and beef until browned.

Add the remaining ingredients. Stir until everything is well combined. Seal the cooker's lid and cook for 20 minutes. Release the pressure manually.

Serve with Mozzarella cheese if desired. Serve.

Old-Fashioned Cassoulet

(Ready in about 30 minutes | Servings 6)

Ingredients

2 tablespoons canola oil

2 pounds pork, cut into chunks

Salt and ground black pepper, to your liking

2 cups beans

1 cup vegetable broth

1 parsnip, chopped

1 carrot, chopped

1 celery stalk, chopped

4 cloves garlic, finely minced

1 small-sized onion, diced

1 teaspoon fennel seeds

1 teaspoon cumin seeds

2 tablespoons dried thyme

2 cups croutons

1 cup cheese, crumbled

Directions

In a skillet, heat canola oil; brown pork chunks on all sides; season with salt and ground black pepper.

Replace the pork to the Instant Pot add the rest of above ingredients, except cheese. Seal the cooker's lid. Next, choose "Stew" setting for 35 minutes. Divide your cassoulet among individual bowls, and serve topped with cheese.

FAST SNACKS

Roast Fingerling Potatoes

(Ready in about 30 minutes | Servings 6)

Ingredients

4 tablespoons canola oil

2 pounds fingerling potatoes

1 sprig thyme

1 sprig rosemary

1/2 teaspoon dried dill weed

3 garlic cloves, with outer skin

1 cup vegetable stock

Sea salt and ground black pepper, to your liking

Directions

Use "Sauté" mode to pre-heat the cooker. Warm canola oil; when the oil is hot, stir in the potatoes, thyme, rosemary, dill, and garlic.

Cook the potatoes, turning occasionally, for about 10 minutes. Now pierce in the middle of each potato with a sharp knife. Add vegetable stock, salt and black pepper to taste.

Choose "Manual" mode and cook for 11 minutes. Afterwards, use quick pressure release. Peel the garlic cloves and smash them. Taste, adjust the seasonings and serve.

Saucy Turkey Wings

(Ready in about 35 minutes | Servings 4)

Ingredients

4 tablespoons butter, at room temperature

4 turkey wings

Salt and ground black pepper, to your liking

1 teaspoon cayenne pepper

1 onion, sliced into rings

1 ½ cups cranberries

1/2 cup orange juice

1 ½ cups vegetable stock

Directions

Use "Sauté" setting and melt the butter. Brown your turkey wings on all sides. Season with salt, black pepper, and cayenne pepper.

Now add the onion rings and cranberries. Pour the orange juice and vegetable stock over all. Close the cooker's lid. Press "Manual" and choose 20 minutes pressure cooking time.

Afterwards, preheat a broiler. Cook the wings under the broiler for about 5 minutes.

While the wings are broiling, press "Sauté" button and cook the sauce uncovered in order to reduce the liquid content. Spoon the sauce over the wings and serve.

Healthy Potato Snack

(Ready in about 15 minutes | Servings 6)

Ingredients

1/4 cup ghee

1 ½ pounds russet potatoes, cut into wedges

Sea salt ground black pepper, to your liking

1/2 teaspoon cayenne pepper

1 teaspoon onion powder

1 teaspoon cumin powder

1/4 teaspoon allspice

1 cup vegetable or chicken broth

Directions

Choose "Sauté" mode and add ghee until it is warmed. Stir in the potatoes; cook for about 8 minutes.

Add the rest of the ingredients. Secure the lid, and press the "Manual" key. Cook for 7 minutes. Transfer to a serving platter and serve.

Saucy Chicken Wings

(Ready in about 15 minutes | Servings 8)

Ingredients

1 tablespoon butter
3/4 cup hot sauce

4 pounds chicken wings, frozen

Directions

Pour the butter and hot sauce into the inner pot of your Instant Pot. Add the wings. Place the lid on cooker, and lock the lid. Press the "SOUP" button.
Serve with your favorite dipping sauce.

Beets with Pine Nuts

(Ready in about 25 minutes | Servings 8)

Ingredients

2 ½ cups water

2 pounds beets

2 tablespoons cider vinegar

2 teaspoons brown sugar

Sea salt and freshly ground black pepper, to your liking

2 tablespoons extra-virgin olive oil

2 tablespoons pine nuts, finely chopped

Directions

Add the water and beets to your inner pot of the Instant Pot. Close lid securely.

Choose "Manual" and cook for 25 minutes. Remove lid. Drain and rinse beets; rub off skins. Cut your beets into wedges. Transfer to a serving bowl.

In a mixing bowl, combine vinegar, brown sugar, salt, black pepper, and olive oil. Drizzle the mixture over prepared beets; toss to combine. Scatter pine nuts over all and serve.

Favorite Steamed Artichokes

(Ready in about 25 minutes | Servings 2)

Ingredients

2 whole artichokes

1/2 lime

White pepper, to taste

1 cup water

Directions

Rinse the artichokes and remove any outer leaves. Now trim off the stem and top third of each artichoke with a sharp knife. Drizzle with lime juice. Sprinkle with white pepper.

Set a steamer basket into your cooker. Pour 1 cup of water at the base of your cooker. Lay the artichokes in the steamer basket and pour in a cup of water.

Close the lid. Choose "Manual" function; adjust the time to 20 minutes. Serve with your favorite dipping sauce.

Sweet Baby Carrots

(Ready in about 20 minutes | Servings 6)

Ingredients

1 tablespoon butter

1 tablespoon brown sugar

1/2 cup water

1/4 teaspoon kosher salt

1 pound baby carrots

Directions

Put the butter, sugar, water and kosher salt into the Instant Pot. Select "Sauté" key and cook for 30 seconds, stirring continuously. Stir in the carrots.

Put the lid on cooker, select "Steam" key, and set the timer to 15 minutes.

Next, uncover and select "Sauté" button. Cook until pot juice has evaporated. Serve.

Marinated Artichoke Appetizer

(Ready in about 15 minutes | Servings 6)

Ingredients

4 large artichokes, trimmed and stems removed

2 tablespoons fresh orange juice

2 teaspoons apple cider vinegar

1/4 cup olive oil

2 cloves garlic, minced fine

1/2 teaspoon dried dill weed

1 teaspoon onion powder

1/2 teaspoon sea salt

1/2 teaspoon fresh ground black pepper

Directions

Place steamed basket in your Instant Pot. Arrange the artichokes, bottom up, in a steamer basket; add 2 cups of water.

Select the "Steam" setting; set cooking time to 8 minutes.

Meanwhile, prepare the marinade. Combine the rest of the ingredients in a mixing bowl.

Cut cooked artichokes in half. Drizzle the marinade over the warm artichokes. Allow the artichokes to sit overnight.

Honey Chicken Wings

(Ready in about 25 minutes | Servings 5)

Ingredients

10 chicken wings

1 teaspoon shallot powder

1/2 teaspoon coriander

1 teaspoon cumin powder

1 teaspoon garlic powder

1/2 cup honey

1 tablespoon apple cider vinegar

Salt and ground black pepper, to your liking

Directions

Preheat your oven to 400 degrees F.

Place chicken wings in your Instant Pot. Place lid on and select the "POULTRY" setting. Reserve the liquid.

Transfer the chicken wings to the oven and roast them until skin is crispy. Remove the chicken from oven and set aside in a baking dish to keep warm.

Add the rest of the ingredients to the pot with chicken broth; push "SAUTE" button. Cook for 10 to 15 minutes, stirring continuously. Pour the sauce over the chicken wings, and serve.

Easy Carrot Snack

(Ready in about 10 minutes | Servings 8)

Ingredients

2 tablespoons butter

1 ½ pounds carrots, cut into matchsticks

1/4 teaspoon baking soda

1/4 cup packed brown sugar

A pinch of salt

1/2 teaspoon grated orange peel

Directions

Place butter in your Instant Pot. Add the carrots along with the remaining ingredients.

Pressure cook for 4 minutes. Serve.

Orange Glazed Sugar Snap and Peas Carrots

(Ready in about 10 minutes | Servings 8)

Ingredients

1 tablespoon butter

1 ½ cups frozen sugar snap peas

1 ½ pounds carrots, cut into matchsticks

A pinch of salt

White pepper to your liking

3 tablespoons orange marmalade

1/2 teaspoon ground ginger

Directions

Simply throw all the ingredients in your Instant Pot.

Pressure cook for 4 minutes. Transfer to a serving bowl and serve.

Sausage Dipping Sauce

(Ready in about 15 minutes | Servings 10)

Ingredients

1 tablespoon butter, at room temperature

1/2 pound ground Italian sausage

1 (28-ounce) can crushed tomatoes

1 onion, chopped

2 cloves garlic, sliced

1 teaspoon dried basil

2 tablespoons flour

Salt and ground black pepper to taste

Directions

Heat the butter in your cooker. Add ground sausage and cook until it is browned. Add the remaining ingredients.

Close and lock the lid; set the timer to 15 minutes. Release pressure naturally. Serve with tortilla chips. Enjoy!

Meatballs with Marinara Sauce

(Ready in about 25 minutes | Servings 12)

Ingredients

1 tablespoon butter

40 frozen meatballs

2 (16-ounce) jars marinara sauce

1 cup vegetable broth

Sea salt and black pepper, to taste

1/4 cup fresh cilantro

Directions

Warm the butter in your cooker on "Sauté" setting. Stir in the meatballs and cook until they are browned. Cook for 2 minutes, stirring frequently.

Add marinara sauce and vegetable broth. Season with salt and black pepper. Close and lock the lid on your cooker.

Set the timer to 20 minutes. Now release the pressure manually. Serve sprinkled with fresh cilantro.

Tomato Dipping Sauce

(Ready in about 25 minutes | Servings 12)

Ingredients

1 tablespoon olive oil

3 cloves garlic

1 shallot, chopped

1 parsnip, chopped

1 carrot, chopped

1 teaspoon basil

1 (28-ounce) can crushed tomatoes

1 cup water

1 teaspoon cayenne pepper

Salt and black pepper, to taste

1 tablespoon parsley

Directions

Click "Sauté" key and warm the olive oil in the cooker. Stir in the garlic and shallot and cook until they are tender, for 1 to 2 minutes.

Add the parsnip, carrots, and basil. Pour in the crushed tomatoes and water.

Close the lid on the cooker. Set the cooker's timer for 20 minutes. Quick release pressure. Season with cayenne pepper, salt, and black pepper.

Sprinkle with fresh parsley. Serve with your favorite dippers such as bread sticks or crackers.

Spicy Tomato Dip

(Ready in about 25 minutes | Servings 12)

Ingredients

2 tablespoons extra-virgin olive oil

1 cup green onion, chopped

2 cloves garlic

1 teaspoon dried oregano

1 teaspoon dried basil

1 teaspoon lemon zest

1/2 teaspoon chili pepper

1 (28-ounce) can crushed tomatoes

1 cup vegetable stock

Sea salt and black pepper, to taste

Directions

Choose "Sauté" setting and heat the oil in the cooker. Stir in green onions and garlic; sauté for 2 minutes or until tender.

Add oregano, basil, lemon zest, and chili pepper. Pour in the tomatoes and vegetable stock. Season with salt and black pepper to your liking.

Cover and cook for 20 minutes. Quick release pressure. Sprinkle with fresh parsley. Serve with dippers of choice.

Party Sausage Dip

(Ready in about 15 minutes | Servings 10)

Ingredients

1 tablespoon lard

1 green bell pepper, diced

1 red bell pepper, diced

1 leek, chopped

2 cloves garlic, sliced

1/2 pound ground Italian sausage

1 (28-ounce) can crushed tomatoes

1/4 cup Kalamata olives

1/2 teaspoon red pepper flakes, crushed

Salt and ground black pepper to taste

Directions

Click "Sauté" and melt the lard. Now sauté bell peppers, leek, and garlic for several minutes. Next, stir in sausage and cook until they are just browned.

Add the remaining ingredients and cover the pot.

Now set cooker's timer for 15 minutes. Release pressure naturally. Serve warm with your favorite dippers.

Meat and Tomato Sauce

(Ready in about 15 minutes | Servings 10)

Ingredients

1 tablespoon olive oil

1 pound lean ground beef

1 pound ground Italian sausage

1 onion, chopped

2 cloves garlic, minced

1/2 cup red wine

2 (28-ounce) cans chopped tomatoes

1 (14-ounce) can chicken broth

1 teaspoon basil

1 teaspoon oregano

1/4 cup heavy cream

Directions

Set the cooker on "Sauté" mode; then, warm olive oil and add meat; cook till it is browned. Reserve 1 tablespoon fat.

Stir in the onion and garlic; let them cook for 1 to 2 minutes, stirring constantly. Deglaze the bottom of your cooker with red wine. Add the canned tomatoes, chicken broth, basil and oregano.

Cover with the lid and set the timer for 8 minutes. Stir in the heavy cream; serve and enjoy.

Buttery Spicy Potatoes

(Ready in about 15 minutes | Servings 8)

Ingredients

8 red potatoes, diced

3 tablespoons butter

2 tablespoon green garlic, minced

Salt and ground black pepper to your liking

Fresh chopped cilantro

Directions

Put a metal rack into the bottom of your cooker; pour in 1/2 cup of water.

Add the potatoes and close the lid; set the timer for 8 minutes. Afterwards, remove the lid carefully. Taste the potatoes for the doneness.

Transfer prepared potatoes to a large-sized serving bowl. Toss them with the remaining ingredients. Enjoy!

Roasted Vegetable Appetizer

(Ready in about 15 minutes | Servings 8)

Ingredients

1 pound Brussels sprouts, trimmed

1/2 head broccoli, broken into florets

1 head cauliflower, broken into florets

1 zucchini, sliced

1 leek, sliced

1 ½ cups carrot, chopped

3 tablespoons butter, melted

3 cloves garlic, sliced

Salt and ground black pepper, to your liking

1/2 cup Parmigiano-Reggiano cheese, grated

Directions

Lay a metal rack in your Instant Pot. Pour in 1 cup of water. Stir in all of the vegetables. Lock the lid, and set the timer to 7 minutes.

Next, remove the lid carefully. While the vegetables are still hot, add butter, garlic, salt, pepper, and cheese; toss to combine. Transfer roasted vegetables to a serving platter. Serve and enjoy!

Brussels Sprout Appetizer

(Ready in about 15 minutes | Servings 6)

Ingredients

2 tablespoons butter

1 small-sized onion, minced

2 cloves garlic, minced

1/4 cup pineapple juice

1 pounds Brussels sprouts, trimmed

Salt and ground black pepper, to your liking

1/4 cup Parmesan, grated

Directions

Select "Sauté" mode, and heat the butter; sauté the onion and garlic for about 2 minutes.

Stir in pineapple juice and Brussels sprouts; stir to combine. Cover and cook for 5 minutes. Carefully remove the lid.

Add the salt, black pepper, and grated Parmesan. Transfer Brussels sprouts to a serving platter and serve.

Italian-Style Tomatoes

(Ready in about 15 minutes | Servings 8)

Ingredients

2 tablespoons olive oil

1 carrot, chopped

2 stalks celery, chopped

1 onion, diced

1 bell pepper, seeded and diced

8 Roma tomatoes, peeled, cored and sliced

1/2 cup water

3 tablespoons brown sugar

1 teaspoon sea salt

1/2 teaspoon ground black pepper

1 teaspoon dried basil

Directions

Choose "Sauté" mode on your cooker. Warm the olive oil in the cooker; then, stir in carrot, celery, onion, and bell pepper. Sauté for 2 to 3 minutes until the vegetables are softened.

Stir in the tomato slices. Add water, brown sugar, sea salt, black pepper, and basil.

Cover and cook for 5 minutes. Afterwards, remove the lid according to manufacturer's directions. Serve.

Artichoke and Spinach Dipping Sauce

(Ready in about 20 minutes | Servings 12)

Ingredients

1 can (14-ounce) artichoke hearts, drained and roughly chopped

1 package (10-ounce) frozen spinach, thawed, drained and chopped

1/2 cup sour cream

2 cups Mozzarella cheese, shredded

1 cup light mayonnaise

1/2 teaspoon salt

1/4 teaspoon ground black pepper

Directions

Set a wire rack in the cooker. Place all the ingredients in a baking dish; stir to combine thoroughly. Then, cover the baking dish with an aluminum foil.

Make a foil sling and lay it on the rack. Place the baking dish on top of the foil. Secure the cooker's lid and set the timer for 10 minutes.

Serve warm with your favorite dippers. Enjoy!

Easiest and Tastiest Hummus Ever

(Ready in about 30 minutes | Servings 12)

Ingredients

1 cup chickpeas

4 cups water

2 tablespoons fresh lime juice

2 garlic cloves, minced

1 tablespoon salt

1/4 cup extra-virgin olive oil

Directions

Add chickpeas and water to your cooker and drizzle with some olive oil.

Secure the lid and cook for 25 minutes. Turn off the heat. Open the lid and drain chickpeas. Transfer them to a food processor, along with lime juice, garlic and salt; blitz the mixture into a smooth puree.

While the food processor is still running, gradually add olive oil. Serve and enjoy!

Green Bean Appetizer

(Ready in about 10 minutes | Servings 6)

Ingredients

1 ½ pounds green beans

2 garlic cloves, minced

1 shallot, minced

1 cup water

1 tablespoon bouillon

1 tablespoon olive oil

Directions

Select "Manual" and set the timer for 4 minutes. Add all the ingredients to the Instant Pot.

Then, carefully remove the lid. Transfer to a large serving platter.

Indian-Style Bean Dip

(Ready in about 20 minutes | Servings 12)

Ingredients

1 pound kidney beans, soaked overnight

3 tablespoons olive oil

1 onion, finely chopped

3 garlic cloves, minced

2-inch piece fresh ginger, grated

3 tomatoes, chopped

1 tablespoon Garam masala powder

1 teaspoon red chili powder

1 teaspoon cumin seeds

2 sprigs coriander leaves, finely minced

1/4 teaspoon salt

Directions

Add kidney beans to a cooker. Choose "Bean" mode and cook until tender.

Meanwhile, in a saucepan, heat olive oil. Then, sauté the onions with garlic, ginger, tomatoes, Garam masala, red chili powder, and cumin seeds.

Next, open the lid; stir the sautéed mixture into your Instant Pot. Add the coriander leaves and salt.

Next, blend this bean mixture in a food processor; work with batches. Serve and enjoy!

Meat Dipping Sauce

(Ready in about 20 minutes | Servings 12)

Ingredients

1 tablespoon vegetable oil

1 cup shallots, chopped

3 cloves garlic, sliced

1 small-sized chipotle pepper, minced

1/2 pound ground meat

1 (28-ounce) can crushed tomatoes

1 teaspoon paprika

Salt and ground black pepper to taste

Directions

First, select "Sauté" mode and melt vegetable oil. Now sauté shallots and garlic for several minutes. Now stir in chipotle pepper and meat; cook until they are browned.

Add the tomatoes, paprika, salt, and ground black pepper; cover your Instant Pot.

Select "Manual"; cook for 15 minutes. Allow the pressure to release gradually and naturally. Serve warm.

Black Bean and Corn Dip

(Ready in about 20 minutes | Servings 16)

Ingredients

1 (15 ounce) can black beans, rinsed and drained

1 tablespoon canola oil

1 onion, finely chopped

3 garlic cloves, minced

1/2 cup fresh corn kernels

1/2 cup mild picante sauce

1 teaspoon celery seeds

1 teaspoon cumin seeds

Sea salt and ground black pepper, to your liking

Directions

First, empty the can of beans into your Instant Pot. Select "Bean" function.

Meanwhile, in a saucepan, cook the remaining ingredients for several minutes or until tender. Carefully open your cooker; add the sautéed mixture to the cooker with beans. Stir to combine. Now, pulse the mixture in your blender or a food processor, working with batches. Serve with corn chips or veggie sticks if desired.

Spicy Green Appetizer

(Ready in about 10 minutes | Servings 6)

Ingredients

1 ½ pounds green beans

1/2 cup green garlic, finely chopped

1/2 cup green onions, finely chopped

1 cup vegetable stock

1 tablespoon canola oil

1 tablespoon rice vinegar

3 tablespoons hoisin sauce

Directions

Fill your Instant Pot with green beans, green garlic, and green onions. Then, pour in vegetable stock. Choose "Manual" function; set the timer for 5 minutes.

Next, remove the cooker's lid according to manufacturer's instructions. Replace prepared beans to a serving platter. Drizzle them with canola oil, rice vinegar, and hoisin sauce. Serve and enjoy!

Classic Corn on the Cob

(Ready in about 10 minutes | Servings 6)

Ingredients

6 ears of corn, shucked

Salt to your liking

Directions

First, break your ears in half. Set a rack in the Instant Pot. Pour 1 cup of water into the base of the pot. Arrange ears of corn on the rack.

Press the "Manual" key for 8 minutes. Lastly, perform a Quick release. Season with salt to your liking and enjoy!

Butter-Lemon Glazed Corn

(Ready in about 10 minutes | Servings 8)

Ingredients

8 ears of corn, shucked

1 tablespoon lemon juice

1/4 cup butter, melted

1 tablespoon fresh parsley, finely chopped

Salt and ground black pepper, to your liking

Directions

Lay a rack in the Instant Pot; then pour in 1 cup of water. Place ears of corn on the rack. Seal the lid.

Select the "Manual" mode; let it cook for 8 minutes. Use Quick release.

In the meantime, in a mixing bowl or a measuring cup, combine the remaining ingredients; mix thoroughly to combine. Toss to coat and serve.

Famous Lemon-Garlic Corn on the Cob

(Ready in about 15 minutes | Servings 6)

Ingredients

6 ears of corn, shucked

2 tablespoons butter, room temperature

2 cloves garlic, minced

1 teaspoon basil leaves, chopped

1 tablespoon lemon juice

Salt and ground black pepper, to your liking

Directions

First, place ears of corn on the metal rack in your cooker. Make sure to add 1 cup of water and seal the lid.

Select the "Manual" setting; adjust cook time to 8 minutes. Carefully open the lid by following manufacturer's instructions.

Meanwhile, heat up the pan over medium heat. Now melt the butter and sauté garlic along with dried basil for several minutes or until they are fragrant. Let it cool slightly; then, add lemon juice, salt, and black pepper.

Transfer prepared ears of corn to a serving platter or divide them among six individual plates. Drizzle the pan sauce over ears of corn and serve.

Perfect Steamed Sweet Potatoes

(Ready in about 15 minutes | Servings 6)

Ingredients

1 cup boiling water

6 sweet potatoes

2 tablespoons extra-virgin olive oil

Directions

Set a trivet at the bottom of your Instant Pot. Add boiling water.

Scrub sweet potatoes and drizzle them with olive oil; wrap sweet potatoes in aluminum foil.

Place sweet potatoes on prepared trivet. Seal the lid; select "Steam" button and set the timer to 15 minutes. Serve warm and enjoy!

Maple Brussels Sprouts

(Ready in about 10 minutes | Servings 4)

Ingredients

2 teaspoons sesame oil

1 cup onion, diced

1/2 cup water

1 tablespoon maple syrup

16 medium-sized Brussels sprouts, cut in half

1 teaspoon cayenne pepper

Sea salt and freshly ground black pepper

Directions

First, set your cooker to "Sauté"; now warm sesame oil; sauté onions for 2 minutes.

In a mixing bowl, whisk water and maple syrup; add your Brussels sprouts to the cooker. Drizzle maple mixture over them and sprinkle with cayenne pepper, salt, and black pepper.

Lock the lid and bring to high pressure for 2 minutes. Quick release the pressure. Serve immediately.

Amazing Broccoli Appetizer

(Ready in about 5 minutes | Servings 4)

Ingredients

3 cups broccoli florets

4 tablespoons vegetable stock

1/2 teaspoon red pepper flakes

1/4 teaspoon salt

1/4 teaspoon black pepper, preferably freshly ground

1/2 teaspoon dried dill weed

1/2 teaspoon dried rosemary

1 teaspoon dried thyme

Directions

Put the ingredients into your cooker.

Bring to HIGH pressure for 1 minute. Next, quick release the pressure. Serve immediately and enjoy!

Bean and Tomatillo Spread

(Ready in about 15 minutes | Servings 10)

Ingredients

1 cup canned beans

1 pound tomatillos, chopped

3 cloves garlic, minced

1 onion, finely chopped

1 teaspoon toasted cumin powder

1 heaping tablespoons fresh basil leaves, chopped

1 heaping tablespoons fresh cilantro leaves, chopped

Juice of 1 lime

1/2 teaspoon cayenne pepper

Salt and ground black pepper, to your liking

Directions

Add beans, tomatillos, garlic, onion, to your Instant Pot. Next, choose "BEAN" function; cook for 10 minutes.

Carefully open the cooker by following the manufacturer's instructions. Mash the bean mixture with a fork or a potato masher. Add the remaining ingredients and stir to combine. Serve.

Mom's Famous Kale Humus

(Ready in about 35 minutes | Servings 12)

Ingredients

4 cups water

1 cup garbanzo beans

1 cup packed kale leaves

2 garlic cloves, minced

1 tablespoon salt

2 tablespoons tahini

1/4 cup extra-virgin olive oil

Directions

Add water and garbanzo beans to your Instant Pot.

Secure the lid; choose "Manual" function and cook for 25 minutes. Turn off the heat. Now drain your garbanzo beans and transfer them to a food processor.

Add kale, garlic, salt, and tahini. Puree until creamy and uniform. Then, gradually pour olive oil in a thin stream. Continue mixing till it reaches your desired texture.

Serve with dippers of choice, such as bread sticks, crackers, veggie sticks, and so on.

Vegan Spinach Dip

(Ready in about 10 minutes | Servings 12)

Ingredients

1 package (10-ounce) frozen chopped spinach, thawed

1 cup silken lite tofu

1 cup Vegan mayonnaise

1 teaspoon Dijon mustard

1/2 teaspoon salt

1/4 teaspoon ground black pepper

Lemon zest, for garnish

Directions

Set trivet in your Instant Pot. Place all the ingredients, except for lemon zest, in a baking dish; now stir with a spoon to combine well. Next, wrap the baking dish in a foil.

Make a foil sling and place it on prepared trivet. Lay the baking dish on the foil sling. Secure the cooker's lid; press "Manual" and set the timer to 8 minutes. Serve sprinkled with lemon zest.

Perfect Pumpkin Hummus

(Ready in about 35 minutes | Servings 16)

Ingredients

4 cups water

1 cup chickpeas

1 cup canned pumpkin puree

2 garlic cloves, minced

A pinch crushed sea salt

1 tablespoon fresh lemon juice

2 tablespoons tahini

1/4 cup olive oil

Paprika, for garnish

Directions

Add water and chickpeas to the Instant Pot.

Cover your cooker and select "Manual" mode; cook for 25 minutes. Turn off the cooker. Now drain your chickpeas; transfer them to a food processor.

Add pumpkin puree, garlic, salt, lemon, and tahini. Puree until the mixture becomes uniform. Slowly add the oil in a thin stream. Continue mixing until you create a silken texture.

Sprinkle with paprika; you can decorate hummus with a few whole chickpeas if desired; serve with veggie sticks.

Chili Pumpkin Hummus

(Ready in about 35 minutes | Servings 16)

Ingredients

1 cup chickpeas

4 cups water

1 shallot, peeled and finely minced

2 garlic cloves, minced

1 cup canned pumpkin puree

1 teaspoon Dukkah spice blend

3/4 teaspoon crushed sea salt

1/2 tsp chipotle chili powder

Pinch of ground cardamom

1 tablespoon soy sauce

1 tablespoon lemon juice

1 teaspoon lemon zest

1 tablespoon cilantro paste

2 tablespoons tahini

1/4 cup olive oil

Toasted pumpkin seeds, for garnish

Directions

Select "Manual" function, and cook chickpeas in water for 25 minutes. Carefully open the cooker and drain the cooked chickpeas; transfer chickpeas to your food processor.

Stir in the shallot, garlic, pumpkin puree, Dukkah spice blend, and sea salt. Mix to combine.

Now add chili powder, cardamom, soy sauce, lemon juice, lemon zest, cilantro paste and tahini. Puree until everything is well combined. Slowly and gradually add olive oil. Continue mixing until everything is well incorporated.

Serve sprinkled with pumpkin seeds and enjoy!

Cremini Mushrooms and Asparagus Appetizer

(Ready in about 10 minutes | Servings 6)

Ingredients

1 cup sliced cremini mushrooms

1 cup scallions, thinly sliced

1 cup asparagus, chopped

1 teaspoon cumin powder

1 teaspoon garlic powder

2 tablespoons water

Sea salt and ground black pepper, to your liking

Directions

Click "Sauté" and cook the mushrooms and scallions until tender or for about 1 minute.

Add the rest of the ingredients. Lock the lid and cook on HIGH pressure; set the timer to 2 minutes. Quick release pressure.

Transfer to a large serving platter and serve.

Squash and Pineapple Treat

(Ready in about 10 minutes | Servings 8)

Ingredients

1 tablespoon olive oil

1 shallot, diced

4 cups summer squash, cut into bite-sized pieces

1 (8-ounce) can pineapple chunks

1/4 cup pineapple juice

2 tablespoons soy sauce

1 tablespoon arrowroot combined with 2 tablespoons water

1 tablespoon brown sugar

Sea salt and freshly ground black pepper, to your liking

Directions

Select "Sauté" function; warm olive oil; now sauté the shallot for 3 to 4 minutes. Add the squash, pineapple chunks, pineapple juice, and soy sauce; stir to combine well.

Next, lock the lid. Choose "Manual" function and cook for 10 minutes. Quick release the pressure.

Combine the rest of the ingredients in a small-sized mixing bowl. Add the mixture to the pot to thicken the liquid. Serve.

Herby Polenta Squares with Cheese

(Ready in about 30 minutes | Servings 6)

Ingredients

2 cups water

2 cups soy milk

1 tablespoon butter, room temperature

1/2 teaspoon salt

1/4 teaspoon cayenne pepper

1 cup dry polenta

Fresh chopped Italian parsley, for garnish

Fresh marjoram, for garnish

Ricotta cheese, for garnish

Directions

Simply fill your Instant Pot with the water, soy milk, butter, salt, and cayenne pepper. Press "Sauté" key.

Gradually stir the polenta into the boiling liquid, stirring continuously. Cover; push the "Manual" button and set the timer for 7 minutes.

Next, release its pressure naturally. Pour the polenta mixture into a baking sheet. Refrigerate it for 20 minutes. Cut into squares and transfer to a plate.

Sprinkle with fresh parsley and marjoram; serve topped with ricotta cheese.

Potato Mash with Marjoram

(Ready in about 15 minutes | Servings 4)

Ingredients

4 medium Yukon Gold potatoes, diced

1 cup vegetable stock

5 cloves garlic, sliced

1/2 cup non-dairy milk

1 teaspoon onion powder

1/2 teaspoon mustard powder

Sea salt and ground black pepper, to your liking

Fresh marjoram, for garnish

Directions

Fill the cooker with potatoes, vegetable stock, and garlic.

Close the lid and select "Manual" function; adjust the time to 4 minutes.

Carefully open the cooker. Mash the potatoes, adding non-dairy milk, onion powder, mustard powder, salt, and black pepper.

Serve immediately garnished with fresh marjoram. Enjoy!

Mashed Potatoes with Hazelnuts and Tarragon

(Ready in about 15 minutes | Servings 6)

Ingredients

6 Russet potatoes, diced

1 cup water

1 bay leaf

1 tablespoon hazelnut oil

1 lemon, zested

1/2 cup soy milk

Sea salt, to your liking

1/4 cup hazelnuts, cracked and toasted

Fresh tarragon sprigs for garnish

Directions

Throw the potatoes along with water and bay leaf into your Instant Pot.

Choose "Manual" and cook for about 4 minutes.

Carefully remove the lid according to manufacturer's directions. Peel and mash cooked potatoes; add hazelnut oil, lemon zest, soy milk, and salt to taste.

Serve sprinkled with hazelnuts and tarragon.

Steamed Cauliflower and Baby Carrots

(Ready in about 10 minutes | Servings 4)

Ingredients

1 cup baby carrots

2 cups cauliflower florets

4 tablespoons water

1/2 teaspoon sea salt

1/4 teaspoon freshly ground black pepper

1 teaspoon tarragon

1/2 teaspoon dried rosemary

Directions

Simply throw all the above ingredients into your Instant Pot.

Press "Steam" button and cook for 3 minutes.

Next, quick release the pressure. Serve warm with your favorite dipping sauce.

Cheesy Corn Dip

(Ready in about 10 minutes | Servings 12)

Ingredients

4 cups corn kernels, frozen

5 green onions, chopped

1 cup sour cream

3/4 cup mayonnaise

Salt and white pepper to taste

1/2 teaspoon paprika

1/4 teaspoon dried dill weed

10 ounces sharp cheese, shredded

Directions

Add corn kernels to your Instant Pot. Choose "Steam" setting and adjust the timer to 3 minutes. Transfer to a large-sized bowl and allow to cool.

Add the remaining ingredients; stir to combine well. Cover the bowl and refrigerate your dip until ready to serve.

Kale and Carrot Appetizer

(Ready in about 10 minutes | Servings 4)

Ingredients

2 tablespoons butter

2 medium-sized sweet onions, finely chopped

3 carrots, cut into matchsticks

10 ounces kale, roughly chopped

1/2 cup vegetable stock

1/2 teaspoon dried dill weed

Kosher salt and ground black pepper, to your liking

1/2 teaspoon red pepper flakes, for garnish

Directions

First, click "Sauté" function and melt the butter. When the butter is melted, toss in sweet onions and carrots. Cook until they're softened.

Add the kale, stock, dill, salt, and ground black pepper. Select "Manual" function and cook for 5 minutes.

Remove the lid and transfer the vegetables to a nice serving bowl. Sprinkle with red pepper flakes and enjoy!

Beets with Walnuts

(Ready in about 30 minutes | Servings 8)

Ingredients

2 pounds beets

2 ½ cups water

2 tablespoons rice vinegar

1 teaspoon lemon zest

1 teaspoon honey

Sea salt and freshly ground black pepper, to your liking

2 tablespoons extra-virgin olive oil

2 tablespoons walnuts, toasted and coarsely chopped

1 teaspoon cumin seeds

Directions

Add the beets and water to the inner pot of your cooker. Close lid securely and select "Manual" setting.

Cook for 25 minutes. Remove lid according to manufacturer's directions. Drain and rinse prepared beets; rub off skins. Slice the beet and replace them to a serving bowl.

In a measuring cup, whisk together rice vinegar, lemon zest, honey, salt, black pepper, and olive oil.

Drizzle the vinegar mixture over the beets in the serving bowl; toss to combine well. Scatter walnuts and cumin seeds over all and serve.

Pumpkin and Cottage Dip

(Ready in about 15 minutes + chilling time | Servings 12)

Ingredients

1/2 cup pumpkin, cut into chunks

3/4 cup Cottage cheese, room temperature

2 teaspoons maple syrup

1/2 teaspoon ground allspice

A pinch of salt

1/4 teaspoon white pepper

Toasted pumpkin seeds, for garnish

Directions

Add pumpkin chunks to the inner pot of your cooker. Press "Steam" and cook for 10 minutes.

Drain pumpkin chunks. Add cheese and beat with a mixer until it is combined. Add maple syrup, allspice, salt, and white pepper; beat until smooth and creamy.

Sprinkle with pumpkin seeds and serve chilled.

Favorite Thanksgiving Dipping Sauce

(Ready in about 25 minutes | Servings 12)

Ingredients

3/4 cup frozen pumpkin chunks

1 cream low-fat cream cheese, softened

1/2 teaspoon salt

1/4 teaspoon pumpkin pie spice

1/2 cup scallions

4 slices bacon

1/2 cup Cheddar cheese, grated

1/4 cup toasted walnuts, roughly chopped

Directions

Throw pumpkin chunks into you Instant Pot. Select "Steam" button and cook for 14 minutes.

Drain the pumpkin chunks and transfer them to a bowl. Beat with an electric mixer along with cream cheese, salt, and pumpkin pie spice.

Now add scallions and bacon to the cleaned inner pot of the cooker. Click "Sauté" and cook until the scallions are tender and the bacon is browned. Crumble the bacon.

Add bacon mixture to the pumpkin mixture. Stir to combine well. Serve garnished with Cheddar cheese and toasted walnuts. Enjoy!

DESSERT RECIPES

Old-Fashioned Coconut Custard

(Ready in about 35 minutes | Servings 8)

Ingredients

2 (14-ounce) cans coconut milk

1 cup whole milk

3 egg yolks

3 whole eggs

1 teaspoon pure vanilla extract

2 cups water

Directions

Pour coconut milk and whole milk into a saucepan; bring to a boil over high heat.

In another bowl, whisk the egg yolks with whole eggs. Now add 2 tablespoons of the warm milk mixture to the whisked eggs; add vanilla and mix until well combined.

Reduce the heat. Transfer the mixture to the simmering milk and stir. Continue simmering for about 4 minutes, stirring frequently.

Next, lightly grease a 6-cup soufflé pan; divide prepared egg-milk mixture among cups. Cover with an aluminum foil.

Pour the water into the cooker. Place a wire rack in your cooker; place the soufflé dish on the rack. Cook for 30 minutes. Serve chilled.

Classic Apple Crisp

(Ready in about 15 minutes | Servings 6)

Ingredients

4 apples, cored, peeled and sliced

1 tablespoon fresh lemon juice

1/2 cup old-fashioned oats

1/4 cup flour

1/4 cup brown sugar

1 teaspoon vanilla essence

1/2 teaspoon grated nutmeg

1 teaspoon cinnamon powder

A pinch of sea salt

4 tablespoons butter

1 cup warm water

Directions

First, sprinkle apples with lemon juice. In another bowl, combine oats, flour, sugar, vanilla, nutmeg, cinnamon powder, salt, and butter. Lay sliced apples in a baking dish. Place oat crisp mixture over it.

Cover baking dish with an aluminum foil. Pour water into the inner pot of the Instant Pot. Place trivet in the pot. Place the baking dish on trivet.

Now lock the lid and press the "BEANS" key; set the timer for 15 minutes. When the steam is completely released, remove the cooker's lid.

Remove the foil and let the dessert rest for several minutes. Enjoy!

Bread Pudding with Golden Raisins

(Ready in about 35 minutes | Servings 6)

Ingredients

6 slices bread, torn into bite-sized pieces

3 cups of milk

3 eggs

1 teaspoon vanilla

A pinch of salt

1/4 cup sugar

1 tablespoon honey

1/4 teaspoon grated nutmeg

Golden raisins, to your liking

Directions

Butter 5 cup bowl. Throw bread pieces into the bowl.

Then make the custard. In a mixing bowl, combine the milk, eggs, vanilla, salt, sugar, honey, and nutmeg.

Pour custard mixture over bread pieces. Now let bread pieces absorb egg-milk mixture. Scatter golden raisins over the top. Cover tightly with a foil that has been greased.

Lay steaming rack in the inner pot. Pour in 2 cups water. Lock the cooker's lid.

Choose "Manual" setting on HIGH; set the timer for 25 minutes. Afterwards, perform a natural pressure release. Serve at room temperature or chilled. Enjoy!

Challah Bread Pudding with Dried Cherries

(Ready in about 35 minutes | Servings 6)

Ingredients

7 slices challah, torn into bite-sized pieces

3 tablespoons butter

2 cups milk

1 cup water

4 eggs

3 tablespoons rum

1/2 teaspoon hazelnut extract

1/2 teaspoon vanilla extract

A pinch of salt

1/4 cup sugar

1 tablespoon honey

1/4 teaspoon grated nutmeg

1/2 cup dried cherries

Directions

Throw challah pieces in a lightly greased baking dish.

Next, make the custard by mixing all the remaining ingredients, except for dried cherries.

Pour custard mixture over challah. Now let challah absorb egg mixture. Scatter dried cherries over the top. Cover with an aluminum foil.

Lay trivet in the inner pot of your cooker. Pour in two cups water. Insert the baking dish and lock the lid.

Select "Manual" function; set the timer to 25 minutes. Lastly, do a natural pressure release. Serve at room temperature.

Amazing Chocolate Cheesecake

(Ready in about 1 hour | Servings 10)

Ingredients

For the Crust:

1 ½ cups almond flour

1/2 cup sugar

1/4 cup coconut oil, room temperature

For the Filling:

1 ½ cups cashews, soaked and drained

1 cup non-dairy milk

1/4 teaspoon cinnamon powder

1/2 cup non-dairy chocolate chips

1/2 teaspoon sea salt

1 teaspoon vanilla essence

2/3 cups sugar

Directions

Mix all the crust items. Press the crust mixture into a silicone cheesecake pan. Press with the back of a spoon and transfer to a refrigerator.

Then, make the filling by mixing all the filling items. Pour the filling over the crust.

Put the trivet into the Instant Pot. Now lower the cheesecake pan onto the trivet. Place IP lid on, and select "MANUAL"; cook for 55 minutes.

Afterwards, let pressure release naturally. Transfer the pan to a cooling rack before serving. Serve well chilled.

Black Chocolate Delight

(Ready in about 15 minutes | Servings 6)

Ingredients

1 ½ cups black chocolate

1 teaspoon almond extract

1 stick butter

1/4 cup all-purpose flour

3/4 cup brown sugar

3 whole eggs

1/2 teaspoon vanilla extract

Directions

In a pan, melt chocolate and butter. Add the remaining ingredients and beat with an electric mixer.

Divide the batter among ramekins. Choose "Manual" and cook for 6 minutes. Quick release pressure and allow your cakes to rest for several minutes before removing from ramekins. Enjoy!

Chocolate Zucchini Bread with Almonds

(Ready in about 40 minutes | Servings 10)

Ingredients

3 eggs

1/2 cup coconut oil, room temperature

1/2 cup applesauce

1 ½ cups sugar

1 teaspoon vanilla paste

2 cups zucchini, grated

2 ½ cups all-purpose flour

1/2 cup cocoa powder

1/2 teaspoon cinnamon powder

1/4 teaspoon grated nutmeg

A pinch of salt

1 teaspoon baking soda

1/2 teaspoon baking powder

1/2 cup almonds, chopped

1/2 cup chocolate chips

Directions

First, beat the eggs, coconut oil, applesauce, sugar and vanilla paste. Stir in grated zucchini.

In another mixing bowl, combine all remaining ingredients. Stir in zucchini mixture; mix to combine well.

Now pour 1 ½ cups of water into the pot; lay the metal rack in the bottom. Pour the batter into a lightly greased pan to fit your Instant Pot. Place the pan on the metal rack.

Click "Manual" and set time to 25 minutes. Natural release pressure for 10 to 15 minutes. Allow the cake to cool before serving. Enjoy!

Rice Pudding with Zante Currants

(Ready in about 30 minutes | Servings 6)

Ingredients

1 ½ cups Arborio rice

A pinch of salt

3/4 cups sugar

5 cups milk

2 eggs

1 cup half and half

1/2 teaspoon ground cinnamon

1/4 teaspoon grated nutmeg

1/2 teaspoon almond extract

1/2 teaspoon vanilla extract

1 cup Zante currants

Directions

In the inner pot, combine, rice, salt, sugar, and milk.

Select the "Sauté" mode. Bring to a boil, stirring constantly, until sugar is dissolved. Then, cover and select the "Rice" mode.

In the meantime, in a mixing bowl, whisk the eggs, half and half, cinnamon, nutmeg, almond extract, and the vanilla extract.

When you hear the beep sound, press "Cancel". Wait 15 minutes, and perform the quick pressure release. While the mixture is still hot, stir in the egg mixture. Now add Zante currants and stir to combine.

Press the "Sauté" key. Cook until the mixture begins to boil. Then, turn off the cooker. Serve at room temperature.

Yummy Dessert Risotto

(Ready in about 20 minutes | Servings 6)

Ingredients

4 cups almond milk

1 ¾ cups rice

1/2 cup coconut

1/4 teaspoon grated nutmeg

1/4 teaspoon ground cinnamon

1/4 teaspoon cardamom

2 ½ cups apples, cored and diced

1/4 cup candied ginger, diced

Directions

Simply throw all of the above ingredients into Instant Pot.

Next, select the "Manual" mode; adjust the time to 12 minutes. Serve at room temperature.

Sweet Peach and Coconut Risotto

(Ready in about 20 minutes | Servings 6)

Ingredients

2 ripe peaches, pitted and halved

4 cups coconut milk

Zest and juice of 1 orange

1 ¾ cups rice

1/2 teaspoon vanilla extract

1/2 cup coconut flakes

1/4 teaspoon nutmeg, preferably freshly grated

1/4 cup candied ginger, diced

Directions

Place all the above ingredients in your cooker.

Choose "Manual" mode; set time to 12 minutes. Serve garnished with whipped cream if desired.

Bread Pudding with Prunes and Pecans

(Ready in about 30 minutes | Servings 6)

Ingredients

4 cups Ciabatta, cubed

1 teaspoon ghee

1 cup almond milk

1 cup whole milk

3 eggs, beaten

1/2 cup prunes, coarsely chopped

1/4 teaspoon grated nutmeg

1/2 teaspoon cinnamon powder

1/4 teaspoon kosher salt

1 teaspoon vanilla paste

Chopped pecans, for garnish

Directions

Pour 2 cups of water into the Instant Pot. Place the steam rack at the bottom.

Add bread cubes to a casserole dish.

In a mixing bowl, combine the remaining ingredients; mix to combine well. Pour this mixture over the bread cubes in the casserole dish. Cover with a wax paper.

Set your cooker to "Steam"; adjust the time to 15 minutes. Next, wait an additional 15 minutes before removing the cooker's lid.

Apricot Oatmeal Dessert

(Ready in about 10 minutes | Servings 4)

Ingredients

4 apricots, pitted and halved

1 cup steel-cut oats

1 cups coconut milk

1/2 teaspoon vanilla paste

2 cups water

1 cup sugar

Directions

Stir everything into the inner pot of your cooker. Choose "Manual/Adjust" mode.

Set the timer to 3 minutes. Open the lid according to manufacturer's directions. Serve garnished with coconut flakes if desired. Enjoy!

Mom's Stuffed Peaches

(Ready in about 15 minutes | Servings 3)

Ingredients

2 cups water

8 cookies, crumbled

2 tablespoons walnuts, chopped

1 teaspoon orange zest

3 peaches, halved and pitted

2 tablespoons butter

Directions

Prepare your cooker by adding the water and the wire rack.

In a mixing bowl, combine the cookie crumbs, walnuts, orange zest. Stuff the peaches and place them on the wire rack; dot with butter.

Close and lock the lid. Choose "Manual" and 4 minutes pressure cooking time. Afterwards, quick pressure release. Serve right away.

Poached Pears in Wine

(Ready in about 15 minutes | Servings 6)

Ingredients

6 firm pears, peeled

1 bottle red wine

4 cloves

1 vanilla bean, slice lengthwise

1 stick cinnamon

1 piece of fresh ginger

1 1/3 cups sugar

1 teaspoon fresh mint

Directions

Arrange the pears in your Instant Pot. Pour the wine into the cooker. Stir in the rest of the ingredients and mix to combine.

Close and lock the lid. Press "Manual" and choose 9 minutes pressure cooking time. Then, perform Quick Pressure Release.

Remove the pears from the cooker. To make the syrup, choose "Sauté", and cook in order to reduce the liquid by half. Serve.

Baked Apples with Raisins

(Ready in about 15 minutes | Servings 6)

Ingredients

6 apples, cored

1/4 cup raisins

1 cup red wine

1/2 cup brown sugar

1/2 teaspoon grated nutmeg

1 teaspoon cinnamon powder

Directions

Lay the apples in the base of your cooker. Add the rest of the ingredients.

Cook for 10 minutes at HIGH pressure. Use Natural release method. Dust with powdered sugar and serve. Enjoy!

Baked Apples with Apricots

(Ready in about 15 minutes | Servings 6)

Ingredients

6 apples, cored

1/2 cup dried apricot, chopped

1/2 cup apple brandy

1/2 cup water

2 star anise pods

1/3 cup honey

¼ cup brown sugar

1 teaspoon cinnamon powder

Directions

Arrange your apples in the base of the Instant Pot. Add the remaining ingredients.

Select "Manual" and set the time to 10 minutes. Perform Natural release method.

Serve dolloped with whipped cream. Enjoy!

Poached Figs with Yogurt Cream

(Ready in about 15 minutes | Servings 4)

Ingredients

1 pound figs

1 cup red wine

1/2 cup honey

1/2 teaspoon grated nutmeg

1/2 cup almonds, toasted and roughly chopped

Directions

Arrange the figs in the bottom of your cooker. Add the rest of the ingredients.

Cover and select "Manual" mode. Now set the timer to 9 minutes pressure cooking time. Use Normal Release method.

Serve with yogurt cream and enjoy!

Cinnamon Bread Pudding with Figs

(Ready in about 15 minutes | Servings 6)

Ingredients

2 cups water

1 teaspoon coconut oil, at room temperature

4 cups stale sweet cinnamon bread, cubed

2 cups almond milk

3 whole eggs, beaten

1/2 cup dried figs, chopped

1/2 teaspoon grated nutmeg

1/2 ground cloves

1 teaspoon cinnamon powder

1/4 teaspoon salt

1/4 teaspoon almond extract

1/2 teaspoon vanilla paste

Directions

Pour the water into the Instant Pot. Place the steam rack on the bottom.

Grease a casserole dish with coconut oil. Add bread cubes to the casserole dish.

In a mixing bowl, combine the rest of the ingredients. Pour the mixture over bread cubes. Cover with wax paper or an aluminum foil.

Select "Steam" mode and adjust the timer to 15 minutes. Serve warm or at room temperature.

Coconut and Mango Rice Pudding

(Ready in about 10 minutes | Servings 4)

Ingredients

3/4 cup rice

1 ½ cups water

1 can coconut milk

1/4 teaspoon salt

1/3 cup brown sugar

1/2 cup half and half

1 teaspoon vanilla paste

1 mango, peeled and cubed

1/4 cup coconut, shredded

Directions

Add rice, water, coconut milk, salt, and brown sugar to your cooker. Bring pressure to HIGH; cook for about 7 minutes.

Unlock the lid, and add half and half, vanilla paste, and mango. Stir to combine. Serve topped with shredded coconut.

Rice Pudding with Blackberries

(Ready in about 15 minutes | Servings 8)

Ingredients

2 cups whole-grain rice

2 cups coconut milk

1/2 cup sugar

A pinch of salt

1 teaspoon cinnamon powder

1 cup blackberries

Directions

Place rice, coconut milk, sugar, salt, and cinnamon powder in your cooker. Choose "Manual" mode; set time to 12 minutes.

Serve garnished with blackberries. Enjoy!

Nutty Carrot and Rice Pudding

(Ready in about 15 minutes | Servings 4)

Ingredients

1 cup white rice

1/2 pound carrots, grated

3 cup water

3/4 teaspoon kosher salt

1/4 teaspoon grated nutmeg

1/4 teaspoon ground cardamom

1/4 teaspoon ground cinnamon

1 tablespoon butter

Mixed nuts, as garnish

Directions

Add all items, except for mixed nuts, to your cooker. Turn your cooker on "Rice" setting.

Afterwards, do a natural pressure release. Serve at room temperature sprinkled with nuts. Enjoy!

Old-Fashioned Lemon Cheesecake

(Ready in about 25 minutes + chilling time | Servings 10)

Ingredients

1/2 cup graham cracker crumbs

2 tablespoons butter, melted

2 tablespoons sugar

For the Filling:

2 (16-ounce) cream cheese, at room temperature

1/2 cup sugar

3 whole eggs

1 tablespoon fresh lemon juice

1 teaspoon lemon zest, grated

1/2 teaspoon vanilla extract

Directions

To make the crust, mix graham cracker crumbs, butter, and sugar in a bowl. Then, press the crust mixture firmly into the spring-form pan.

In another bowl, beat together cream cheese and sugar until smooth and very creamy. Fold in the eggs (one at a time), lemon juice, lemon zest, and vanilla. Pour batter into the prepared crust.

Pour 2 cups of water into your cooker; insert the trivet in the bottom of the cooker. Now lower the cheesecake on the trivet. Lock the lid in place.

Choose "Manual" setting, and bring it to HIGH pressure for 15 minutes. Lastly, allow the pressure to come down naturally.

Then, remove the lid and refrigerate your cheesecake for at least 4 hours. Enjoy!

Coffee Can Sweet Bread

(Ready in about 1 hour 25 minutes | Servings 10)

Ingredients

1/2 cup milk

1/4 cup white sugar

1/2 stick butter

1 tablespoon active dry yeast

2 cups all-purpose flour

A pinch of salt

2 eggs

Butter

3 tablespoons all-purpose flour

Directions

In a saucepan, combine the milk, sugar and butter over medium heat. Now stir in dry yeast.

In a mixing bowl, combine together two cups flour and salt. Fold in the eggs and the yeast mixture. Then, turn dough out onto a lightly floured surface; knead until the dough becomes elastic.

Cover and allow the dough to rest in a warm place for about 1 hour.

Butter and flour a coffee can that will fit into your cooker. Add 8 cups of water to the cooker. Replace the dough to the coffee can. Cover with a foil.

Cover with the lid and press "Manual" button; cook for 15 minutes. Remove the bread from the can with a knife. Serve.

Honey Rice Pudding with Dates

(Ready in about 25 minutes | Servings 6)

Ingredients

1/2 cup sugar

A pinch of salt

1 ½ cups Arborio rice

5 cups milk

2 eggs

1 cup half and half

1 tablespoon honey

1 cup dates, chopped

1 teaspoon cinnamon powder

1/2 teaspoon cardamom

Directions

In the inner pot, combine sugar, salt, rice, and milk

Choose the "Sauté" mode; bring to a boil. Stir to dissolve the sugar. Next, choose "Rice" button.

Meanwhile, whisk the eggs, half and half, and honey. Next, use the quick pressure release and remove the lid. Add the egg mixture to the cooker. Add dates, cinnamon, and cardamom.

Choose the Sauté function. Cook until the mixture begins to boil. Serve right now.

Festive Caramel Cheesecake

(Ready in about 40 minutes | Servings 10)

Ingredients

For the Cake:

1 ½ cups finely crushed crackers

4 tablespoons butter, melted

2 cups Ricotta cheese, softened

1/2 cup sugar

1/4 cup sour cream

1 tablespoon flour

1 teaspoon vanilla paste

1/2 teaspoon cinnamon powder

2 whole eggs

For the Topping:

1/2 cup caramel sauce

1 teaspoon cardamom

Directions

Oil a spring-form pan with cooking spray. Cover with a piece of parchment paper and spray it. Set the pan aside.

In a mixing bowl, combine the crumbs and butter. Press the mixture into the bottom of the pan. Set aside.

Then, beat the cheese and sugar with an electric mixer. Add the sour cream, flour, vanilla, and cinnamon. Fold in the eggs; mix until smooth and creamy. Pour the mixture into the prepared crust in the pan.

Pour two cups of water into the bottom of the cooker. Place the trivet on the bottom. Place the pan on the trivet.

Next, secure the lid and choose "MANUAL" function. Set the timer to 35 minutes. Spread caramel sauce evenly over the cake. Sprinkle with cardamom. Refrigerate your cheesecake overnight.

Royal Peach and Vanilla Custard

(Ready in about 40 minutes + chilling time | Servings 6)

Ingredients

4 cups whole milk

1/3 cup caster sugar

3 egg yolks

3 whole eggs

Freshly grated nutmeg

1/2 teaspoon grated orange zest

1 teaspoon pure vanilla extract

2 cups water

1 cup peaches, chopped

Directions

Add milk and sugar to a saucepan, and cook over medium-high heat, bringing to a boil.

In a separate mixing bowl, beat the egg yolks with whole eggs. Then, add two tablespoons of the warm sugar-milk mixture to the beaten eggs; add nutmeg, orange zest, and vanilla and mix until well combined.

Turn the heat to medium-low and continue simmering for about 4 minutes, stirring continuously.

Then, oil a soufflé dish with a non-stick cooking spray; pour the mixture into the dish. Cover with an aluminum foil.

Pour the water into the bottom of your Instant Pot. Place the trivet at the bottom; lay the soufflé dish on the trivet. Cook for 30 minutes. Allow to cool completely and add chopped peaches.

Transfer to a refrigerator to chill for several hours. Serve and enjoy!

Honey and Pear Pudding

(Ready in about 15 minutes | Servings 4)

Ingredients

2 ripe pears, cored and diced

4 cups milk

2 tablespoons tangerine juice

1 ¾ cups rice

1/2 sugar

1/2 teaspoon hazelnut extract

1/2 teaspoon vanilla extract

1/4 teaspoon nutmeg, preferably freshly grated

2 tablespoons honey

Directions

Simply throw all the above ingredients, except for honey, in your Instant Pot.

Choose "Manual" setting; set the timer to 12 minutes. Serve drizzled with honey and enjoy!

Pineapple Custard

(Ready in about 45 minutes + chilling time | Servings 6)

Ingredients

4 cups almond milk

1/2 teaspoon grated orange zest

1/3 cup sugar

1 teaspoon vanilla extract

3 whole eggs

2 cups water

3 egg yolks

1 cup pineapple chunks

Directions

Warm almond milk and sugar in a pan over medium-high heat; bring to a boil.

In a mixing bowl, thoroughly whisk whole eggs and egg yolks. Then, add 2 tablespoons of the warm milk mixture to the whisked eggs; add orange zest and vanilla; mix until everything is well combined.

Reduce the heat to medium-low; let it simmer for 3 to 4 minutes, stirring frequently.

Then, coat a soufflé dish with melted butter; pour prepared custard mixture into the soufflé dish. Cover with a foil.

Add the water to the bottom of your Instant Pot. Lay the metal rack at the bottom; lay the soufflé dish on the metal rack. Cook for 30 minutes. Cool completely before adding the pineapple chunks.

Serve well chilled and enjoy.

Carrot Pudding with Raisins

(Ready in about 20 minutes | Servings 6)

Ingredients

3 cups water

1 ½ cups carrots, grated

1 cup rice

1/2 cup sugar

3/4 teaspoon a pinch of salt

1/2 teaspoon ground cinnamon

1/4 teaspoon ground cloves

1 tablespoon coconut oil, softened

1 cup raisins

Directions

Add all items to your Instant Pot. Now choose "Rice" mode.

Perform a natural pressure release. Serve at room temperature or chilled. Enjoy!

Poached Apples and Apricot

(Ready in about 20 minutes | Servings 4)

Ingredients

4 firm apples

8 dried apricot halves

1 cup red wine

1/2 cup honey

1/2 teaspoon cinnamon powder

4 whole cloves

Directions

Place the apples in the bottom of your Instant Pot. Arrange the apricots around the apples. Pour in the wine.

Add honey, cinnamon powder, and cloves. Cover with the lid; choose "Manual" function. Set the timer to 9 minutes. Afterwards, perform Normal release method. Serve with ice cream.

Poached Plums and Nectarines with Cream

(Ready in about 15 minutes | Servings 6)

Ingredients

1 pound plums

1/2 pound nectarines

1 cup white wine

1/2 cup sugar

1 tablespoon honey

1 vanilla bean, split lengthwise

1/2 cinnamon stick

Whipped cream, for garnish

Directions

Put the plums and nectarines into your cooker. Pour in the wine.

Add the remaining ingredients. Cover and select "Manual" mode. Adjust the timer to 9 minutes.

Afterwards, use Normal release method. Serve with whipped cream.

Tropical Rice Pudding

(Ready in about 15 minutes | Servings 6)

Ingredients

4 cups milk

1 ¾ cups long-grain white rice

1/2 cup sugar

2 tablespoons tangerine juice

1/2 teaspoon vanilla extract

1/4 teaspoon grated cloves

2 tablespoons honey

1 cup mango

1/2 cup papaya

Directions

Throw all the above items, except mango and papaya, in your Instant Pot.

Select "Manual" mode; adjust the timer to 12 minutes. Serve topped with mango and papaya. Enjoy!

Poached Dried Fruit

(Ready in about 10 minutes | Servings 6)

Ingredients

1 ½ pounds mixed dried fruits

1 cup cranberry juice

1/4 cup sugar

1 vanilla bean, split lengthwise

2-3 cloves

1/2 cinnamon stick

Plain yogurt, to serve

Directions

Simply throw mixed dried fruits in your cooker. Add the rest of above ingredients.

Put the lid on and select "Manual" function. Adjust the timer to 9 minutes.

Lastly, use Normal release method. Serve garnished with plain yogurt.

Pear Crisp with Almonds

(Ready in about 20 minutes | Servings 8)

Ingredients

4 pears, cored and cut lengthwise into 1/2-inch-thick slices

1 tablespoon fresh lemon juice

1/2 cup old-fashioned oats

1/4 cup flour

1/4 cup sugar

1 teaspoon grated orange zest

1 teaspoon vanilla paste

1/2 teaspoon almond extract

1 teaspoon cinnamon powder

3 cloves

1/4 teaspoon kosher salt

4 tablespoons unsalted butter

1 cup warm water

Roughly chopped almonds, as garnish

Directions

Drizzle the pears with lemon juice. In a bowl, mix oats, flour, sugar, orange zest, vanilla paste, almond extract, cinnamon, cloves, salt, and unsalted butter. Lay prepared pears in a baking dish. Place prepared crisp mixture over the pears. Sprinkle with almonds.

Pour water into your cooker. Place a metal rack in the bottom of the inner pot. Cover baking dish with a foil and transfer it to the prepared metal rack.

Now lock the lid; use "BEANS" button and adjust the timer to 15 minutes. Afterwards, remove the cooker's lid according to manufacturer's instructions. Serve at room temperature. Enjoy!

Festive Dessert with Prunes and Pecans

(Ready in about 55 minutes | Servings 8)

Ingredients

2 sticks butter	A pinch of salt
1 cup sugar	1 teaspoon orange zest
1 cup self-rising flour	1/2 cup prunes, chopped
1 ½ teaspoons baking powder	1/2 cup pecans, chopped
3 whole eggs	1 tablespoon orange liqueur
1 teaspoon ground ginger	Double cream, for garnish

Directions

First of all, beat together the butter and sugar in a dessert bowl. Add the sifted flour and baking powder. Now whisk the eggs vigorously. Add the whisked eggs to the mixing bowl.

Stir in ground ginger, salt, and orange zest. Next, add prunes, pecans, and orange liqueur.

Add 2 cups of water to the Instant Pot's inner pot. Place a rack inside, and place the dessert bowl on top.

Select "Manual" function, HIGH pressure, and 50 minutes. Meanwhile, whisk double cream.

Press "Cancel" and check for the doneness of your dessert. Decorate the pudding with cream and serve.

Cheesecake with Raspberry Sauce

(Ready in about 35 minutes | Servings 10)

Ingredients

1 ¼ cups graham cracker crumbs

5 tablespoons butter, at room temperature

1 pound cream cheese

1/2 cup sugar

2 eggs

1/4 cup sour cream

1 tablespoon lemon zest, finely grated

2 tablespoons flour

1/2 teaspoon vanilla extract

Raspberry sauce, for garnish

Directions

First, add 2 cups of water to your cooker. Now set a rack into the cooker.

Mix graham cracker crumbs and the butter until everything is well combined. Grease the inside of your springform pan and press the crumb mixture into the bottom of the pan.

In a food processor, beat the cream cheese together with sugar; process until smooth. With the processor running, slowly add the eggs (one at a time). Now stir in sour cream, lemon zest, flour, and vanilla. Process until everything is well mixed.

Pour the batter into the pan. Next, using a foil, form a sling that will hold the pan. Lower the springform pan into the cooker. Lock the lid.

Select "Manual" key. Cook at HIGH pressure for 25 minutes. Uncover and remove the pan. Allow to cool completely before serving. Serve with raspberry sauce.

Frozen Lime Cheesecake

(Ready in about 35 minutes + chilling time | Servings 10)

Ingredients

1 ¼ cups digestive biscuits, crumbled

5 tablespoons butter, at room temperature

1 pound full-fat cream cheese

1/3 cup caster sugar

2 whole eggs, room temperature

1/4 cup sour cream

Zest and juice from 2 limes

1 tablespoon lemon zest, finely grated

2 tablespoons flour

1/2 teaspoon grated ginger

1/2 teaspoon anise seeds

1/2 teaspoon vanilla extract

Directions

In a bowl, combine crumbled biscuits and butter. Lightly grease the inside of a springform pan with non-stick cooking spray. Now press the biscuit mixture into the bottom of the spring-form pan.

Next, add 2 cups of water to your Instant Pot. Now lay trivet at the bottom of the cooker.

In a food processor, mix the cream cheese together with caster sugar; process until creamy and smooth. Fold in the eggs, one at a time.

Add the rest of the ingredients. Pulse until everything is well blended.

Pour the batter into the springform pan. Cook at HIGH pressure; set the timer to 25 minutes. Wrap your cheesecake in a foil and freeze overnight. Serve.

Dried Fruits Compote

(Ready in about 10 minutes | Servings 8)

Ingredients

4 cups water

6 dried figs, halved

6 dried apricots, halved

2 cups dried cherries

1/2 cup caster sugar

1 vanilla pod

2 tablespoons crystallized ginger, chopped

2 sprigs fresh mint

Directions

Place all items in an ovenproof dish. Place trivet in the bottom of your Instant Pot. Lay the dish on the trivet.

Select "STEAM" mode. Now set the timer for 5 minutes.

Afterwards, use the steam release. Serve warm.

Spicy Berry Compote

(Ready in about 10 minutes | Servings 8)

Ingredients

1 cup red currants

1 cup black currants

1 cup strawberries

4 cups water

1/2 cup sugar

1/2 teaspoon cardamom pods

1/2 teaspoon cloves

1 teaspoon cinnamon powder

1 vanilla pod

Directions

Simply throw the ingredients in an ovenproof dish.

Set trivet into your cooker. Place the dish on the trivet. Choose "STEAM" button and cook for 5 minutes. Then, use the steam release.

Serve warm or at room temperature with vanilla ice cream if desired.

Rustic Apple Compote

(Ready in about 10 minutes | Servings 8)

Ingredients

1 pound apples, cored and diced

6 dried apricots, halved

1 tablespoon brandy

1/2 cup sugar

1/2 teaspoon cloves

A pinch of salt

1 cinnamon stick

1 vanilla bean, split in half

Directions

Put all the above ingredients into a steel bowl.

Set a metal rack in the bottom of the Instant Pot. Place the steel bowl on the metal rack.

Choose "STEAM" button and cook for 5 minutes under HIGH pressure. Then, use the steam release.

Serve warm or at room temperature, sprinkled with chopped pecans if desired.

Cheesecake with Cranberry Topping

(Ready in about 35 minutes + chilling time | Servings 12)

Ingredients

For the Cake:

4 tablespoons butter, melted

1 ½ cups biscuits, roughly broken

1/2 cup sugar

2 cups cream cheese, softened

1/4 cup sour cream

1/2 teaspoon cinnamon powder

1/4 teaspoon anise seed

1 tablespoon flour

2 whole eggs

For the Topping:

1 ½ cups cranberries

1 cup golden caster sugar

Cold water

1 tablespoon ground arrowroot

Directions

In a bowl, combine the butter with biscuits. Spread the mixture around the bottom of a lightly springform pan.

Next, beat the sugar and cream cheese with an electric mixer. Add the sour cream, cinnamon, anise seed, and flour. Fold in the eggs, one at a time; continue to mix until it is creamy. Pour the mixture into the prepared crust.

Add 2 cups water to the cooker. Lay the rack on the bottom. Then, lay the pan on the rack.

Cover the cooker with the lid and choose "MANUAL" mode. Set the timer to 35 minutes. Refrigerate your dessert overnight.

Meanwhile, you can make the compote; place the cranberries, sugar, and 1 cup of water in a saucepan; then, bring to a simmer for 5 minutes, stirring periodically.

Then, mix the arrowroot with 2 tablespoons of cold water; add the mixture to the saucepan. Cook for 2 more minutes, stirring regularly. Allow the topping to cool completely.

Spread the topping over your cheesecake and serve chilled.

Chocolate and Honey Rice Pudding

(Ready in about 20 minutes | Servings 4)

Ingredients

1 ¾ cups rice

4 cups milk

Zest of 1 lemon, grated

1/2 cup sugar

1/2 teaspoon hazelnut extract

1/2 teaspoon vanilla extract

1/2 cup chocolate chips

2 tablespoons honey

Directions

Simply throw your ingredients, except for chocolate chips and honey, in your cooker.

Choose "Manual" function; adjust the time to 12 minutes. Remove the lid according to manufacturer's instructions. Stir in the chocolate chips; gently stir to combine.

Divide your pudding among individual bowls. Drizzle with honey and enjoy!

Chocolate Hazelnut Crunch Pudding

(Ready in about 30 minutes | Servings 6)

Ingredients

2 tablespoons cocoa powder

4 cups milk

1 cup rice

1/4 teaspoon grated cloves

1/2 cup sugar

1 teaspoon vanilla extract

2 ounces bittersweet chocolate, chopped

1/2 cup hazelnuts, toasted and coarsely chopped

1 tablespoon egg white, lightly beaten

4 teaspoons sugar

Directions

In the inner pot of your Instant Pot, place cocoa powder, milk, rice, cloves, sugar, and vanilla.

Then, select "Manual" function; now cook for 12 minutes. Carefully remove the cooker's lid. Stir in the bittersweet chocolate.

Then, start making the Hazelnut Crunch by preheating your oven to 300 degrees F. Toss together hazelnuts, egg white, and sugar. Spread the mixture on a baking sheet.

Bake your crunch, stirring regularly, for about 15 minutes. Allow the crunch to cool completely.

Serve prepared pudding topped with hazelnut crunch. Enjoy!

Banana-Vanilla Rice Pudding

(Ready in about 15 minutes | Servings 6)

Ingredients

1 cup basmati rice

1 cup water

3 cups vanilla rice milk

1/3 cup sugar

1/4 teaspoon kosher salt

1 teaspoon vanilla extract

4 ripe bananas, divided

Ground cardamom, for garnish

Directions

Add rice, water, vanilla rice milk, sugar, and salt to your Instant Pot.

Push "Manual" button and use [+ -] function to select 12 minutes. Afterwards, remove the cooker's lid.

Let the pudding rest for 5 to 10 minutes before releasing pressure. Add vanilla extract and 2 mashed bananas. Stir to combine. Cut two remaining bananas into thin slices.

Divide the pudding among serving bowls; serve topped with banana slices and ground cardamom. Enjoy!

Star Anise Chocolate Cake

(Ready in about 20 minutes | Servings 10)

Ingredients

1 ½ cups black chocolate chips

1 stick butter

1 cup sugar

1 teaspoon anise seeds

1/2 teaspoon grated ginger

1/2 teaspoon grated nutmeg

1/4 cup flour

3 eggs

Icing sugar, for garnish

Directions

Microwave the chocolate chips and butter until they are completely melted. Add sugar, anise seeds, ginger, nutmeg, flour and eggs. Beat until everything is well mixed or until there are no lumps.

Pour the batter into a buttered cake pan. Insert the trivet into your Instant Pot. Pour in 2 cups of water. Place the cake pan on the trivet.

Cook 6 minutes on "Manual" mode. Afterwards, perform quick release. Let it cool completely. After that, invert the cake onto a serving platter and dust it with icing sugar. Enjoy!

Strawberry Tapioca Pudding

(Ready in about 10 minutes | Servings 4)

Ingredients

1/3 cup seed tapioca pearls, soaked

1/2 cup water

1 ¼ cups whole milk

1/2 cup sugar

1/2 orange, zested

1 vanilla bean, split lengthwise

1 cup strawberries, trimmed

Directions

Prepare your cooker by adding 1 cup of water; then, place steamer basket in the bottom and set it aside.